The third chronicle of

Hugh de Singleton, surgeon

MEL STARR

MONARCH
BOOKS

Oxford, UK & Grand Rapids, Michigan, USA

First published in the UK in 2010 by Monarch Books
(a publishing imprint of Lion Hudson plc)
Wilkinson House, Jordan Hill Road, Oxford, OX2 8DR, England
Tel: +44 (0)1865 302750 Fax: +44 (0)1865 302757
Email: monarch@lionhudson.com
www.lionhudson.com

ISBN 978 1 85424 974 6

Distributed by:
UK: Marston Book Services, PO Box 269, Abingdon, Oxon, OX14
4YN
USA: Kregel Publications, PO Box 2607, Grand Rapids, Michigan
49501
Scripture quotations taken from the Authorized Version of the
Bible (The King James Bible), the rights in which are vested in
the Crown, are reproduced by permission of the Crown's Patentee,
Cambridge University Press.
The text paper used in this book has been made from wood
independently certified as having come from sustainable forests.

Cover design by Emma De Banks.

British Library Cataloguing Data
A catalogue record for this book is available from the British
Library.
Printed and bound in the UK by MPG Books Ltd.

For Fran and Larry

Acknowledgments

In the summer of 1990 my wife Susan and I discovered a lovely B&B in the village of Mavesyn Ridware. The proprietors, Tony and Lis Page, became friends. We visited them again in 2001, after they had moved to Bampton. I saw that the village would be an ideal setting for the tales I wished to write. Tony and Lis have been a wonderful resource for the history of Bampton. I owe them much.

When Dan Runyon, Professor of English at Spring Arbor University, learned that I was writing *The Unquiet Bones*, he invited me to speak to a fiction-writing class about the trials of a rookie writer. Dan sent some chapters to his friend Tony Collins. Thanks, Dan.

And many thanks to Tony Collins and the fine people of Monarch for their willingness to publish an untried author.

Thanks go also to Spring Arbor University student Brian Leyder, who suggested the title for Master Hugh's third chronicle.

Modern Oxford resembles the medieval city, but there have been many changes. Streets often bear different names than they did six hundred years ago. Dr John Blair, of Queen's College, has been a great help in navigating the differences between the modern and the medieval. However, if the reader becomes lost in medieval Oxford's narrow lanes the fault is mine, not Dr Blair's.

Mel Starr

Glossary

Angelus bell: Rung three times each day – dawn, noon, and dusk. Announced the times for the Angelus devotional.

Assart: Turning unused or "waste" land into cultivated farmland.

Bailiff: A lord's chief manorial representative. He oversaw all operations, collected rents and fines, and enforced labor service. Not a popular fellow.

Banns: A formal announcement, made in the parish church for three consecutive Sundays, of intent to marry.

Braes: Medieval underpants.

Calefactory: The warming room in a monastery. Benedictines allowed the fire to be lit on 1 November. The more rigorous Cistercians had no calefactory.

Candlemas: 2 February. The day marked the purification of Mary. Women traditionally paraded to church carrying lighted candles. Tillage of fields resumed this day.

Canon: A priest of the secular clergy who lived under rules comparable to monastic orders. Did not usually minister to the commons.

Chauces: Tight-fitting trousers, often parti-colored (having different colors for each leg).

Claret: Yellowish or light-red wine from the Bordeaux region.

Coney: Rabbit.

Cordwainer: A dealer in leather and leather goods imported from Cordova, Spain.

Cresset: A bowl of oil with a floating wick used for lighting.

Curate: A clergyman who often served as an assistant to the rector of a parish.

Dexter: A war horse, larger than pack-horses and palfreys. Also called a destrier. Also the right-hand direction.

Dower: The groom's financial contribution to marriage, designated for the bride's support during marriage and possible widowhood.

Dowry: A gift from the bride's family to the groom, intended for her support during marriage, and widowhood, should her husband predecease her.

Egg leaches: A very thick custard, often enriched with almonds, spices, and flour.

Farthing: One fourth of a penny. The smallest coin.

Free companies: At times of peace during the Hundred Years' War, bands of unemployed knights would organize themselves and ravage the countryside. France especially suffered.

Galantyne: A sauce made with cinnamon, ginger, vinegar, and breadcrumbs.

Gathering: Eight leaves of parchment, made by folding the prepared hide three times.

Groom: A lower-ranking servant to a lord. Often a teenaged youth. Occasionally assistant to a valet. Ranked above a page.

Hallmote: The manorial court. Royal courts judged free tenants accused of murder or felony. Otherwise manor courts had jurisdiction over legal matters concerning villagers. Villeins accused of murder might also be tried in a manor court.

Kirtle: The basic medieval undershirt.

Lammas Day: 1 August, when thanks was given for a successful wheat harvest. From the Old English "loaf mass".

Liripipe: A fashionably long tail attached to a man's cap.

Lych gate: A roofed gate in the churchyard wall under which the deceased rested during the initial part of a burial service.

Mark: 13 shillings and 4 pence – 160 pence.

Marshalsea: The stable and associated accoutrements.

Martinmas: 11 November. The traditional date to slaughter animals for winter food.

Maslin: Bread made with a mixture of grains, commonly wheat with barley or rye.

Matins: The first of the day's eight canonical hours (services). Also called Lauds.

Nones: The fifth canonical office, sung at the ninth hour of the day (about 3 p.m.).

Oyer et terminer: To hear and determine.

Palfrey: A gentle horse with a comfortable gait.

Pannage: A fee paid to the lord for permission to allow pigs to forage in an autumn forest.

Pottage: Anything cooked in one pot, from the meanest oatmeal to a savory stew.

Prebend: A subsistence allowance granted to a clergyman by a parish church.

Sacrist: A monastic official responsible for the upkeep of the church and vestments, and time-keeping.

St Catherine's Day: 25 November. St Catherine was the most popular female saint of medieval Europe. Processions were held in her honor on her feast day.

St Stephen's Day: 26 December.

Set books: The standard texts used by medieval university students.

Solar: A small private room, more easily heated than the great hall, where lords often preferred to spend time in winter. Usually on an upper floor.

Subtlety: An elaborate dessert, often more for show than consumption.

Terce: The canonical office (service) at 9 a.m.

Toft: Land surrounding a house, in the medieval period often used for growing vegetables.

Valet: A high-ranking servant to a lord – a chamberlain, for example.

Vigils: The night office, celebrated at midnight. When it was completed, Benedictines went back to bed. Cistercians stayed up for the new day.

Villein: A non-free peasant. He could not leave his land or service to his lord, or sell animals without permission. But if he could escape his manor for a year and a day, he would be free.

Whiffletree: A pivoted swinging bar to which the traces of a harness are fastened and by which a cart is drawn.

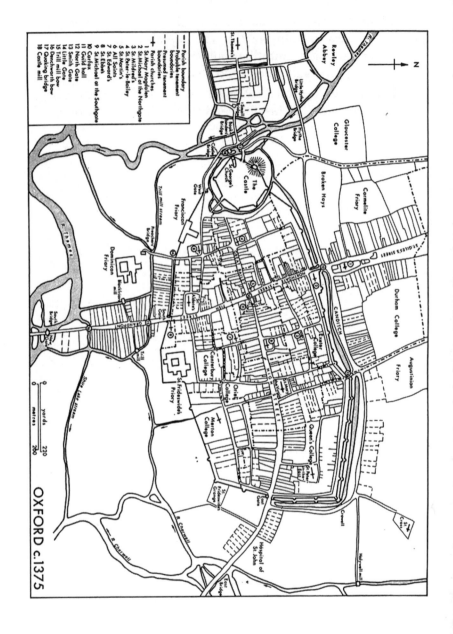

OXFORD c.1375

Key:

- ✝ — Parish boundary
- ─ ─ — Probable tenement boundaries
- ─ ─ ─ — Presumed tenement boundaries
- ✝ — Parish churches

1 St Mary Magdalen
2 St Michael at the Northgate
3 St Mildred's
4 St Martin's
5 St Peter-le-Bailey
6 All Saints
7 St Edward's
8 St Ebbe's
9 St Michael at the Southgate
10 Carfax
11 Guild hall
12 North Gate
13 Smith Gate
14 Little Gate
15 Trill mill bow
16 Denchworth bow
17 Quaking bridge
18 Castle mill

Chapter 1

I had never seen Master John Wyclif so afflicted. He was rarely found at such a loss when in disputation with other masters. He told me later, when I had returned them to him, that it was as onerous to plunder a bachelor scholar's books as it would be to steal another man's wife. I had, at the time, no way to assess the accuracy of that opinion, for I had no wife and few books.

But I had come to Oxford on that October day, Monday, the twentieth, in the year of our Lord 1365, to see what progress I might make to remedy my solitary estate. I left my horse at the stable behind the Stag and Hounds and went straightaway to Robert Caxton's shop, where the stationer's comely daughter, Kate, helped attract business from the bachelor scholars, masters, clerks, and lawyers who infest Oxford like fleas on a hound.

My pretended reason to visit Caxton's shop was to purchase a gathering of parchment and a fresh pot of ink. I needed these to conclude my record of the deaths of Alan the beadle and of Henry atte Bridge. Alan's corpse was found, three days before Good Friday, near to St Andrew's Chapel, to the east of Bampton. And Henry, who it was who slew Alan, was found in a wood to the north of the town. As bailiff of Bampton Castle it was my business to sort out these murders, which I did, but not before I was attacked on the road returning from Witney and twice clubbed about the head in nocturnal churchyards. Had I known such assaults lay in my future, I might have rejected Lord Gilbert Talbot's offer to serve as his bailiff at Bampton Castle and remained but Hugh the surgeon, of Oxford High Street.

Kate promised to prepare a fresh pot of ink, which

I might have next day, and when she quit the shop to continue her duties in the workroom I spoke to her father. Robert Caxton surely knew the effect Kate had upon young men. He displayed no surprise when I asked leave to court his daughter.

I had feared raised eyebrows at best, and perhaps a refusal. I am but a surgeon and a bailiff. Surgeons own little prestige in Oxford, full of physicians as it is, and few honest men wish to see a daughter wed to a bailiff. There were surely sons of wealthy Oxford burghers, and young masters of the law, set on a path to wealth, who had eyes for the comely Kate. But Caxton nodded agreement when I requested his permission to pay court to his daughter. Perhaps my earlier service to mend his wounded back helped my suit.

I left the stationer's shop with both joy and apprehension. The joy you will understand, or would had you seen Kate and spent time in her presence. I was apprehensive because next day I must begin a thing for which I had no training and in which I had little experience. While at Balliol College I was too much absorbed in my set books to concern myself with the proper way to impress a lass, and none of those volumes dealt with the subject. Certainly the study of logic avoided the topic. Since then my duties as surgeon and bailiff allowed small opportunity to practice discourse with a maiden. And there are few females of my age and station in Bampton.

I made my way from Caxton's shop on Holywell Street to Catte Street and thence to the gate of Canterbury Hall, on Schidyard Street. As I walked I composed speeches in my mind with which I might impress Kate Caxton. I had forgotten most of these inventions by next day. This was just as well.

Master John Wyclif, former Master of Balliol College and my teacher there, was newly appointed Warden of Canterbury Hall. Several months earlier, frustrated at my inability to discover who had slain Alan the beadle and Henry atte Bridge, I had called upon Master John to lament my ignorance and seek his wisdom. He provided encouragement, and an empty chamber in the Hall where I might stay the night, safe from the snores and vermin at the Stag and Hounds.

When I left him those months earlier he enjoined me to call when I was next in Oxford and tell him of the resolution of these mysteries. At the time of his request I was not sure there ever would be a resolution to the business.

But there was, and so I sought Master John to tell him of it, and seek again his charity and an empty cell for the night. The porter recognized me, and sent me to Master John's chamber. I expected to find him bent over a book, as was his usual posture when I called. But not so. He opened the door to my knock, recognized me, and blurted, "Master Hugh... they've stolen my books."

The greeting startled me. I peered over the scholar's shoulder as if I expected to see the miscreants and the plundered volumes. I saw Master John's table, and a cupboard where his books were kept. Both were bare. He turned to follow my gaze.

"Gone," he whispered. "All of them."

"Who?" I asked stupidly. Had Master John known that, he would have set after the thieves and recovered the books. Or sent the sheriff to do so.

"I know not," Wyclif replied. "I went to my supper three days past. When I returned the books were gone... even the volume I left open on my table."

Master John is not a wealthy man. He has the living of Fillingham, and the prebend of Aust, but these provide a thin subsistence for an Oxford master of arts at work on a degree in theology. The loss of books accumulated in a life of study would be a blow to any scholar, rich or poor.

"The porter saw no stranger enter or leave the Hall while we supped," Wyclif continued. "I went next day to the sheriff, but Sir John has other matters to mind."

"Sir John?"

"Aye. Roger de Cottesford is replaced. The new high sheriff is Sir John Trillowe."

"He offered no aid?"

"He sent a sergeant 'round to the stationers in the town, to see did any man come to them with books he offered to sell. Two I borrowed from Nicholas de Redyng. He will grieve to learn they are lost."

"And the stationers... they have been offered no books?"

"None of mine missing. And Sir John has no interest, I think, in pursuing my loss further."

The colleges have always wished to rule themselves, free of interference from the town and its government. No doubt the sheriff was minded to allow Canterbury Hall the freedom to apprehend its own thief, without his aid or interference.

"How many?"

"My books? Twenty... and the two borrowed."

I performed some mental arithmetic. Master John read my thoughts.

"The books I borrowed from Master Nicholas... one was Bede's *Historia Ecclesiastica*, worth near thirty shillings. One of mine was of paper, a cheap-set book, but the others were of parchment and well bound."

"Your loss is great, then. Twenty pounds or more."

"Aye," Wyclif sighed. "Four were of my own devising. Some might say they were worth little. But the others... Aristotle, Grosseteste, Boethius, all gone."

Master John sighed again, and gazed about his chamber as if the stolen books were but misplaced, and with closer inspection of dark corners might yet be discovered.

"I am pleased to see you," Master John continued. "I had thought to send for you."

"For me?"

"Aye. I have hope that you will seek my stolen books and see them returned to me."

"Me? Surely the sheriff..."

"Sir John is not interested in any crime for which the solution will not bring him a handsome fine. Rumor is he paid King Edward sixty pounds for the office. He will be about recouping his investment, not seeking stolen books.

"And you are skilled at solving mysteries," Wyclif continued. "You found who 'twas in Lord Gilbert's cesspit, and unless I mistake me, you know by now who killed your beadle and the fellow found slain in the forest. Well, do you not?"

"Aye. It was as I thought. Henry atte Bridge, found dead in the wood, slew Alan the beadle. Alan had followed him during the night as Henry took a haunch of venison poached from Lord Gilbert's forest, to the curate at St Andrew's Chapel."

"Venison? To a priest?"

"Aye... a long story."

"I have nothing but time, and no books with which to fill it. Tell me."

So I told Master John of the scandal of the betrayed confessional of the priest at St Andrew's Chapel. And of the blackmail he plotted with Henry atte Bridge – and Henry's brother, Thomas – of those who confessed to poaching, adultery, and cheating at their business.

"I came to Oxford this day to buy more ink and parchment so I may write of these felonies while details remain fresh in my memory."

"And what stationer receives your custom?"

"Robert Caxton. It was you who sent me first to Caxton's shop. You knew I would find more there than books, ink, and parchment."

"I did? Yes, I remember now telling you of the new stationer, come from Cambridge with his daughter... ah, that is your meaning. I am slow of wit these days. I think of nothing but my books."

"You did not guess I might be interested in the stationer's daughter?"

"Nay," Wyclif grimaced. "I surprise myself for my lack of perception. You are a young man with two good eyes. The stationer's daughter..."

"Kate," I said.

"Aye, Kate is a winsome lass."

"She is. And this day I have gained her father's permission to seek her as my wife."

Master John's doleful expression brightened. The corners of his mouth and eyes lifted into a grin. "I congratulate you, Hugh."

"Do not be too quick to do so. I must woo and win her, and I fear for my ability."

"I have no competency in such matters. You are on your own. 'Tis your competency solving puzzles I seek."

"But I am already employed."

Master John's countenance fell. "I had not considered that," he admitted. "Lord Gilbert requires your service... and pays well for it, I imagine."

"Aye. I am well able to afford a wife."

"But could not the town spare you for a week or two, until my books are found? Surely a surgeon... never mind. You see how little I heed other men's troubles when I meet my own."

"All men think first of themselves. Why should you be different?" I asked.

"Why? Because my misplaced esteem tells me I must. Do you not wish the same, Hugh? To be unlike the commons? They scratch when and where they itch and belch when and where they will and the letters on a page are as foreign to them as Malta."

"But... I remember a lecture..."

Wyclif grimaced.

"... when you spoke of all men being the same when standing before God. No gentlemen, no villeins, all sinners."

"Hah; run through by my own pike. 'Tis true. I recite the same sermon each year, but though we be all sinners, and all equally in need of God's grace, all sins are not, on earth, equal, as they may be in God's eyes. Else all punishments would be the same, regardless of the crime."

"And what would be a fitting penalty for one who stole twenty books?"

Wyclif scowled again. "Twenty-two," he muttered. "My thoughts change daily," he continued. "When I first discovered the offense I raged about the Hall threatening the thief with a noose."

"And now?"

Master John smiled grimly. "I have thought much on that. Was the thief a poor man needing to keep his children from starvation, I might ask no penalty at all, so long as my books be returned. But if the miscreant be another scholar, with means to purchase his own books, I would see him fined heavily and driven from Oxford, and never permitted to study here again, or teach, be he a master."

"Both holy and secular wisdom," Wyclif mused, "teach that we must not do to another what we find objectionable when done to us. No man should hold a place at Oxford who denies both God and Aristotle."

"You think an Oxford man has done this?"

Wyclif chewed upon a fingernail, then spoke. "Who else would want my books, or know their worth?"

"That, it seems to me, is the crux of the matter," I replied. "Some scholar wished to add to his library, or needed money, and saw your books as a way to raise funds."

As it happened, there was a third reason a man might wish to rob Master John of his books, but that explanation for the theft did not occur to me until later.

"I am lost," Wyclif sighed. "I am a master with no books, and I see no way to retrieve them."

I felt guilty that, for all his aid given to me, I could offer no assistance to the scholar. I could but commiserate, cluck my tongue, and sit in his presence with a long face.

The autumn sun set behind the old Oxford Castle keep while we talked. Wyclif was about to speak again when a small bell sounded from across the courtyard.

"Supper," he explained, and invited me to follow him to the refectory.

Scholars at Canterbury Hall are fed well, but simply. For this supper there were loaves of maslin – wheat and barley – cheese, a pease pottage flavored with bits of pork, and tankards of watered ale. I wondered at the pork, for some of the scholars were Benedictines. Students peered up from under lowered brows as we entered. They all knew of the theft, and, I considered later, suspected each other of complicity in the deed.

A watery autumn sun struggled to rise above the forest and water meadow east of Oxford when I awoke next morning. Wyclif bid me farewell with stooped shoulders and eyes dark from lack of sleep. I wished the scholar well, and expressed my prayer that his books be speedily recovered. Master John believes in prayer, but my promise to petition our Lord Christ on his behalf seemed to bring him small comfort. I think he would rather have my time and effort than my prayers. Or would have both. Prayers may be offered cheaply. They require small effort from men, and much from God. The Lord Christ has told us we may ask of Him what we will, but I suspect He would be pleased to see men set to their work, and call upon Him only when tasks be beyond them.

I thought on this as I walked through the awakening lanes of Oxford to Holywell Street and Robert Caxton's shop. Was it really my duty to Lord Gilbert which prevented me from seeking Wyclif's stolen books, or was I too slothful to do aught but pray for their return? I did not like the answer which came to me.

As I approached the stationer's shop I saw a tall young man standing before it, shifting his weight from one foot to the other. The fellow was no scholar. He wore a deep red cotehardie, cut short to show a good leg. His chauces were parti-colored, grey and black, and his cap ended in a long yellow liripipe coiled stylishly about his head. The color of his cap surprised me. All who visit London know that the whores of that city are required by law to wear yellow caps so respectable maidens and wives be left unmolested on the street. He was shod in fine leather, and the pointed toes of his shoes curled up in ungainly fashion.

The fellow seemed impatient; while I watched he strode purposefully past Caxton's shop, then reversed his steps and walked past in the opposite direction, toward my approach. I drew closer to the shop, so that at each turn I could see his face more clearly. His countenance and beard were dark, as were his eyes. The beard was neatly trimmed, and his eyes peered at my approach from above an impressive nose – although, unlike mine, his nose pointed straight out at the world, whereas mine turns to the dexter side. He seemed about my own age – twenty-five years or so. He was broad of shoulder and yet slender, but good living was beginning to produce a paunch.

I slowed my pace as I approached the shuttered shop. Caxton would open his business soon, and I assumed this dandy needed parchment, ink, or a book, although he did not seem the type to be much interested in words on a page.

I stood in the street, keeping the impatient coxcomb company, until Robert Caxton opened his shop door and pushed up his shutters to begin business for the day. The stationer looked from me to his other customer and I thought his eyes widened. I bowed to the other client and motioned him to precede me into the shop. He was there before me.

The morning sun was low in the southeast, and did not penetrate far into the shop. But dark as the place was, I could see that Kate was not within. He of the red cotehardie saw the same, and spoke before I could.

"Is Mistress Kate at leisure?" he asked.

Caxton glanced at me, then answered, "Near so. Preparing a pot of ink in the workroom. Be done shortly."

"I'll wait," the fellow said with a smile. "'Tis a pleasant morning. And if Kate has no other concerns, I'd have her walk with me along the water meadow."

He might as well have swatted me over my skull with a ridge pole. My jaw went slack and I fear both Caxton and this unknown suitor got a fine view of my tonsils.

Robert Caxton was not so discomfited that he forgot his manners. He introduced me to Sir Simon Trillowe. A knight. And of some relation to the new sheriff of Oxford, I guessed.

When he learned that I was but a surgeon and bailiff to Lord Gilbert Talbot, Sir Simon nodded briefly and turned away, his actions speaking what polite words could not: I was beneath his rank and unworthy of his consideration.

"We heard naught of you for many months, Master Hugh," Caxton remarked.

This was true. I had neglected pursuit of Kate Caxton while about Lord Gilbert's business in Bampton. And, to be true, I feared Kate might dismiss my suit should I press it. A man cannot be disappointed in love who does not seek it.

"No doubt a bailiff has much to occupy his time," the stationer continued.

Sir Simon doubtless thought that I was but a customer, not that I was in competition with him for the fair Kate. He would learn that soon enough.

The door to Caxton's workroom was open. Kate surely heard this exchange, which was a good thing. It gave her opportunity to compose herself. A moment later she entered the shop, carrying my pot of promised ink, and bestowed a tranquil smile upon both me and Sir Simon. I smiled in return, Trillowe did not. Perhaps he had guessed already that it was not ink I most wished to take from Caxton's shop.

"Mistress Kate," Sir Simon stepped toward her as she passed through the door. "'Tis a pleasant autumn morn... there will be few more before winter. Perhaps we might walk the path along the Cherwell... if your father can spare you for the morning."

With these words Trillowe turned to the stationer. Caxton shrugged a reply.

"Good." Sir Simon offered his arm and, with a brief smile and raised brows in my direction, Kate set the pot of ink on her father's table and took Trillowe's arm. They departed the shop wordlessly.

Caxton apparently thought some explanation in order. "You didn't call through the summer. Kate thought you'd no interest. I told her last night you'd asked to pay court. But Sir Simon's been by a dozen times since Lammas Day... others, too."

"Others?"

"Aye. My Kate does draw lads to the shop. None has asked me might they pay court, though. But for you."

"Not Sir Simon?"

"Nay. Second son of the sheriff, and a knight. He'll not ask leave of one like me to do aught."

"And Kate returns his interest?"

Caxton shrugged. "She's walked out with him three times now. A knight, mind you. And son of the sheriff. Can't blame a lass for that."

"No," I agreed.

"Can't think how his father'd be pleased, though. A stationer's daughter! A scandal in Oxford Castle when word gets out, as it surely has, by now," Caxton mused.

"Aye. What lands his father may hold will pass to his brother. The sheriff will want Sir Simon seeking a wife with lands of her own."

I hoped that was so. But if a second or third son acts to displease his father, it is difficult to correct him. How can a man disinherit a son who is due to receive little or nothing anyway? So if a son courting Kate Caxton displeased the sheriff of Oxford, such offense might escape retribution. This thought did not bring me joy.

Chapter 2

Nothing much else of that day in Oxford brought joy, either. Even Caxton's refusal to accept payment for parchment and ink could not raise my spirits. I trudged through the mud to the Stag and Hounds, retrieved Bruce from the stables, and from the old horse's broad back watched as the castle keep faded into the distance while we two, horse and rider, sauntered past Oseney Abbey toward Bampton and home.

I arrived at the castle at the ninth hour, in time for supper. Lord Gilbert was in residence, so this was a more elaborate meal than when he resided at another of his castles, with several guests, and many grooms and valets occupying lower tables.

A groom brought an ewer, basin, and towel to the high table and I washed the dust of the Oxford Road from my face and hands. The water was pleasingly scented with mint.

I had enjoyed no dinner that day, so as soon as Lord Gilbert's chaplain offered thanks to our Lord Christ for the meal I broke the loaf of wheaten bread before me, spread butter on the fragments with my knife, and set about calming my growling stomach.

It was during the third remove, a game pie, that I noticed Lady Petronilla peering at me from the other end of the high table. There are, I believe, subtle signals of sorrow which women perceive more readily than men. I was unaware that my discontent was plain to another. And to Lord Gilbert it was not.

The game pie this day seemed beneath the cook's usual standard. I had little desire to finish my portion. And the subtlety also seemed to lack appeal. Perhaps the wheaten loaf poisoned my appetite.

Three days later, after a supper of eels baked in vinegar and spices, pike in galantine, and salmon in syrup, John the chamberlain approached me as I entered my chamber. Lord Gilbert, he said, was in the solar and would see me.

A blaze in the fireplace both lit the solar and warmed it against the chill of an autumn evening. Lady Petronilla glanced up at me from her needlework as John ushered me into the chamber, and Lord Gilbert looked my way briefly before continuing his conversation with Sir Watkin Kidwell, a guest to whom I had been introduced at Tuesday supper when I returned from Oxford.

I stood, confused about the summons, until Lord Gilbert nodded toward a bench which rested, unoccupied, between him and Lady Petronilla. This seat was pleasingly near the fire, and while I sat a groom replenished the logs to the accompaniment of a great salvo of sparks which swirled up the chimney. I was tired, and had recently supped. The combination produced drowsiness. I feared I might topple into the fire.

The hum of conversation ceased. I awoke from my lethargy to see Sir Watkin rise, bow, and bid Lord Gilbert and Lady Petronilla "Good night." I stood, perhaps a bit wobbly, to honor Sir Watkin's departure, as did Lord Gilbert.

When the guest had departed Lord Gilbert resumed his chair and motioned me back to my bench. I drew it away from the fire, for the logs recently placed on the blaze were now burning furiously.

"Lady Petronilla," Lord Gilbert began, "would have me speak to you."

Lady Petronilla looked up briefly from her work and smiled from under lowered brows. I could not guess why she thought conversation necessary, but her gentle smile reassured me that the discussion was probably not going to center upon some malfeasance on my part. Few men enjoy a command to meet with their employer, and I admit to some apprehension when John delivered

Lord Gilbert's summons. I had been reluctant, two years past, to accept Lord Gilbert's offer to become bailiff of his Bampton estate. But now I found myself equally reluctant to leave the post should Lord Gilbert have detected some dereliction on my part.

It was not Lord Gilbert, but his wife, who had detected a change in my manner, and it was this she had noted and urged her husband to investigate. Therefore my summons this evening.

"M'lady," he continued, "believes some thing is amiss with you, and would have me seek it out."

"Amiss, m'lord?"

"Aye." Lady Petronilla laid her work in her lap and spoke. "You were laughing and in good spirit when you departed for Oxford Monday. But since your return you are morose. I have watched you at table... you eat but little. I told m'lord, 'Some mishap has overtaken Master Hugh while at Oxford.'"

"M'lady," Lord Gilbert interjected, "has a meddlesome imagination."

"Meddlesome I am not," Lady Petronilla barked. "I am... observant."

"Aye," Lord Gilbert chuckled and nodded toward me. "She is that."

"I told m'lord 'tis not good for a young man, so full of life and joy one day, to be so glum the next."

"And I told her this was not our concern." He paused. "She disagreed."

Lady Petronilla nodded and pursed her lips.

"So I have called you here to learn what has gone amiss in Oxford. Or," he hesitated, "to learn if my wife's imagination has..."

"'Tis no imagining," Lady Petronilla rejoined.

Lord Gilbert was to my right hand, Lady Petronilla to my left. Their dispute caused my head to swivel. I made no reply to Lady Petronilla's assertion, but she would not accept my silence.

"Come, Master Hugh. When a young man cannot finish a tasty game pie for his supper, or salmon in syrup, then something is much awry."

"Hmm," Lord Gilbert muttered, pulling at his beard. "This is true? You did not finish your salmon?"

"He did not."

"I have never known you to reject a salmon. M'lady speaks true… What troubles you, Hugh?"

I dislike encumbering others with my own misfortune. And I have observed that, on most occasions, others prefer not to share the burden anyway. I hesitated to reply.

Lady Petronilla understood what my silence implied.

"You do not protest, Master Hugh. So 'tis true. Were it not so, you would be quick to object."

"It is a matter for my own concern," I finally replied. "I do not wish to vex others."

"I told you 'twas so," Lady Petronilla said triumphantly to her husband. Lord Gilbert raised one eyebrow and went to pulling at his beard. These mannerisms I knew well. He stroked his chin when deep in thought, and raised an eyebrow when puzzled. This last expression I had tried to emulate. Unsuccessfully.

"It is not good for a man to carry his worries alone," Lord Gilbert remarked. "You have no wife to share your sorrows."

"Or joys," Lady Petronilla smiled.

"'Tis more difficult for you, of course… finding a wife. You must search her out for yourself. Our fathers," Lord Gilbert smiled at his wife, "placed us together. For the which I am grateful, as is, I trust, m'lady."

Lady Petronilla beamed in reply. This conversation had somehow got around to wives and marriage. Perhaps Lord Gilbert had an intuition that a young man's woe might have to do with a lass.

"I would be much pleased to find a good wife," I agreed. "I know that marriage may bring sorrow, but bachelorhood brings little joy."

"Well," Lord Gilbert chuckled, "you had best get you back to Oxford. You will not find her in Bampton Castle…

nor anywhere in the town, I think."

"But I have duties here."

"What? Michaelmas is long past. The harvest is in, and John Holcutt has matters well in hand for winter. You are at leisure to pursue your own ends and seek a wife. A prosperous burgher's daughter, I think, or, with luck, the only child of a knight, with lands she might bring with her."

Lady Petronilla nodded agreement. Gentlemen and their ladies are much alike. Get land; this is nearly all they think on. Kate Caxton will have small dowry, I think. Her father is a burgher, but I am not privy to the depth of his purse. Knowing Lord Gilbert as I do, however, should he lay eyes on Kate, he will approve my choice.

My choice. Little good my decision would do me now, with the handsome Sir Simon Trillowe in pursuit of Kate.

"You have friends in Oxford," Lord Gilbert continued. "Surely some will know of a suitable lass."

"Perhaps more than one might suit," Lady Petronilla smiled. "'Tis always good to have a choice in such matters."

Lord Gilbert frowned at this remark. "You would have preferred a choice?"

"You think I did not have one?" she rejoined. "Our fathers placed us together, 'tis true, but my father would not match me with a man I rejected."

"So you..."

"Aye," Lady Petronilla smiled. "My father knew who I would have and who I would not."

"There were others you would have accepted? Who?"

"I will say no more," she laughed, "but that choice of a spouse is good. Neither you nor Master Hugh need know more."

"Master Wyclif is a friend, is he not?" Lord Gilbert returned to his subject. "You should seek him and learn if he knows of suitable maids about Oxford."

"But m'lord," Lady Petronilla scoffed, "Master John

is a bachelor scholar. What will he know of marriageable maids?"

"He has lived in Oxford many years, and even scholars, with their noses pressed to their books, have two eyes and can appreciate a comely lass, and two ears and can hear of virtue."

Lady Petronilla had no reply to this logic, so returned to her needle. I decided to speak plainly to Lord Gilbert.

"I visited Master John Monday eve. He is much distressed. Some thief has stolen his books."

Lord Gilbert raised both eyebrows. "Indeed? He has told the sheriff of the loss?"

"Aye. Sir John Trillowe is newly appointed High Sheriff of Oxford. He seems little interested in seeking stolen books."

Lord Gilbert's eyes narrowed and his lips compressed to a fine line. "He would not."

"You know Sir John?"

"I do."

I awaited an explanation of Lord Gilbert's expression when he heard the name. None was forthcoming, but I knew my employer well enough to know that he must think little of this new sheriff. In the past two years I had found Lord Gilbert's estimation of other men to be fair, so was prepared to think little of a man I had never met. I had met his son. An acorn does not fall far from the oak. But I am prejudiced.

"Master Wyclif has no clue as to who has taken his books?" Lord Gilbert continued.

"None."

He raised an eyebrow and went to tugging at his chin, but it was Lady Petronilla who spoke: "Is not Master Wyclif a favorite of Duke John?"

"Aye," Lord Gilbert replied. "The Duke of Lancaster is Master Wyclif's patron. The scholar comes from lands in Yorkshire which are in the Duke's gift."

"I wonder," Lady Petronilla laid her needlework in her lap and looked up, "that Master Wyclif does not seek help from Duke John. Surely the king's son should have ways and means to find stolen books."

"The Duke will be in London, enjoying his palace, or at Pontefract. I think he cares little for books... although he might be pleased did another discover the thief and return the books to his favorite." As he said this Lord Gilbert went to pulling at his chin again.

"Master Hugh, you have few duties now 'til hallmote. And you are proven adept at solving mysteries. Perhaps you should return to Oxford and seek Master Wyclif's books."

"And while he is there," Lady Petronilla added, "he might also seek a wife. I cannot tell which may be easier to discover."

Before I could think of an objection Lord Gilbert spoke again, and my fate was sealed. "I think John of Gaunt would be much pleased to learn 'twas my bailiff who discovered the thief who stole his favorite's books."

Lord Gilbert, Third Baron Talbot, is one of the most powerful nobles in the realm. But even he would like the good will of John of Gaunt, Duke of Lancaster, son of the King Edward that now is, and brother of the King Edward to be, the fourth of that name, the Black Prince.

In matter of fact, with the old king ill, and the Black Prince often waging war in France, it is Duke John who runs the kingdom. So some say. But not where others may hear.

"John Holcutt is competent to deal with the manor. And I will remain until St Catherine's Day. So that's settled, then. Nothing to keep you. You may be off tomorrow. Take Arthur, if you wish. Might be well to have an assistant along. Arthur's no fool, and worth three in a fray, should you find the felons and they not wish to surrender their loot."

I awoke next morning, cold, at the ringing of the Angelus Bell. The Church of St Beornwald is several hundred paces north of Bampton Castle, but the dawn was still and sound carried well. I thought how pleasant it would be to have a good wife to warm my bed on such mornings. This musing was not new to me, and brought no joy, for as I tossed in my cold bed I thought on Lady Joan Talbot, now the Lady de Burgh, and of Kate Caxton.

The fire in my chamber was but black coals. A few embers glowed when I blew on the ashes; enough that I was able to resurrect the blaze with a few carefully placed splinters and then two logs. My feet were cold on the flags, so I climbed back into my bed until the fire might warm the chamber. Cold as the bed was, it was warmer than the floor.

After a loaf of maslin and a wedge of cheese I mounted Bruce, the old gelding Lord Gilbert had assigned to my use, and Arthur climbed astride an ancient palfrey which had once borne Lady Petronilla. Riding the shaggy old beast did not seem to displease Arthur. Most grooms, when forced to travel, must do so afoot. I slung a leather-and-wood box containing my surgical instruments, and a pouch of herbs, across Bruce's broad rump. What use these might be to me I did not know, but I dislike being without my implements.

A slanting sun illuminated the tops of the oaks in Lord Gilbert's forest to the west of Bampton as Arthur and I rode under the portcullis and set off toward Mill Street and the bridge over Shill Brook. It was a fine day for travel, did a man have a joyous reason and pleasant destination in mind. I had neither.

Lord Gilbert had set me to a task for which I felt unequal. And the pursuit of Kate Caxton, which a week past brought cheer when I thought on it, now lay leaden on my heart.

Villeins and tenants were busy in the fields we passed. Wheat and rye had been sown, and oxen and the occasional horse drew harrows across the fields to cover the seed with soil. Children shivered in the morning air, their fists filled with rocks to toss at birds which would steal the seed before the harrow could do its work.

Acorns and beech nuts had fallen, so swineherds had driven their hogs into the forest for pannaging. The pigs might regret their appetite on Martinmas. Pigs are much like men. Or perhaps men are like pigs: we think little of what today's pleasure may cost tomorrow.

The sky was pale blue and the sun lacked warmth. It was not only swine which roamed the forest. Tenants and villeins also stalked the woodland, gathering fuel for the winter soon to be upon us.

The tower of Oseney Abbey was a welcome sight when it appeared above the trees which lined the Thames. I appreciated the gift of Bruce, the old dexter which had borne Lord Gilbert at the Battle of Poitiers, but I have never become inured to the saddle. True, it is better to ride than walk sixteen miles. Better yet to stay home at Bampton Castle and have neither sore rump nor legs.

But I had a duty to Lord Gilbert, and, indeed, to Master Wyclif as well. By the time Bruce clattered across the Castle Mill Stream Bridge I was resolved to exert myself in the matter of Master John's books. And in the matter of Mistress Kate Caxton, also. But I admit I felt more confidence regarding the discovery of missing books than the winning of a fair maid. Thieves are more predictable than a lass.

Canterbury Hall owns no stable, so Arthur and I left our beasts at the Stag and Hounds. Oxford's streets were crowded as we walked south toward St John Street and Canterbury Hall. Perhaps among the throng was a thief, or more than one. How I was to find him I knew not.

The porter at Canterbury Hall recognized me and sent me straightaway to Master Wyclif's chamber. Arthur had walked before me as we pressed through the crowd on the High Street, but trod respectfully behind after we approached the porter. Arthur is a good man to have about when it is necessary to make a path through the throng. He is not so tall as me, but weighs, I think, two stone more. His neck is as thick as my thigh.

The scholar was absent. There was no response to my knock on his chamber door. The Michaelmas Term was begun, so I assumed Master John to be at his work, lecturing students. Perhaps he had been at the business long enough that he could carry on without his set books.

While I stood, uncertain, before the door I heard a voice raised in argument. Cells for the students of Canterbury Hall lined the enclosure opposite the warden's chamber, and a kitchen and hall closed the western side of the yard. Three glass windows gave light to the interior of this hall, and although they were closed to the autumn air, they permitted the sound of angry dispute to flood the enclosure.

Arthur also heard the argument and peered at me under a furrowed brow. I left Master John's door and walked to the nearest of the three windows. Arthur followed.

From beside the window I could hear the dispute plainly. I had the gist of the quarrel in less time than it takes to pare a fingernail. The inhabitants of the Hall were divided into two opposing camps, each accusing the other of complicity in the matter of their warden's stolen books. Occasionally I thought I heard Master John over the din, trying to calm the debate. A man might as well try to arrest the wind as silence an Oxford scholar who wishes to make known his opinion.

In addition to the three windows, the east wall of the hall included a door. It was behind me as I stood at the window, so I heard, rather than saw, the door open abruptly and immediately slam shut. Arthur and I turned and watched Master John stalk across the yard toward his chamber. He had not seen us against the wall, for the open door blocked his view, although the afternoon sun bathed the enclosure in a golden glow.

Wyclif did not hear us follow; he was muttering to himself as he strode. So he pushed through his chamber door and slammed it in our faces unknowingly. Arthur stared goggle-eyed, first at me, then at the door. I was accustomed to scholarly disputes. Indeed, I had shouted my way through several in my youth. But such discord was new to Arthur. He thought he was to spend some days in the peaceful company of scholars and masters. But there are few men so disputatious as scholars. Arthur was learning this and the knowledge startled him. I think had I released him at that moment he would have sought out the Stag and Hounds, mounted the old palfrey, and scurried off for Bampton.

I rapped on Master John's chamber door and a heartbeat later it was flung open.

"What?!" Wyclif roared, then clamped his lips shut when he saw it was me. "I beg pardon, Master Hugh. I thought... never mind what I thought. Come in."

Master John held open the door and stood to one side as a welcome. Arthur, his cap in his hands, followed me into the gloomy chamber. The scholar had had no time, and perhaps no desire, to light a cresset to bolster the thin light of a late October afternoon which managed to penetrate the chamber through a single narrow window.

There were but two benches in the room. Arthur noted this and stood aside, in a shadowy corner, as Wyclif motioned to a bench and sat silently upon the other. Neither of us spoke for a moment.

"You forgot some business in Oxford?" Master John finally asked.

"No. I am come to offer my service, as you desired, in the matter of your stolen books."

"Ah," Wyclif smiled. "Some good tidings for a change."

"You have made no progress in discovering the books, or who it was who took them?"

"None. And the issue divides the Hall... more so than it already was."

"I... we, uh, overheard some debate just now."

"Hah. Debate. Indeed, Master Hugh, you are a tactful man. The monks and seculars are at each other's throats, each thinking the other's responsible."

"And you," I asked, "what think you?"

Wyclif was silent, his lips pursed and brow furrowed. The only sound was Arthur shifting his weight from one foot to another.

"Thinking on my loss leaves an ache, so I try not to think on it at all."

"You are successful?"

"Nay," Wyclif grimaced. "'Tis sure that the more a man tries not to consider a thing, the more he will so do."

"You think much on the loss, then?"

"Aye, but to no purpose."

The ringing of a small bell interrupted our conversation. "Supper," Master John muttered. "I care little for food this day, but you and your man are hungry, surely. Come."

Wyclif led the way from his chamber across the yard to the hall. The scholars who preceded us there were in muttered conversation but fell silent when they saw Master John's scowl.

Supper was a pottage of peas, leeks, and white beans, with a maslin loaf, wheat and rye. Saturday is a fast day. Nevertheless I detected a few bits of bacon flavoring the pottage. A man watching might have thought this a monastic house where the residents observed silence while in the refectory. There was no resumption of the afternoon argument. The scholars ate warily, one eye on their fellows, the other on Master John.

Arthur and I ate heartily. We'd enjoyed no dinner. We might have dined at the Stag and Hounds when we left the horses, and, indeed, Arthur had peered beseechingly at me as we left the place. But I have dined many times at the Stag and Hounds. Too many times.

It was dark when we left the hall. A sliver of moon gave enough light that I did not stumble on the cobbles of the yard. Arthur did. The ale served with supper was fresh. Arthur drank copiously.

Master John led us to his chamber, and while he lighted a cresset I resumed my bench and Arthur took his place in the corner. But he did not remain standing. His back slid down the wall until he was seated in a crouch on the flags. He released a contented belch as the descent concluded.

"Lord Gilbert has released you to do service for me?" Wyclif inquired.

"Aye."

"I am in his debt."

"Not yet. I have found no books nor a malefactor."

"Ah, but you will. I have faith."

Arthur greeted Master John's judgment with a snore. The scholar smiled and peered into the corner where Arthur sat, elbows on knees and head on arms.

"You will be weary from your journey this day. I will have straw brought to the guest's cell for your man and you may seek your rest. Time enough on the morrow to begin your search."

Chapter 3

Scholars at Canterbury Hall take no morning meal. So when Arthur and I left our cell and made our way to Master John's chamber, my stomach growled as loudly as Arthur's snores. Arthur seemed not to notice.

Master John was awaiting my arrival. His door squealed open on rusty hinges a heartbeat after I rapped my knuckles upon it. Why, I wondered, must those hinges protest so? Canterbury Hall and its buildings were but four years old. A scholar's life is consumed with the ethereal, I think, while the realities are as lost to him as feathers upon the breeze. Greasing hinges is, to Master Wyclif, a gossamer reality.

"Master Hugh, you slept well?"

"Aye," I lied.

"I did also. For the first time in many days. You will soon find my books."

I was not so confident as Master John, but saw no purpose in disillusioning the hopeful scholar.

"You did not rise for Matins," Wyclif observed. "And I was loath to wake you. You must have rest, and your wits about you, if you are to find my books."

"If I am to do so I must first know all that happened the day they went missing. Especially I would know of any event out of the ordinary."

Master John scratched the back of his head, thought for a moment, then replied, "'Twas a normal day. A lecture in the morning. After dinner a disputation... which was a little less disputatious, perhaps, than ordinary."

"How so?"

"Canterbury Hall is a new foundation, created by the Archbishop four years past. 'Twas begun with good intentions," Wyclif sighed, "but as with many noble designs, things have gone much awry.

"The Archbishop's plan was to bridge the gap at Oxford between monks and secular fellows. So Canterbury Hall is to have four monks, from Canterbury, and eight secular scholars. There were four wardens before me, in but four years. The first was a monk of Canterbury. The secular scholars drove him out. The next were seculars, and the monks would not have them."

"There is much discord in the house?"

"Ha," Wyclif sniffed. "I have tried to calm my charges, but my soft answers have not turned away wrath. They argued before I came, and they will continue no matter what I do. The monks are particularly contentious. They wished for another of their house to be appointed warden. When this was not so they became angry. And as the secular fellows outnumber them two to one, they feel any criticism as a disparagement which must be promptly answered, else their antagonists will overwhelm them."

"And now each faction accuses the other of stealing your books?"

"Aye. You overheard yesterday's dispute?"

"We did."

"As I am no monk, the secular fellows are convinced 'tis the monks who have done this... to force me out."

"And you, what do you think?"

"Monks or seculars," Wyclif mused, "it must be one or the other guilty."

"Not some thief from outside the Hall?"

"The porter saw no stranger about the Hall."

"It was while you were at supper they were taken?"

"Aye."

"So had some miscreant been about, it might have been too dark for the porter to see him?"

"Aye," Wyclif agreed.

"Them scholars' gowns is black," Arthur commented from his corner. "Make 'em hard to see of a night... did a man not want to be seen."

"While you supped, did any leave the table, seculars or monks?"

"Nay," Wyclif spoke firmly. "'Tis a puzzle. No stranger sought entrance from the porter, nor was any such seen about. So the deed must have been done by one within the Hall. But we were all at supper."

"Your logic, Master John, is impeccable, as always. But it must be flawed. Even though all of your scholars, secular and monks, were at table, it seems sure that one of them, at least, gave guidance in this matter."

"To whom?"

"Ah, you have me there. This is what I must search out. The porter says none were about, but as all the residents of the Hall were at their meal, there was surely one, or more, to do the theft."

Master John went to scratching the back of his head again. "Aye, it must be as you say. But why, if the thief was a stranger to the Hall, must it be a scholar gave direction?"

"How would an alien know which chamber was yours, or know the value of your books... or know that you kept them in your chamber rather than in the library?"

"An' 'twould take more'n one, I'm thinkin'," Arthur commented. "I seen scholars carryin' books on the street. One thief didn't get many books away by hisself. How many was took?"

"Twenty-two," I replied.

"One thief didn't get twenty-two books over the wall," Arthur declared.

Over the wall! A man wearing a scholar's black gown could go over the wall near where Master John's chamber butted against it. Such a man might pass about the yard in little danger of being seen. The porter would be looking out from the gatehouse toward St John's Street. The scholars would be at their meal.

"Come," I urged, and led the way from Master John's chamber into the yard. The scholar and Arthur followed obediently into the morning sunlight, questioning expressions upon their faces.

There were but three short lengths of the Canterbury Hall wall which were exposed to the yard. Most of the wall formed the exterior of the hall, the kitchen, the scholars' cells, and the chapel. But on either side of the entrance gate the interior of the wall was exposed, and on the south extension there was a short length of open wall, between Master Wyclif's chamber and the hall. I turned my steps in that direction.

The cobbled yard extended here to the wall. I studied the cobbles, and looked to the top of the wall. The stones were silent.

The wall about Canterbury Hall is not imposing. I stood on my toes, reached as high as I could, and came within a hand's breadth of the top of the enclosure. A man would need but a short ladder to climb over the wall, but the cobbles at my feet would leave no mark if a ladder had once rested there. Outside the wall, however, might be another matter.

Master John and Arthur studied me while I studied the wall and the cobbles at its base. While I examined the wall a bell rang from the nearby priory Church of St Frideswide. I recognized the bells. I had heard them ring out to summon students to battle during the St Scholastica Day riots, when I was new to Oxford as a student at Balliol College.

"Time for mass," Wyclif explained. Arthur and I followed him to the chapel as scholars left their cells and moved silently across the yard to join our small procession.

I could not keep my thoughts on worship. My mind reviewed what I had learned of Canterbury Hall, which was little enough. I pondered monks and antagonistic secular scholars, the weight of twenty-two books, and ladders.

My brooding mist dissolved when Master John concluded his sermon, performed the kiss of peace, and then passed the gospel to the scholars who, each in turn, also kissed God's word. I watched intently to see did any shy from this duty. For a man to kiss the gospel while he hid evil in his heart would be a grave sin, as all present in the chapel, even Arthur, knew. My hope for easy resolution of theft was frustrated. All kissed the holy book with fervor. Either all were innocent of complicity in larceny, or one, at least, had no fear for his soul.

It was time for dinner when mass was done. I began to recognize the diet of Canterbury Hall. The meal was another pease pottage with a maslin loaf, cheese, and ale. The pottage was flavored again with bacon, and the ale was fresh. The meal was hot, tasty, and filling. But a man could soon become weary of the fare. Perhaps this was one reason the scholars of Canterbury Hall were so contentious.

It was the work of the fellows to take down the tables after the meal. During the week the benches would then be arranged for disputation, and the tables set up again for supper. There would be no debates this day; it was Sunday. But the tables were stacked against the wall regardless of the day.

The work was none of Master John's, so he left the hall immediately after his dinner was finished. I followed, and Arthur trudged behind. The tedium of the diet at Canterbury Hall seemed not to affect Arthur's appetite. I believe he would have preferred to stay for another bowl of pottage.

Master Wyclif turned and spoke when we were well away from the hall and any listening ear. "You spoke of ladders," he reminded me.

"Indeed. But if a ladder was propped against the inner side of the wall, it would leave no mark against the cobbles. We must go out and inspect the outer side of the wall."

We did. But before we passed through the gate I stepped off the distance from the end of Master John's chamber to the front wall, on Schidyard Street; seventeen paces. Outside the wall, at the corner where south and east walls meet, I began to step off the distance, and stopped when I completed seventeen paces.

This experiment was also a disappointment. There

were no cobbles here, outside the wall, but if a ladder was recently placed here the mark was lost in the foliage which found the warmth of a sun-warmed south wall agreeable.

I was unwilling to give up the search so easily. A closer inspection was needed. I knelt and on hands and knees inspected the ground about the base of the wall. I assumed a ladder tall enough to top the wall would have its base one pace or a little more from the foot of the wall. So it was along such a line I searched. Arthur grasped my intent and wordlessly joined me in examining the sod. This was a fruitless enterprise. We gained only soiled hands and stained chauces at the knees.

Arthur's remark that a thief or two had come over the wall had seemed to me so likely that I was reluctant to give up the theory, although I had found no evidence that it was so.

"Nothing, eh?" Wyclif observed.

I shook my head, brushed mould from hands and knees, and turned my gaze to the nearby structures which lay close to the south wall of Canterbury Hall. Of these there were few. Three houses stood between Canterbury Hall and the town wall, where the wall abutted St Frideswide's Priory. These housed, I assumed, three families and their businesses.

The buildings were much alike; two stories, with shops and workrooms below, the family living quarters above. They were of timber, wattle and daub. Two had recently thatched roofs; one roof, however, was old and decayed and whoever slept beneath it was going to awaken often in a damp bed. Whatever business occupied these homes, it was seemingly enough to keep them, but not enough to bring prosperity. In difficult times like this, perhaps that is all a man can ask of his craft.

A muddy lane led from Schidyard Street and gave access to these structures. As the homes faced this lane, it was the tofts at the rear of the houses which abutted the south wall of Canterbury Hall.

The tofts were not large, nor were they walled. They

appeared to be cultivated. Indeed, the last of the season's cabbages and turnips were yet unharvested from the toft nearest Schidyard Street.

No sound of labor or commerce came from the houses. This was the Lord's Day. The inhabitants were enjoying their day of rest.

I turned to Master John, ready to acknowledge defeat, when my eye scanned the side of the middle house. A ladder lay on the turf close by the west wall of the structure. It was in shadow, nearly invisible as it lay, one side on the earth, the other propped low against the side of the house.

I pointed to the ladder: "Look there." Arthur and Master John followed my arm, then turned to me. A look of triumph flickered across the scholar's face.

"Whose houses are these?" I asked.

"A cobbler and two who deal in wool... yarn spinners."

"The middle house?"

"A yarn-maker, I think. The fellow's wife and daughters card and comb and work the distaff. The husband busies himself with buying and selling."

The middle house featured the decaying roof. "I think wool may not provide much custom," Master John observed.

"Nay," Arthur agreed. "Not since the great dyin'. Them as is dead have no need o' new garments, an' them as live can wear what the dead need no more."

I walked across the muddy toft to the rear of the yarn-spinner's house and rapped upon the door. I heard a bench scrape across a flagged floor – perhaps there had once been more prosperity in this house than at present – and the door cracked open. The man who stood in the opening was clearly puzzled to have callers in his toft. He peered from me to Arthur to Master John. I thought a flash of recognition crossed his features when he saw Master Wyclif.

"The ladder which lays aside your house, for what is it used?"

The fellow was puzzled by my question. Why should three men, one in the black gown of a scholar, approach his home through the toft on a quiet Sunday afternoon and enquire about a ladder?

"'Tis the thatcher's," he answered. "Me roof is bad. Needs redone afore winter."

The questioning look never left the man's face while he provided this simple answer. He surely sought some reason why three strange men should enquire about a ladder.

"You need to borrow a ladder?" he finally asked. "Thatcher won't mind, I'm thinkin', so long as it's back 'ere when he begins work."

"When will that be?"

"Soon, I 'ope. Thought he was to begin last week."

"How long has the ladder been here?"

"Dropped it off with a cart-load of reeds near a fortnight past. Reeds is out front. 'Ope 'e gets round to me roof soon, 'fore November rains set in."

"Does the ladder lay now just as it did when the thatcher left it?"

"Dunno... paid no heed."

"Would you come and have a look?"

"Aye. What's all this about?" The yarn-spinner peered at Master John. "You be of Canterbury Hall?"

"I am," Wyclif replied.

"Thought I seen you there. Does the Hall need a ladder, the thatcher won't mind yer usin' 'is... won't know of it anyway, so long as you bring it back."

The four of us passed the corner of the house and gazed upon the ladder. "Is it as it was when the thatcher left it?" I asked.

"Can't say. Paid no mind." The puzzled expression returned to the fellow's face as he realized we intended to borrow no ladder. An explanation was in order.

"Property has gone missing from Canterbury Hall. 'Tis possible some felon used a ladder to get over the wall, just there." I pointed to the wall, some twenty paces away.

Understanding, then apprehension washed across the yarn-spinner's countenance.

"I'm an honest man, an' no thief," he protested.

"We do not accuse you," I assured him, "but it's possible the stolen goods were taken by one who gained entrance to the Hall over the wall."

"An' so you want to know has the ladder been moved?" The yarn-spinner grasped my intent. "I been busy with work. Gave no thought to the thatcher's business... 'E hasn't begun yet, so..."

The man's voice trailed off with his thoughts.

"Have you seen, in the past fortnight, any man walking along the wall?"

"Nay. None pass there. Where would a man go did 'e walk behind me toft along that wall? His journey would lead 'im no place."

"No place an honest man need go," Arthur added.

We stood between the yarn-spinner's house and that of the cobbler as we discussed ladders and walls. While we spoke my gaze drifted over the town wall to the water meadow to the south and the willows lining the banks of the Cherwell. Two figures walked there; a woman dressed in a long cotehardie of blue, and a man wearing parti-colored chauces, a red cotehardie, and a cap ending in a long yellow liripipe. The couple were two hundred paces from me, and walking away, so I could not see their faces. I did not need to.

The sight of Kate and Sir Simon caused me to lose the thread of our conversation. The others noted this and followed my eyes to the south. We four stared at the strolling pair, and Arthur began to sing in a cracked voice, "It was a lover an' his lass, with a hey, with a ho, with a hey nonnny, nonny, no."

The yarn-spinner and Master John chuckled at this wit. Then Wyclif noticed my face and fell silent.

I turned my face from Kate Caxton to the riddle before me: Master John's missing books. Any man who had seen Mistress Kate might wonder that I was able to do so. Truth is, the resolve did not last long.

I have found it helpful when faced with a puzzle to write of events and possible solutions, placing my thoughts on parchment. Doing so keeps my mind ordered, and some minor incident, when inked on parchment, can take on new significance.

So as Master Wyclif, Arthur, and I trudged along the wall and back to the porter and the gatehouse, I asked Master John for parchment, quill, and ink. Also for a table and bench. These were brought to the guest chamber. I set Arthur free for the afternoon, told Master John of my intent, and until the tenth hour sat scratching my thoughts on parchment. I wondered if I was wasting parchment. And yes, more than once my thoughts strayed to Kate Caxton.

Master John's books were gone, likely taken by more than one man. The porter, did he speak truthfully, saw no one enter the hall. The scholars, both monks and seculars, were at supper when the thieves struck. But these felons knew where to go, so some knowledge of the Hall might have been passed to them. Or perhaps the thieves were formerly attached to Canterbury Hall. Or perhaps they were simply in luck when they entered Master John's chamber.

Arthur's guess that a ladder was used to gain entrance had seemed worth pursuing, but when the wall and grounds about it were examined no sign of a ladder's use was found. Nevertheless, a ladder was readily available. But would a thief, intent on stealing Master John's books – a thing which must have been contemplated for many days – know that the thatcher's ladder would be conveniently propped against the yarn-spinner's house? Perhaps, if a ladder was used, the thieves brought their own, and the presence of the thatcher's ladder was but coincidence.

To what man would the books be most valuable? A scholar, surely. Or who would most like to see Master John bereft of his volumes? Oxford is a den of scholarly vipers, each seeking eminence above others. Did some master take this way to avenge himself against a slight from Wyclif?

"Too many folk here in a hurry," Arthur announced, breaking upon my thoughts as he entered the guest chamber. "Even on the Lord's Day, scurryin' 'ere an' there. Bampton be more to my likin'."

His remarks concluded, Arthur sat heavily upon the other bench and stared at me, then at the parchment before me. What I had written there was meaningless to him, but he peered at the writing with a confident expression, as if the mystery of stolen books could be explained through the mystery of writing.

I laid the quill aside, picked up the parchment, and told Arthur, "Here are no answers, only questions."

"An' when you find answers to the questions, you find books, eh?"

"Aye. And not all of the questions need answers. Only the proper questions must be explained."

"Trouble is," Arthur observed, "you don't know yet of the questions you writ which ones 'tis need answers. That right?"

"Aye. I must choose what I will search for first – books, or the thief who plundered them. If I find the thief, I will then find the books. But the act of thievery is past, so how I am to trace the felon I do not know. If I find the books, I might then learn who it was who took them, and how, for the books are surely not destroyed, and are searchable."

"Seems to me," Arthur replied, "what Master Wyclif wants most is his books. Did he never know the thief he'll be satisfied, long as 'e has 'is books. T'other hand, 'e'd not be pleased to know who 'twas took 'em did 'e never see 'em again."

Arthur made sense. Find the books. See justice for the thief after. If the books were ever offered for sale, my work would be easier. If they had become part of some scholar's library, I must fail. How could I inspect every library in every house and hall and college in Oxford?

The first thing to do was to visit the stationers of Oxford and leave with each a list of the stolen volumes. I sought Master John and procured another sheet of parchment upon which I made seven lists of the stolen works. This business I did not conclude until the sun was below Oxford's rooftops and the bell rang for supper. I include the list:

Rhetoric: Aristotle
Perspective: Witelo
Institutes: Priscian
Categories: Aristotle
Ethics: Aristotle
Metaphysics: Aristotle
Sentences: Lombard
Topics, Books 1, 2, and 3: Boethius
Topics, Book 4: Boethius
Elements: Euclid
Almagest: Ptolemy
Historia Scholastica: Comestar
Commentary on Aristotle's "Physics": Grosseteste
Commentary on Posterior Analytics: Grosseteste
De causa dei: Bradwardine
Holy Bible
De Actibus Animae: Wyclif
De Logica, three volumes: Wyclif
Borrowed:
Moralia on Job: Gregory the Great
Historia Ecclesiastica: Bede

Chapter 4

Arthur and I set off Monday morning to visit the stationers and booksellers of Oxford. Of such establishments there had been six when I was a lad at Balliol College. I assumed Caxton's shop would make seven. I was wrong.

I determined to visit the other stationers first, as I hoped there might be other business to detain me at Caxton's. I left the sixth list at a shop on the Northgate Street, and passed two other stationers new to me before Arthur and I arrived at Holywell Street before Caxton's open shutters. I must copy two more lists.

We entered the shadowed shop and blinked in the dim interior. Caxton, behind his desk, looked up, saw me, and spoke a greeting. I thought I saw something of pleasure and relief in his eyes, but perhaps my vision was but obscured by the shadows.

"Master Hugh," Caxton greeted me as he rose from his bench. "I am pleased to see you again. I feared, with winter near upon us, you might not call again 'til May."

"I have business in Oxford," I replied.

"Always business, Master Hugh? Never pleasure?"

"Ah, well, I had hoped to combine the two."

"Perhaps hope is not enough, Master Hugh. Perhaps you should be more businesslike in seeking pleasure."

I was well rebuked.

"Business before pleasure. I have a list of books stolen from Master John Wyclif near a fortnight past." I handed the summary to Caxton and he held it close before his nose to read. "Twenty-two books missing. Has any man wished to sell a volume from the list?"

Caxton read the list carefully before he answered.

"A sergeant asked the same ten days ago, but he had no list. A penniless scholar wished to sell a copy of Ovid's *Metamorphoses* last week, but that is not on your list, and he has not returned. I think another stationer made better offer. But no... none of these have been offered. If so any are, I am to seek you straightaway, is this not so?"

"Aye. Master John has asked my assistance, and Lord Gilbert has commissioned me to seek books and felons."

Arthur stood behind me, cap in hand, in the door of the shop, during this conversation. So it was that when Kate slipped past him she could not see into the dim interior of the building to see who it was who spoke to her father. Arthur is so constructed as to block a view quite well.

Arthur's place also obstructed my sight, so when Kate put her hand to mouth and blurted, "Master Hugh!" I was as startled as she. And she was but a dark shape in the door, the bright street and city wall behind her. But a pleasing shape.

An awkward silence followed, finally broken when Caxton announced that he had business to attend to in the workroom. Arthur may not read words on a page, but he can read the times. He advised that he was off to the Stag and Hounds to see to the horses and disappeared through the shop door as Caxton vanished into his workroom.

I managed to stammer a greeting and express pleasure that I should find Kate well. Perhaps that was an assumption, but she certainly appeared well.

"I thought, after last week, you might not return," she replied. "I am pleased to be wrong."

My wits were scrambled. This was not a new experience when in the presence of a comely maid. I managed to speak the wrong words. "I... uh, have business in Oxford... for Master John Wyclif."

Her countenance fell. "Oh. I thought, perhaps..."

I saw my error and hurried to undo it. "I was pleased when this duty brought me to Oxford, for there is another matter here which calls for my attention."

"What are these two matters, Master Hugh?"

"I seek a thief, and have designs to become one myself."

Kate had moved to stand beside the open shutter. My words puzzled her. Her eyebrows rose and forehead furrowed.

"I will explain. Master John Wyclif, newly appointed warden of Canterbury Hall, has suffered a grievous loss. Twenty-two books of his were stolen from his chamber a fortnight ago while he was at supper."

"You think the thief may try to sell the stolen books?" she mused.

"Aye. I have brought your father a record of the missing volumes. But none have been offered him for sale."

"And what of the other business which brings you to Oxford? You seek to become a thief? I am at a loss, Master Hugh."

"Aye, a thief. A thing may be stolen yet violate no law."

"You speak in riddles," she pouted.

"I will make me plain. I seek to steal a heart."

"Ah... you speak aright, Master Hugh. Against such a theft there is no law, although mayhap a lifetime of penalty result."

"Penalty?"

"Indeed. Dare a man steal a maid's heart, he will own an obligation his life long... although some husbands there may be who do not see it so."

"Perhaps some husbands see such an obligation as onerous, rather than a delight."

"So you seek such an obligation and think gaining it a joy?"

"I do, and I would."

"Then the maid is to be congratulated, I think, should you succeed in this theft."

"I trust she may always think so."

"But perhaps theft is unnecessary. Perhaps a heart may be given, and need not be stolen."

"'Twould surely be best, I think."

"And what progress have you made in these matters?"

"Little, I fear. I have left a register of the stolen volumes with most of Oxford's stationers. But there are two more since I was in attendance at Balliol College... and your father. So I must prepare two more lists."

"If the thief took the books for his own library, what then?" Kate asked.

"This is a worry. Should none of the missing works appear at an Oxford stationer for sale, then I am at a loss. I will vex myself no more at present, and allow concern for the future to care for itself. Our Lord Christ said, 'Sufficient to the day is the evil thereof.'"

"And the heart you would steal... has this been chosen?" She could not hide a smile as she spoke.

"Aye, it has. But I am not a practiced thief, and know little of how such robbery may be accomplished. I thought to walk the water meadow on the banks of the Cherwell to think on it. There is a path there, I have heard. Would you accompany me?"

"I will, Master Hugh, does my father not need me."

Robert Caxton did not need his daughter for any pressing business, and I caught a glimpse of him peering out from his workroom door as Kate and I left the shop.

We strolled east on Holywell Street to Longwall Street, past the Trinitarian Friars and St John's Hospital, thence to the Cherwell and its fringe of willows at the East Bridge. The grass of the water meadow was short, cut for winter fodder and now but brown stubble. Across the meadow I could see, past the town wall, the wall of Canterbury Hall and the houses which stood before it. These structures lay upon rising ground, and so overlooked the town wall. To the west of Canterbury Hall the spires of St Frideswide's Priory Church rose toward the heavens.

My attention was drawn to the three houses abutting Canterbury Hall. Three men crawled about the roof of the center dwelling. The yarn-spinner would soon have a new roof.

Kate followed my eyes and noted also the activity two hundred paces to the north. I had turned my gaze back to the sluggish stream. Moving water has always held attraction for me, whether the muddy Wyre, near my childhood home at Little Singleton, or Shill Brook, at Bampton. But Kate was yet observing the thatchers and so saw as one lost his grip near the peak of the roof, slid down the slope, and dropped from the eave to the ground. I heard her catch her breath as this mishap, unknown to me, unfolded before her eyes. I turned and saw her hand rise to her lips.

"What has happened?"

"A thatcher has fallen from that rooftop just now. I saw him drop. Come... your skills may be needed."

Kate grasped my arm and drew me in haste from the path and across the brown stubble of the meadow to the Southgate and thence up to St Frideswide's Lane, leading east around the priory.

The fallen thatcher had been lifted to a sitting posture when Kate and I reached him. His companions were attempting to discover the extent of his injury, but this was obvious. He clutched his left shoulder with his right hand and cried imprecations whenever his companions touched the offended spot. The thatcher, I guessed, had fallen upon his shoulder and broken his collarbone, or perhaps dislocated the shoulder, or maybe both.

I had some experience with dislocated shoulders, having restored Bampton's miller from such an injury, but had never treated a broken collarbone. Indeed, little treatment is possible for such a hurt.

As we came upon the fallen thatcher he was loudly berating the friend who had unwisely sought to examine the injury. His cries included utterances unsuited for a maid's ears, but Kate did not blush. Rather, she pushed me toward the thatchers and spoke:

"We saw your friend fall. This is Master Hugh de Singleton, a surgeon. Perhaps he may serve..."

"A surgeon?" one repeated. "Aye, that we do need. Aymer, do you hear? The lad's a surgeon. Fix you up in no time."

Aymer seemed unimpressed with this announcement and continued to groan and voice anathema against the roof which had tossed him to the ground.

Aymer's companions stood away from him and I knelt before him in their place. He quieted and peered at me, propped up now by his right hand upon the earth behind him.

The fall had dropped the thatcher nearly before the cottage door. As I went to my knees to inspect the injury, I saw the yarn-spinner and his wife, attracted from the distaff by the commotion, observing the scene from the open door.

"You struck the ground upon your shoulder?" I asked.

"Aye," he grimaced. "'Eard somethin' pop, like, when I hit. Don't remember nothin' else 'til the lads sat me up."

"Can you move the fingers of your left hand?"

Aymer looked to his hand, wiggled the fingers, and seemed astonished that they functioned well.

"What did I do to meself?"

"I believe you have broken your collarbone, and perhaps suffered a dislocated shoulder as well. I must conduct an examination to be certain."

"Can you do aught for me?"

"Aye... when I have learned the nature of your injury."

"Best have at it then."

I took the thatcher's left wrist in my hands and squeezed. He made no response. I moved the pressure up his arm to the elbow. Still he made no complaint.

"You have broken no bone below the elbow," I told him.

I then pressed firmly upon his bicep. The fellow winced. "You feel pain there?" I asked.

"Nay, not in me arm. But when you pulled on me arm, me shoulder hurt."

"'Tis as I thought. But I must make one more test to see did you dislocate your shoulder. This may distress you some."

I took the man's shoulder joint between the fingers of both hands and pressed to see was the joint as God made it. Aymer drew in his breath sharply, but made no other complaint. It was his good fortune I needed to make no other examination. The shoulder was not out of joint.

"'Tis my belief," I said as I stood to my feet, "that you have broken your collarbone and this is your only injury. Such a fracture can heal, but you may do no work until Christmastide. Your shoulder must be held immobile for many weeks."

Aymer frowned, and peered up at me with concern and question in his eyes. "'Ow do I do me work?"

"You do not... until Christmastide."

Aymer looked up to his cohorts. They stared back silently. No offer of aid was made. From Michaelmas to Christmas must surely be the busy season for a thatcher, when folk renew their roofs for winter with reeds cut at end of summer.

I turned to the yarn-spinner, observing from his door, and asked him to draw a bench to his door where I might set my patient. I had had enough of kneeling in the mud to inspect the injury.

A bench was provided, and the two undamaged thatchers assisted Aymer to it. But for his tender shoulder the fellow seemed whole enough and did not wince as he was helped from the mud to the bench.

I asked the yarn-spinner for a length of cloth. It need not be linen or wool. A cheap hempen fabric would suit. While the man entered his cottage to seek out such a fragment I left my patient, with assurance that I would soon return to set his fracture aright, and with Kate at my side walked 'round the Canterbury Hall wall to the entrance gate.

Kate was required to await my return outside the gate at the porter's hut. No women are permitted in Canterbury Hall's precincts so that the monks there remain unsullied by their presence. Some monks seem well sullied even without females at hand. But it is true, the sight of Kate might well cause a man to reconsider his vows.

I went to the guest chamber and from my box I drew two pouches. One contained the dried and pulverized seeds and root of hemp, the other dried, pounded lettuce. I returned forthwith to Kate, who surely felt out of place standing unaccompanied before the gate to Canterbury Hall. There were women of Grope Lane who stood so near Balliol College when I was a student. I did not wish Kate to be associated with their employment.

Together we hurried down Schidyard Street to the yarn-spinner's cottage. My patient sat where I left him. The yarn-spinner stood behind with a length of brown hempen fabric. I asked the man for a cup of ale. He frowned at this added expense for his roof, but grudgingly entered his cottage and returned a moment later with what appeared to be a cup of well-watered ale. Watered or not, it would serve.

I emptied part of both pouches, hemp and lettuce, into the cup and stirred the mix with a splinter of broken reed from the thatchers' work. This I gave Aymer to drink.

"This potion will dull the pain when I must prod your shoulder to see the bones set firm against one another," I explained.

Aymer took the cup with his good hand and, watered though it was, drank the potion down with approval, and a belch when he had drained the cup.

"The remedy will take effect in an hour or so. I will have you wait upon the bench, your back to the cottage wall. Your friends may be about their work while you rest here. I will be about my business and return when 'tis time to see to the injury."

I saw one of the thatchers turn and grin toward the other. If the fellow deduced my business, it was no concern to me. I offered my arm to Kate and we set off down the muddy path to St Fridewide's Lane, Fish Street, the water meadow, and the path along the Cherwell.

"Will the thatcher's shoulder mend?" Kate asked as we stumbled across the stubble.

"Aye, does he do as he is told and leave his work so the fracture will heal."

"So 'tis a break, then?"

"I cannot be sure 'til I feel my way across his shoulder."

"And this examination will be painful?"

"Aye. But the hemp and lettuce potion will diminish the hurt. Some."

We regained the path, and reversed our direction, walking in silence for a time along the stream, ducking under the occasional low-hanging willow branch.

"The theft you intend... when will you strike?" Kate asked.

"Soon, I think. Time lost in such a venture may never be reclaimed, and I have squandered much already."

We came to the end of the path, where the Cherwell flows under the East Bridge, and turned to walk back through the Eastgate to the town and my patient.

"There is time," I said, "to return you to your father before I see to the thatcher. Or, if you wish, you may accompany me while I see to him and we will return to Holywell Street after."

"I will remain with you. I think my father had no pressing work for me this day."

It was as I expected. When I put my fingers to Aymer's collarbone I felt the fractured ends move under my touch. And the shoulder was swelling, turning red and purple beneath the skin. Aymer gasped as the broken bones grated against each other. I have used hemp and lettuce before, with good result. God provides much for men to ease their suffering in this world. But he has provided nothing which will end all suffering. So Aymer's pain was less than might have been, but was real enough. Pain is God's way of telling us not to do some things again. Surely Aymer, when he is next upon a roof, will take more care.

The break was clean, so far as my probing fingers could discover. I placed the fractured ends of the broken collarbone together so well as I could, which was not difficult, as the bone is but beneath the skin in that place. I also had in my pouch a vial of oil of rue, mixed with oil of ginger root. This concoction I rubbed gently about the thatcher's swelling shoulder. Both rue and ginger relieve pain, but rue must not be applied alone or blisters will rise where it touches the skin, and the cure becomes worse than the complaint.

When I had the bones in place I set Aymer's arm across his stomach and made a sling from the hempen home-spun the yarn-spinner had produced. I supported Aymer's arm in the sling, tied it behind his neck, and pronounced the work complete.

"You must take care to keep your arm in the sling 'til St Stephen's Day. You may then return to your work, but take care, even so. Where the bone has knit it will be weak for many months even after the sling may be discarded."

"'Til when?"

"You should be near good as new by Candlemas."

The thatcher shrugged, and winced, as his injury taught him that he must in future express himself in another way.

"'Ow much do I owe ye?" he asked, rising tentatively from his bench.

This thatcher was not a wealthy man. His chauces were torn from close contact with the reeds and stained, and his cotehardie was faded and threadbare. "Ha'penny for the potion, and a farthing to the yarn-spinner for his ale and hempen cloth."

It was now past noon, and my growling stomach reminded me of the time. I waited while the thatcher explored his purse for coins, and when he had done and placed a ha'penny in my hand I offered my arm to Kate and we set off for Holywell Street and her father's shop.

"I fear this morning's distraction will cause your father concern."

"He will understand, when he learns the cause of our delay. After all, it was your skills gave him relief for the wound which troubled his back."

"He may be concerned for his dinner."

"There is a capon in the pot, which I set to stewing this morning. What of your dinner, Master Hugh?"

"I will return to Canterbury Hall."

"It may be that the scholars there will have taken their meal already."

"The cook will find something for me, I think."

"The capon is fat. You shall dine with father and me."

Kate spoke this not as an invitation, but as a conviction. A capon seemed to me an improvement to the usual pottage and loaf at Canterbury Hall. I made no objection.

We walked through the Smithgate on to Holywell Street but forty paces from Caxton's shop. As we did a figure appeared in the door, leaving the place. The man was tall, with a close-trimmed dark beard, wore parti-colored chauces, a green cotehardie, and a yellow liripipe coiled about his head.

Sir Simon Trillowe saw us approach and frowned mightily, so that his dark brows met above his nose. He took no step in our direction but stood fast before the shop and observed us through narrowed eyes.

"Sir Simon," I greeted him with a bow.

Trillowe made no reply to me, but turned to Kate and spoke. "Mistress Kate... your father said you were out. Perhaps I am too late to ask if we might walk again along the Cherwell?"

"Aye, Sir Simon. I am needed this afternoon in the shop."

Trillowe smiled grimly at Kate, glared at me, and strode west toward Canditch and the castle.

It was well past noon and the bell at the Augustinian Friary rang for nones when Kate, her father, and I sat at the workroom table for our dinner. The capon had stewed all morning in a broth with turnips and leeks and was delicious. I did not wish to be thought a glutton, so contented myself with a modest portion. But when I had finished Kate spooned out another helping to my bowl.

I protested, but she knew it was but for courtesy and ladled the bowl full. Robert Caxton looked up from his own spoon with a benign expression. I was pleased that the stationer did not seem to think I was presuming upon either his dinner or his good nature.

While we ate Kate told her father of the injured thatcher and my ministrations to him.

"'Tis a good thing to be able to help men so," Caxton affirmed between bites of turnip. "My back seems now good as ever since you drew the splinter from it."

"Father kept the splinter," Kate laughed, "and shows it to all who are willing to hear the tale of his wound."

I was pleased to learn that word of my skills might thus become known, but it seems unlikely that an injured man would forsake the physicians and surgeons of Oxford to seek me at Bampton. It is good when men speak well of you, even if no profit follow.

I was reluctant to leave the stationer's shop when the meal was done. Had you seen Kate and spent time in her presence you would understand. I have written these words before. They bear repeating. And lurking in my mind was an apprehension that Sir Simon might return while I was away.

Nevertheless I bid Kate and her father "good bye" – after praising the meal. Kate can cause a man to forget himself, but I kept enough of my wits about me that I remembered to thank her for dinner.

Only after I left the stationer's shop did I think of Arthur. I have written that Kate had such an effect upon me. Perhaps Arthur had gone to the stables behind the Stag and Hounds and seen to our horses. Then he might have dined at the inn. Or perhaps he returned to Canterbury Hall and was fed there. I set my feet toward Canterbury Hall. If I did not find Arthur there, he might return later and find me.

I found him. Arthur had drawn a bench from the guest chamber and sat upon it against the chamber wall, drowsing in the afternoon sun. I might have some worry for his welfare, but it was clear he had little concern for mine. Considering the company in which he last saw me, this was understandable.

Arthur became aware of my approach, and jerked upright when he saw me. He seemed abashed that I had found him lazing in the sun, but I hold nothing against a man who seeks the simple pleasures God provides when no duty calls him.

"Are the horses well?" I asked.

"Aye. They be fine. An' Mistress Kate?" Arthur grinned.

"Likewise. There are more stationers in Oxford than when I last resided in the town. I must copy two more lists."

"What do you want of me? Can't serve with copyin'."

Arthur has many skills, but dealing with books and words on a page are not among them. I thought of another employment for him.

"Go to Northgate Street, and perhaps the castle foregate, and keep your ears open. It seems unlikely that a despoiler of books would seek to sell them there. But I have few other plans. Perhaps a careless thief may let a word slip, and it be repeated."

Many days had passed since the theft. If a robber wished to sell his plunder he would surely do so straightaway, not wait near a fortnight. Or would he? I had no better notion, so Arthur set off and I went to the guest chamber to copy two more lists.

I might have saved ink, parchment, and time. The stationers to whom I took the lists had not been presented any of the books registered, although both gave ready assurance that, should a volume from the list be offered, they would report the business to me at Canterbury Hall. I had no reason to doubt their word, but it occurred to me as I departed the second stationer on Great Bailey Street that, for a share of the profit, a man might close his eyes to the misdeeds of a felon. There was little I could do about that. No man can change the nature of another. Only the Lord Christ can do so, and then only if the one whose soul is altered be willing.

There was again a pease pottage with leeks and maslin loaves for supper. I thought of the meal I might have enjoyed at Bampton Castle had I supped there rather than Canterbury Hall. But was I in Bampton I would not have enjoyed time and dinner with Kate Caxton. Most things worthwhile have a price.

The Angelus Bell ringing from the Priory Church of St Frideswide awoke me next morning. The tolling had not the same effect on Arthur. The man could sleep through our Lord's return.

I had become accustomed to breaking my fast with cheese and a loaf fresh from the Bampton Castle oven. I did not enjoy setting about my day with an empty stomach. Arthur agreed on this matter, but while we were guests at Canterbury Hall we must observe the regimen. This was to me further proof that I had made the proper choice when I decided I would not seek a position in the Church. Although I suppose as secular clergy with my own parish I might eat when I chose.

This day I decided to visit the monastic houses in Oxford to learn if any had recently been offered books. I sent Arthur again to the marketplace and castle foregate to listen.

The great Benedictine House in Oxford is Gloucester College. I set my feet for Stockwell Street, and arrived as the chapel bell chimed for Terce. I waited until the service was done, then sought the college librarian. The monk in charge of the college volumes was a genial fellow, well fed, who peered at me with watery eyes made weak from much attention to his manuscripts.

I did not think it necessary to provide such a man with a list of Wyclif's stolen books. He would be familiar with all the missing volumes, and most assuredly his library would include the missing titles, with the possible exception of Bede's work, which is rare and valuable.

The fellow had been offered no books, as I expected. But he readily agreed to send word to Canterbury Hall should he be approached to buy.

I returned to the Hall for my dinner. Arthur was there before me, and eager for his meal, which this day was not a pottage, but egg leaches for a first remove and eels baked in ginger for the second remove. This was a pleasant change from the Hall's normal fare. Arthur approved. He grinned at me from the far end of the table, his cheeks bulging with eels. A groom at Bampton Castle might share in egg leaches, but would never enjoy eels in ginger.

Chapter 5

I went in the afternoon to the Franciscan and Dominican Houses where friars who seek degrees at Oxford reside while at their studies. It would be a waste of parchment to write more than that they had no knowledge of Master John's books. And yes, they would send word to Canterbury Hall should any man offer to sell. But for my dinner this was a wasted day.

The cook, I think, decided he must atone for dinner. Supper this day was a white pottage of oats and leeks. Arthur ate two bowls of the stuff, but when I finished my portion I felt I should whinny like a horse did I consume more.

I had no opportunity before supper to question Arthur about his day, but did so as soon as we retired to the guest chamber after supper. I lit a cresset and asked Arthur of town gossip. He removed his cap, brushed thinning hair with thick fingers, and spoke.

"Buy a man a cup of wine at tavern an' he'll be glad to tell what 'e knows. There be many folk in Oxford don't abide by what the priests tell 'em," he began. "But you'll not be carin' about all that."

"Aye. Spare me the details of Oxford's sins. I once lived here, remember?"

"Oh, aye. Well, 'tis known about town that you seek Master Wyclif's books. 'Eard it spoke of three, four times."

"So the theft is known?"

"Aye. Not as most on Northgate Street or the castle forecourt care 'bout that. Most is like me, see, an' books is no good to 'em.

"Strange thing. Some young gentlemen was passin'

by the castle forecourt an' two was badgerin' the other. Said as how he looked a fool, chasin' a tradesman's daughter, an' her then tossin' 'im aside for a bailiff. They came near to blows. Figured I knew who was spoke of."

"Did one of these fellows have a dark beard, trimmed short, and wear a yellow cap with a liripipe coiled about his head?"

"Aye. 'Twas him the others nettled. Had 'is hand to 'is dagger before the others left off."

Sir Simon had lowered himself to court a burgher's daughter. To be rejected would injure his pride. He would blame me. Perhaps I should be on my guard.

I left Arthur to report on my progress, or lack of it, to Master John. I found him seated in his chamber, a candle before him and a borrowed book open on the table. He did not seem surprised when I told him I had no better idea now how to seek his books than the day before.

Arthur was snoring upon his pallet when I returned to the guest chamber. This music, and my thoughts, kept me awake long into the night. The sacrist of St Frideswide's Priory was rousing the canons for vigils before I slept.

There was yet Rewley Abbey and Oseney Abbey, and the friaries of the Carmelites, the Augustinians, and the Trinitarians to visit. I resolved to seek Master John's volumes in these houses next day if Arthur learned nothing more in another day of attending to Oxford gossip. While he did so I resolved to pursue another mystery: women.

I awoke with the Angelus Bell from St Frideswide's Priory to a cold, drizzling morning. Arthur was not pleased that I sent him to the castle forecourt on an empty stomach on such a day. I told him to return and we would meet for dinner. I did not tell him the business I intended to pursue. I should have.

I wrapped my cloak about me and set off for Holywell Street. This cloak was of fur, a gift from Lord Gilbert two years past as part of my wages for accepting the post of bailiff on his Bampton estate.

I had seen others peer enviously at me when I wore the garment through Oxford's streets. Such a coat was beyond my station. Let them stare. I was warm and dry.

I made my way up Catte Street, passed through the Smithgate, and had walked but two or three paces east on Holywell Street when three men stepped before me and blocked my way. My first thought was that I had been accosted by thieves and was about to be robbed of my purse. A second thought caused me to realize this was not likely. It was not the dark of night, when felons might be abroad, but day, and the men who obstructed me were not poorly dressed, as one might expect of a man willing to risk his neck to have another man's coins.

One of the three stepped toward me and demanded my name. I told him. He next asked my destination. I told him that, as well. He then asked about my coat; where had I come by it? When I told him it was a gift he rolled his eyes and turned to his companions.

One of these was a man of about my size and age. Which is to say he was some above average in height and slender. The leader of the three turned to this fellow and spoke:

"Sir William, is this the coat?"

"Aye, the very one."

The leader of this band was a brawny fellow, not of my height, but he surely outweighed me by two stone or more. He was of Arthur's size and shape. He grasped my shoulders and before I could react, so surprised was I, he spun me about and his companions stripped my coat from me.

"You are arrested," the leader told me harshly.

"Of what am I accused?" I replied, somewhat stupidly as I think back on it.

"Hah... do not take us for fools. You have stolen Sir William's fur coat."

"Not so," I replied with some heat. My wits were returning and my temper was aroused. "'Twas a gift from Lord Gilbert Talbot."

I thought the fellow hesitated for a moment. Perhaps it was my imagination. "And why should a lord give a fur coat to you?"

While I engaged the leader in this conversation Sir William was inspecting my coat. "This is my coat, Sir Thomas," he said firmly.

Sir Thomas, who still gripped my arm, turned back to me. "You were a fool to steal such a coat, and twice a fool to walk along the Cherwell with a maid where another might see you wearing a stolen coat."

I opened my mouth to protest but before I could speak the third member of the group, a short, round fellow, seized my free arm and with Sir Thomas began dragging me down Canditch toward the Northgate. A crowd of onlookers gaped at the scene, believing, I am sure, that some miscreant had been apprehended.

Sir Thomas and his silent companion alternately dragged and shoved me through the streets to Oxford Castle. Once there I was taken through stone passageways to a chamber I knew well, the anteroom and clerk's office for the sheriff of Oxford, where two years past Margaret Smith and I convinced Roger de Cottesford and a judge of the King's Eyre that they must release Thomas Shilton. Standing beside the clerk was a man I knew. Sir Simon Trillowe grinned thinly at me behind hooded eyes.

"Inform Sir John that we have caught the thief," Sir Thomas told the clerk. The man rose silently from his place, opened the heavy door behind him, and did so.

The Sheriff of Oxford appeared in the doorway moments later. His stout body nearly filled it. Small, dark eyes peered at me from a florid face which featured a large, hooked nose. He was Sir Simon's father. The nose left no doubt of that.

"Here is the stolen coat," Sir Thomas proclaimed, standing aside so Sir John could see my cloak in Sir William's hands. "We found the thief on Holywell Street, as Sir Simon said we might."

Sir Simon dropped his eyes and bowed slightly toward Sir Thomas. The smile remained upon his lips and I knew why I was apprehended and charged. What I might do to free myself was not so evident.

"'Tis yours, surely?" the sheriff asked Sir William.

"Aye. There is no doubt. A London furrier made it for me two years past. Twelve shillings it cost me."

Sir John turned to me with glaring eyes. "What have you to say for yourself?"

"The man lies... or is mistaken. His only true words are that the coat was indeed made by a London furrier. But it was made for Lord Gilbert Talbot."

"Then why would you have it?"

"A gift from Lord Gilbert. He wished me to serve him as bailiff at his Bampton estate and offered a fur coat to persuade me to agree to the post."

"He lies," Sir Simon said. Until these words he had lounged against the chamber wall, pleased with my discomfort. "I've seen Sir William with this very coat these past two years."

Sir John turned again to me and spoke through thin lips. "I think it odd that Lord Gilbert would give such a coat to a... a bailiff. I know Lord Gilbert. He is a parsimonious fellow. I doubt he owns such a coat for his own shoulders."

"Then send for him and ask," I challenged.

"I see no need to trouble Lord Gilbert when I have before me two witnesses who say you are a thief."

The sheriff turned to his clerk and spoke. "Fetch the gaoler." To Sir Thomas he said, "We are fortunate the county court is assembled this week. Trial in this matter will be Friday. Be he guilty, we may hang him Saturday."

I had no doubt but Sir Simon and his friends would make certain that I would be condemned. I tried again to convince Sir John to consult Lord Gilbert.

"Unless you send to Lord Gilbert," I cried, "you will do murder come Saturday. I am no thief. I am in Oxford to seek thieves... those who have stolen Master John Wyclif's books. And Master John has seen me wear this coat. He also can tell you 'tis mine, not Sir William's."

"Master Wyclif?" Sir John pursed his lips. "Troublesome fellow."

As the sheriff delivered this opinion his clerk appeared with a slovenly man I assumed to be the gaoler.

This conjecture was quickly proven correct. The fellow lifted shackles and chain in his left hand and expertly bolted the irons about my wrists before I could react. What good reacting might have done I cannot tell.

I was led from the clerk's chamber, through the gallery, to a stone staircase. Shadows there were dark. I could not see where the staircase ended for the gloom. The gaoler gave me a shove when he detected my reluctance and as I took the first step I heard laughter echo down the corridor from the clerk's anteroom.

I found the bottom step more by feel than by sight. The gaoler, perhaps accustomed to the shadows in which he worked, shoved me a few paces past the last step, then stopped before an indentation in the stones which, when my eyes grew more familiar with the dark, I saw to be a door.

Before I could draw another breath I heard the door swing open and received another shove which propelled me into a cell darker even, was that possible, than the corridor in which a moment before I was standing.

The gaoler slammed the door shut behind me and replaced the bar. How many men, I wondered, have heard that same sound while standing in this place? Perhaps Thomas Shilton, imprisoned on my mistaken testimony, occupied this very cell. He emerged unscathed when I learned my error. Would I escape also? This seemed doubtful, for those who placed me here knew I was no thief and if they were in error seemed glad of it.

The cell was not utterly dark. Near the top of the vaulted ceiling a slit was cut into the wall, perhaps three fingers high and a forearm long. Dim light penetrated the cell through this aperture. It perhaps opened to some shaded part of the castle yard. The slit was too high to reach, and it would have been of no use to try. Even a man as slender as I could get no more than a hand through the opening. And then only if his wrists were unshackled. Mine were not.

Some previous occupant of the cell had tried, I think, to enlarge the slot. As my eyes grew accustomed to the place I could see about the hole rounded and chipped edges to the stonework. Some wretch, bound for the gallows, had discovered some tool with which he had chiseled away at the opening. Perhaps he had scraped at the stone with the irons about his wrists. I forced the thought from my mind. I did not wish to consider how a man might tear flesh from hands and fingers in such a futile effort.

Some wretch! I was now that wretch. Did not the sheriff predict the gallows for me come Saturday? It was Wednesday. I had three days to live, did not Lord Gilbert or Master John intercede for me. Why should they? They did not know where I was, nor did any other who might be minded to aid me. So I thought.

The gloom of my spirit matched the gloom of my cell. No friend knew of my plight, and those who put me in this place would not tell them. No, this was not true. There was a friend who knew of my affliction. I knelt in the rotten rushes covering the dirt floor of the cell and called upon the Lord Christ to free me from my unjust captors. Perhaps, I hoped, He had already noted my misfortune and set a plan in motion for my freedom. But it would do no harm to remind Him of my trouble in case other matters had captured His attention. An unwelcome thought came to mind. If the Lord Christ loved and served me only so much as I loved and served Him, where then might I be?

From this point I must tell the tale as it was told to me. For two days I lived in the cell beneath Oxford Castle, awaiting my fate, unknowing of the answer to my prayers taking place outside the castle walls. I was fed stale bread, thin pottage, and foul water. I would not again complain of the cook at Canterbury Hall.

Arthur returned to Canterbury Hall for his dinner with information he thought I would be pleased to learn. But the bell rang for dinner and I did not appear. Arthur saw no reason to go hungry just because I was tardy, so sat at his place at the low end of the table and devoured two bowls of pottage with little concern for me. He told me later he assumed I had again found my dinner with Kate Caxton.

Sir Thomas Barnet, justice of the peace and he who apprehended me on the Holywell Street, was known to several onlookers at my arrest. One of these had business with Robert Caxton, and was on his way to the stationer's shop when he saw me confronted and dragged off to the castle. This tale he reported to the stationer. Kate overheard his account.

When, for the second day, I did not call at the shop, Kate became uneasy. The customer who told of my arrest was not close enough to the scene to hear of that with which I was charged, but he saw that the man seized was tall and wore a fur coat – which had been stripped from him. Kate knew I owned such a garment.

I did not appear at Canterbury Hall for my supper and Arthur knew something was amiss. He did not know where I might have gone in search of books, but did know where I might have gone in search of a maid. Although darkness was settling upon Oxford, Arthur hastened to Holywell Street. Be there a man safe from attack on a dark street, that man is Arthur. He wears the blue and black livery of Lord Gilbert Talbot. Few men wish to anger a powerful lord, even if they may not know the noble's colors, by attacking one of his servants. Grooms seldom own much worth taking, and Arthur is a powerful man, worth two in a brawl.

So he went unmolested to the stationer's shop where, after some pounding upon the door, Robert Caxton opened to him. My disappearance, and the arrest of a young man wearing a fur coat on the Holywell Street, caused much consternation at the stationer's shop that night. Arthur would have gone to the castle then, but Caxton persuaded him that he would not be received, the gate being closed for the night.

Arthur told me he spent a sleepless night, and at dawn ran to Canterbury Hall, pounded upon Master Wyclif's chamber door, and together they returned to Caxton's shop. The four then hurried to the castle and entered as a warder drew up the portcullis.

Kate said it took some time to find the sheriff. They discovered a man who directed them to the clerk's anteroom, but the sheriff was not in. They waited. When Sir John arrived he dismissed their plea for my release. He told Master John that I had been arrested and charged on presentment of evidence. He, himself, had seen the evidence. Trial would be tomorrow. Had Master John evidence he wished to set before the court, he might do so on the morrow.

The clerk showed them firmly from his office, and it was Kate who, in the castle forecourt, turned to Arthur and bid him ride to Bampton for Lord Gilbert. The county court might dismiss Robert Caxton, Kate, Arthur, even Master Wyclif, but the court would hear Lord Gilbert Talbot.

I knew nothing of this. The slot in my cell appeared in ghostly light to announce dawn, but I had no other way to learn the time. The bells of Oxford which rang for holy office could not penetrate to my place.

The gaoler returned as the light from my thin embrasure began to fade. I heard him lift the bar and the door creaked open. A bowl of cold pottage and a cup of foul water appeared in the opening. The door banged shut before I could rise from the malodorous rushes which I had gathered in one corner of the cell as my bed.

I felt no hunger. Two spoonfuls of the cold pottage and a sip of water were all I could manage. If a man were to stay long in such a place the diet might kill him before he went to the gallows.

Arthur went from the castle to the Stag and Hounds, retrieved his old palfrey, and set off across Castle Mill Stream bridge and Oseney Island as fast as the ancient beast could trot. So he told me.

By the time Arthur saw the spire of the Church of St Beornwald rise above the forest east of Bampton it was too late to return to Oxford that day. John the chamberlain ushered him to the solar, where Lord Gilbert and Lady Petronilla are pleased to sit by the fire of an evening.

Lord Gilbert heard Arthur's tale with rising fury, swore vengeance against Sir John did harm come to me, and sent Arthur first to the kitchen, for his supper, then to the marshalsea with orders to have five coursers and Arthur's palfrey ready and saddled at dawn.

The rising sun was yet but a glow above the naked branches of the forest to the east of Bampton, and the Angelus Bell ringing to announce the dawn, when Lord Gilbert, Arthur, and four other grooms thundered across the bridge over Shill Brook and rode east toward Oxford. Arthur's palfrey could not keep up the pace, but he followed with as much haste as the old beast could manage.

About the time Lord Gilbert was rattling the planks of Shill Brook bridge I was looking up to the place in my cell where dawn showed the location of the slot and the world beyond. This day the county court would find me guilty of theft. Of this I was certain, for none who knew of my innocence knew of my peril. So I believed. I knelt again on the rushes, as I had done often the day before, and asked the Lord Christ to spare me. If He chose not to do so, then I asked that I might go to my death as a Christian, bearing no unforgiven malice toward those who sought my death. Which of these requests He would find most difficult to perform I knew not.

I had not been shaved since Tuesday, and my chauces and cotehardie were wrinkled from sleeping in them and stained from lying upon the filthy rushes which were my bed. I looked a thief even was I not. Certainly Sir Thomas, Sir Simon, and Sir William hoped my disheveled appearance would lead others to accept my guilt.

I ran fingers through my hair, made myself as presentable as I could, and awaited summons to my doom. I had no way to judge the time, but thought it must be near to the sixth hour when I heard the gaoler lift the bar and squealing hinges respond.

I had seen no daylight for two days. The courtroom into which the gaoler shoved me was lit by a row of south windows. I blinked in the light and it was some moments before I saw Kate, her father, and Master John standing near the back of the hall. Their dour expressions did little to lighten my spirits, although Kate did manage a fleeting smile and fluttered her fingers in my direction. My eyes turned to others in the chamber and I saw Sir Simon scowling at me. He had observed Kate's greeting.

I blinked my way, still shackled, to the accused's box with more joy in my heart than another in my place might have felt. While stumbling up the stairway from the cells I had thought of a way to escape the gallows. In time Lord Gilbert would learn of my plight and see me freed. Until then, if it be necessary, I would plead Benefit of Clergy.

No man who can read and has his wits about him should ever face the gallows for felony. Even should the county court or the King's Eyre find him guilty, and guilty he may be, can he read from the Bible and plead Benefit of the Clergy, he will escape the hangman. What punishment a consistory court might demand would be small indeed compared to a noose. The Church hangs no man.

The bailiff shouted for silence and the din subsided. "Oyez," he cried. "All good and worthy men are called to hear the charge against Hugh de Singleton."

The judge took his place – he was none other than Sir Thomas Barnet. The king's statute of four years past gives justices of the peace the power to apprehend and try felonies in accordance with writs of *Oyer et terminer*. It was sure now I must plead Benefit of the Clergy, for there was no jury in the box to hear my plea.

Sir Thomas called Sir William to testify, which he did convincingly. Sir Thomas held out my coat. Sir William drew close to inspect it and pronounced it his own. Sir Simon was next called, and swore that he had seen his friend, Sir William, wear this very coat for two years, since his return from London, where he had joined his father, who had been called to Parliament.

"Do you answer this charge?" Sir Thomas growled and glared at me. His countenance could leave no doubt in the spectators' minds of his opinion.

"I am not guilty of this charge," I replied with as much resolve as I could muster. "The coat is my own.

'Twas a gift two years past from Lord Gilbert Talbot, as I told you two days past. You had but to send for him to know the truth, which you would not do, for truth is a thing you wish to evade."

"Silence!" Sir Thomas roared. "There are laws to deal with those who impugn the court and its officers. You have answered the charge; you will say no more."

"He may not, but I will," said a voice from the rear of the chamber. It was Master John. He pushed his way through onlookers to Sir Thomas' bench and spoke again. "I have testimony to give in this case," he declared.

"Oh? And who are you?"

"I am John Wyclif, Warden of Canterbury Hall."

I saw Sir Thomas look to Sir Simon and Sir William and shrug. They bent their heads together while Sir Thomas granted Master John permission to speak. He could do no other, for an accused man is allowed to bring three witnesses to court to testify on his behalf.

"Say what you will."

"Master Hugh speaks the truth. The coat is his and was a gift of Lord Gilbert Talbot to induce him to accept the post of bailiff on Lord Gilbert's Bampton estate. I have seen him wear this coat when he called on me here, in Oxford."

"You claim that Sir Simon, son of the sheriff, speaks perjury?" Sir Thomas asked, incredulity in his voice.

"Aye, he does. Or he cannot recognize one fur from another."

Laughter passed through the hall at this, but neither Sir Simon nor Sir William smiled.

"No other witnesses being present," Sir Thomas bellowed over the snickering, "I will consider a verdict."

Silence descended upon the court. Sir Thomas gave indication of thoughtful meditation. I knew this but artifice. My fate was already determined. So Sir Simon thought.

Sir Thomas looked up from studying his hands. His audience took this as a sign that he was prepared to announce a verdict. He was.

"In the matter of Hugh de Singleton," he announced grimly, "I find the defendant guilty as charged."

"Sir Thomas," I cried over the uproar which followed. "I claim Benefit of the Clergy."

That silenced the crowd.

"Very well," Sir Thomas looked to his bailiff. "Bring a Bible from St George's Church."

St George's Church is upon the grounds of Oxford Castle. The bailiff returned with the Holy Book in but a few moments and placed it upon the bench before Sir Thomas. He opened it at random, scanned a page, then demanded that I approach.

"To claim Benefit of the Clergy you must read a passage of Holy Writ to my satisfaction. Come and read where my finger points."

I did so. Sir Thomas had opened to the Book of Isaiah, chapter nine, verse eighteen. I read the verse:

Succensa est enim quasi ignis impietas:
Veprem et spinam vorabit,
Et succendetur in densitate saltus,
Et convolvetur superbia fumi.

When I had done I returned to my box. Sir Thomas stared gravely at the Bible, then at me, and then spoke. "Benefit of the Clergy is denied. You made errors in the passage."

"Not so!" roared Master John. "I know that scripture well. Master Hugh read it properly. 'Tis you who are in error!"

"Be silent," Sir Thomas barked. "You do not decide matters of law in this court. That is my bailiwick."

Sir Thomas turned again to me. "Hugh de Singleton, you are found guilty of theft. This court..."

A tumult from beyond the hall interrupted Sir Thomas as he was about to pass sentence upon me. I heard the echo of several agitated voices. These increased in volume rapidly.

The door at the rear of the chamber crashed open and Lord Gilbert Talbot strode into the court. His beefy face was livid above his beard, his apparel dusty. Spectators at the rear of the chamber, who had expected to hear me sentenced to the gallows, melted back from the agitated noble as ice from a flame.

Lord Gilbert spoke no word, but strode purposefully toward Sir Thomas. Three blue-and-black-clad grooms walked grim-faced behind him.

Lord Gilbert stopped before Sir Thomas, stood arms akimbo, and nodded toward me. "I am told you charge my bailiff with stealing his own coat!" he thundered.

Sir Thomas surely knew who addressed him, but in a bid to collect his thoughts said, "Who... who are you?"

"Gilbert, Third Baron Talbot. Who are you, to try my bailiff?"

"I am Sir Thomas Barnet, justice of the king's peace... with powers of *Oyer et terminer.*"

"Indeed. And who is it says this coat," Lord Gilbert lifted it from the bench, "is his and not Master Hugh's?"

Sir Thomas turned to peer at Sir William and Sir Simon. They appeared willing to dissolve into the stonework, was such a thing possible.

"Uh... 'tis... uh, much like my coat, I, uh... which was stolen a fortnight past," Sir William finally stammered.

"Careless of you, to leave a valuable garment laying about where a thief might make off with it. Where did you leave it? In the stews?"

Onlookers snickered again, much to Sir William's discomfort. Sir Thomas, his voice and vanity returning, roared out for silence. Laughter and chattering did finally subside, but not promptly. Sir Thomas' influence seemed waning.

Lord Gilbert stared at Sir William. "Where is it you purchased this coat you claim as yours?"

"Uh, London, m'lord."

"London, you say? Who was the furrier," he challenged, "and upon what street is his shop?"

"Uh... I do not remember, m'lord."

"Hah," Lord Gilbert snorted. "Then tell of what fur this coat is made."

"Uh… 'tis weasel, m'lord."

"Weasel, is it? Tell me, Sir William, do you possess lands worth four hundred marks per year?"

"What matter his wealth?" Sir Thomas spluttered.

Lord Gilbert turned from Sir William to face Sir Thomas. A look of incredulity lifted both eyebrows.

"What matter? Surely, Sir Thomas, as one sworn to uphold the King's statutes, you know of the sumptuary laws made these two years past. No knight may wear fur of weasel or ermine unless he be worth four hundred marks per year. Sir William, I ask you again, be your worth four hundred marks per year?"

"Uh… nearly so, m'lord," the fellow stammered.

"Nearly so?" Lord Gilbert rumbled. "Then if this coat be truly your own, you are in violation of the ordinance. But, you say, you cannot remember the furrier. I can. This coat is of dyed fox, and 'twas made by Andrew Adrian, of Walbrook Street. Sir Thomas, if you look inside the coat you will see Master Adrian's mark: two 'A's, embroidered in gold thread inside the left breast. Look and see if 'tis not so," he demanded.

I remembered the letters well but had never known their meaning and thought they were an elaborate "G" and "A". It was well I did not know the meaning. I might have told when protesting my arrest. Then in court Sir William would not have twitched in ignorance before Lord Gilbert.

Sir Thomas reached reluctantly for the coat before him on the bench. It was as if he thought the foxes it was made from might return to life and snap at his fingers. The chamber grew silent as he lifted the garment, peered at the lining, then looked to Sir William. I saw a smile cross Lord Gilbert's florid face and he folded his arms across his chest.

"Uh, I remember now," Sir William blurted. "Aye… 'twas Andrew Adrian, of the Walbrook Street who made my coat. I asked it be dyed to resemble weasel. I, uh, wished to be thought… uh, above my station," he admitted.

"But…" Sir Thomas protested. Before he could say

more Lord Gilbert spoke again.

"The letters embroidered there are not twin 'A's, are they, Sir Thomas?"

"Nay."

"They are 'G' and 'A', for Geoffrey Adrian... of Watling Street, not Walbrook Street, as Sir William so mistakenly now remembers. Your memory, Sir William, is exceeding poor for one so young."

Onlookers guffawed again. This time Sir Thomas was not so quick to silence the mirth. He knew it would do no good.

It was Lord Gilbert who quieted the spectators, and without a word. He turned and glowered at the observers and all fell silent.

"You are a justice of the King's peace... is this not so?" Lord Gilbert growled at Sir Thomas.

"Aye, m'lord."

"By king's writ you have power of *Oyer et terminer*." Lord Gilbert stood, arms akimbo again, was silent for a moment, then spoke quietly but with menace. "Then set this man free. There is mischief here for you to discover. That coat," he pointed to the garment before Sir Thomas, "was not stolen by Master Hugh, but 'twas about to be stolen from Master Hugh by that thief." He pointed to Sir William, who seemed ready to shrink behind Sir Simon.

The hall was silent. All awaited Sir Thomas' response. My heart skipped several beats before Sir Thomas spoke.

"My Lord Gilbert persuades me that Master Hugh de Singleton is wrongly... uh, mistakenly accused of theft. The charge is dismissed."

I looked to Lord Gilbert with a smile of gratitude. When I glanced back at the bench Sir Thomas was gone, about to pass through a door at the side of the hall. My coat lay on the bench, and I moved to retrieve it.

From the corner of my eye I saw Sir Simon and Sir William edging furtively along the wall toward the same door which had swallowed Sir Thomas. They had twice Sir Thomas' distance to cover, and another also saw their attempt to flee the chamber.

"Halt!" Lord Gilbert bellowed. They halted, eyes wide with concern. A knight should not display fear, but Lord Gilbert is of such rank and stature that even a true knight might regret causing him displeasure.

Sir Simon and Sir William stood motionless, backs against the stone wall of the chamber. Lord Gilbert advanced toward them and did not halt until his face was but a palm's width from Sir William's nose. He spoke in a whisper, but my hearing is yet acute, and Lord Gilbert's whisper, when he is angry, might deafen a man at ten paces. Lord Gilbert was indeed angry.

"What Sir Thomas may make of your perjury I know not. But this I know; do you seek to do ill again to my bailiff, I will see you suffer for it. And do not send some companion to revenge yourself on Master Hugh. Any harm which comes to him I will construe as from you. Is this understood?"

Sir William gulped air and nodded. Lord Gilbert then turned to Sir Simon, who had observed this threat with detachment. Lord Gilbert said no more, but simply glared at Sir Simon under dark brows. The man finally spoke: "Aye, m'lord."

Chapter 6

We made a procession leaving the court chamber; Lord Gilbert, me, the grooms, Kate and her father, and Master Wyclif. Our parade did not halt until we reached the castle forecourt, where a groom had remained with the horses. As we entered the forecourt Arthur arrived upon his wheezing palfrey. Lord Gilbert turned to me and spoke.

"This business is a puzzle to me. Why did that scoundrel accuse you of stealing his coat when he knew it was not so? Has he aught against you?"

"Sir William? Nothing, I think."

Lord Gilbert frowned and pulled at his beard. "Then why did he wish to see you entertain the commons with the sheriff's dance?"

"'Twas not Sir William, I think, who desired that end, but Sir Simon."

"The sheriff's son? What have you done to raise his choler? Has this to do with Master Wyclif's books?"

"Nay. I think not."

"But that was the business which brought you to Oxford, was it not? What else might provoke Sir Simon's wrath?"

"There was other business brought me here. You and the Lady Petronilla advised me on the matter."

"We did?"

"Aye. You suggested I seek a wife in Oxford."

Understanding washed across Lord Gilbert's square face. "Ah... and that quest has caused this trouble?"

"I fear so, m'lord. Sir Simon and I court the same maid."

"Hmm. Sir Simon is a proud man. Like his father."

The others of our party were privy to this conversation. One of them spoke. "No more, m'lord," Kate said.

Lord Gilbert peered over my shoulder at Kate Caxton, then met my eyes. "This is the lass?"

"Aye," I grinned. I thought I understood Kate's words and could not suppress my joy.

Lord Gilbert inspected Kate again. I turned to follow his gaze and saw her blush and curtsey in response to his scrutiny. His eyes, I thought, lingered upon her longer than was meet. Like most of his station, Lord Gilbert admires a fine horse and a comely lass. Men of any rank are much the same.

It seemed to take Lord Gilbert some effort to draw his eyes from Kate and turn them again to me. I understood his trial. I have the same difficulty when in her presence.

"I applaud your choice, Master Hugh," he beamed. "I would hear when the banns will be read."

"Ah... my suit is not yet come to such a happy conclusion, m'lord."

"No matter, no matter. Lady Petronilla will know of it so soon as may be. Your chamber off the hall in the castle will be too small for a man with a family, I think. We will move you back to Galen House. What say you, Hugh? Will that suit?"

Nobles believe they must order all men's lives, else the world come undone. But, it is true I had had similar thoughts regarding my habitation should my pursuit of Kate Caxton succeed.

"Well? Cat got your tongue?" Lord Gilbert laughed when I hesitated to reply.

"Nay, m'lord. It would suit very well... but other matters come first."

"Aye, indeed. Have faith, Hugh," he clapped me upon my back, "and seek your future. God will grant it, I think, to so loyal a servant of His as you."

I did not reply to that assertion. It seems to me God does not always grant the requests even of His saints. The Apostle Paul sought the removal of his "thorn in the flesh", but the plea was not granted.

Robert Caxton's head swiveled from me to Lord Gilbert and back again. As Lord Gilbert put foot to stirrup I turned to the stationer to see the effect of this conversation. I was gratified to see a smile play across his lips.

Lord Gilbert and the grooms, but for Arthur, mounted their steeds and clattered across the cobbles. Arthur, Robert Caxton, Master John, and I seemed drawn to the same theme and turned as one toward Kate. Whether she was yet crimson from Lord Gilbert's examination or blushed anew, I know not. An awkward silence followed, until Master John, rarely lost for words, spoke.

"I must return to Canterbury Hall. Hugh, after you have seen Mistress Kate to Holywell Street I would speak to you about the books. But no need for haste," he added before he turned away.

Arthur glanced about him briefly, decided that it was not so long past dinner that he could not discover a morsel at Canterbury Hall kitchen, and announced that he would accompany Master John and leave the palfrey at the Stag and Hounds. I offered my arm to Kate and we set off behind her father for Holywell Street.

We walked silently until our steps took us from the Canditch to Holywell Street. I searched my mind for some light topic of conversation but nothing offered. This was not the first time I found myself so. The presence of a comely lass will usually strike me dumb. Perhaps Kate had worked this distraction on other lads and understood the effect.

"'Twas Sir Simon, you think, who set the plot against you?" she offered.

"Aye, so I believe."

"Because of me, then."

"The evil another does cannot be laid to you."

"I should not have agreed when he first began his suit... but he did not seem a wicked sort then."

"What man would show the baseness in his soul when in pursuit of a maid?"

"'Tis later, I think, when the maid becomes a wife, that she knows all about her husband," Kate sighed.

"A man also, will not truly know his wife 'til they be wed," I agreed.

"Aye," Kate sighed. "It is a wonder folk wed at all... such are the hazards."

"Are there no rewards?"

She was silent for several paces, and slowed her steps so that her father was two houses ahead before she replied. "I think, if the proper mate be found, the risks in marriage be small and the compensation be great."

"We are of like mind," I replied. "I remember my parents' hall, before the great death. There was much bliss in their eyes when they were together at table, or of an evening by the fire."

"It was so with my father and mother," Kate replied with somber tone. "I was small when my mother perished, but I remember. 'Tis why I seek a man like my father."

"A stationer?"

"Nay," she laughed. "It is not the ink on a man's fingers which draws me."

"Then what?"

"It is a man's right to rule his house, yet I would seek a husband who will govern justly, as did my father."

"I wish you success. Your beauty will attract many suitors. You may sort through the swarm until you find such a fellow."

"Perhaps I have already done so... and 'tis not Sir Simon," she said firmly.

"It would give me joy to know it was so. I know I have many challengers for your hand. I wish for no new suitors for competition."

"A suitor? Why, Master Hugh, do you speak of a suit?"

"Has your father not told you? I asked his permission to pay you court. Did he not say so?"

Kate averted her eyes, and color again rose in her cheeks. "Aye. I jest with you. He did so."

"And your response?"

"You ask me to uncover a secret between a man and his daughter?"

"Nay... but I would know your heart. Do I have grounds for hope, or do I squander my time and affection?"

We had reached Caxton's shop, and stopped before the open door whence the stationer had entered a moment before.

"Your hope is pleasing to me, Master Hugh. Do not think otherwise."

"Then I am Hugh, not Master Hugh."

"Very well, you shall be Hugh, 'til God and Holy Church make you my master."

"God and Holy Church? You have also a choice in the matter, Kate."

"My choice is made," she whispered, and held my arm close.

"Shall I then speak to your father?"

"It would please me."

And so my happiness was sealed while Kate and I walked the Holywell Street to her father's shop. In but half a day I had gone from fear for my life to success in love. I was much pleased with the turn in my fortune.

We entered the shop as Caxton raised his shutters and prepared to tardily open his shop for the day. Kate looked up to me with expectation, then announced that she would prepare a meal. She disappeared through the open door to the workroom and left me standing before her father. We exchanged stares. It was my obligation to begin this conversation. I sorted through remarks I might make to open the parley. None seemed to suit. Generations of young men have faced the same trial. Caxton guessed at my distress and eased it.

"We are relieved, Kate and I, that Lord Gilbert arrived in Oxford in time." In time for what he did not say, nor did he need to.

"As am I," I smiled.

"We slept little last night. Kate shed many tears when she learned you were arrested."

No man wishes to be the cause of his beloved's tears, and I was about to say so when Caxton added, "She sobbed that she was to be made a widow before she might be a bride."

Caxton had pushed open a door. I was not so addled that I could not see and walk through it.

"It is of this I would speak. You agreed I might pay court to Kate. I have done so, and she approves my suit." I swallowed the frog in my throat and pressed on. "I wish to make her my wife."

Caxton peered somberly at me. "She approves?"

"She does."

"Will you continue to seek Master Wyclif's books and be wed also?"

"I have thought on that," I admitted. "I have no home in Oxford for a bride, and cannot seek stolen books from Bampton. Does Kate agree, we may have betrothal and read the banns so soon as she may wish, and be wed when I conclude the business of Master John's books."

"You believe this will be soon?"

"Kate will be incentive to make it so," I smiled.

"There must be time to discuss dowry and like matters," Caxton replied. "No need for haste."

That was his opinion, but not necessarily my own.

The stationer turned toward the workroom door and called for his daughter. Kate appeared immediately in the door. I think she had been pressed against the doorframe, listening while we spoke of her future.

"Kate, Master Hugh asks for your hand. Will you have him for your husband?"

"Aye, father, I will." She did not hesitate.

"Then I consent and offer my blessing." Caxton smiled, then turned quickly and busied himself at a shelf stacked with parchment gatherings.

Another awkward silence followed. How does a man know what to say at such a time? He has no experience nor practice for the moment. Voices from the street intruded upon the stillness, and I entertained the odd thought that, given twenty years or so, God willing,

I might be in Caxton's place.

Kate broke the hush. "A pottage is warming on the hearth, and there is a loaf and cheese for our dinner."

A man might turn from warmed pottage, but not after eating molding bread and drinking foul water for two days. Kate ladled the pottage into three bowls, broke the maslin loaf, and directed me to take a place at the workroom table. Caxton spoke a prayer over the simple meal, asking the Lord Christ to bless the food and our marriage, and thanking him for intercession and my freedom from Oxford Castle. The pottage was liberally flavored with pork, and was delicious. Or was it Kate, gazing at me from across the table, that was tasty? Perhaps my senses were confused.

I remained at the shop after dinner to discuss betrothal with my future father-in-law. Upon Sunday the priest at St Peter-in-the-East Church would announce to the parish the forthcoming marriage of Kate Caxton and Hugh de Singleton. Before this priest we would pledge to marry. There would be ample witnesses, and the banns might be first read then as well.

The banns must be read in Bampton, also, as the Church of St Beornwald was my parish. And when wed, in Bampton we would live. I wished for the marriage to take place in Bampton, and thought the stationer might object, but he was amenable.

I did not expect a great dowry to accompany Kate. The lass was gift enough. But Caxton offered a house in Oxford, also on the Holywell Street. This house was one of three he had purchased when he came from Cambridge to set up his business here. One house was his shop and home, the others he rented. It was one of these he offered as Kate's dowry. I was much pleased. The income from such a house, twenty shillings each year, would be a welcome addition to the stipend Lord Gilbert provided.

For Kate's dower I offered twelve shillings. When we made Galen House our home Kate would have a toft, so I also offered to buy for her a rooster and a dozen hens.

I have heard that there is often much vigorous

bargaining before dowry and dower are agreed upon and a wedding may proceed. Perhaps such is the case when each party brings great wealth to the marriage. Kate and I could not do so. Robert Caxton and I came to agreement in little more time than it has taken me to write of the covenant.

I would have enjoyed speaking more to Kate that day, but she might not have thought the same. I reeked of the cell and its filth, and was unshaven. I requested of Caxton that he tell his daughter of the terms of her betrothal, and that I would join her on Sunday at St Peter's Church whence we would make pledge to each other. Tomorrow I would be about seeking Master Wyclif's stolen books. For this work I had new ardor. When the thieves were found I would be free to take a bride and return to Bampton.

The kitchen at Canterbury Hall provided two buckets of hot water. In one I soaked my filthy clothes and in the other I scrubbed the Oxford Castle gaol from my flesh. I had thought to scrape the stubble from my chin, but decided to leave it. Perhaps I would grow a beard. I was soon to be wed, no longer to be thought a lad. And a beard might remind me of lessons learned in the dungeon of Oxford Castle. It was not clear what these lessons might be, but when I discovered them the beard might serve to remind me of them.

Master Wyclif provided a scholar's robe for the afternoon while my kirtle, chauces, and cotehardie dried in the pale autumn sun. Arthur had watched my purification wordlessly. When I was done with the work and adjusting the robe, he spoke.

"Near forgot, with all that's happened since, but I learned a thing in castle forecourt the day you was took to gaol. Don't know as it has to do with Master Wyclif's books... but you said to tell you of aught I heard."

"I did. What news?"

"Where the forecourt verges on Great Bailey Street a pieman has a stall. Mostly pie, little meat."

"You purchased one?"

"Aye. Wanted to stand close an' hear 'im gossip with regular customers."

"He has regular customers for meatless pies?"

"Aye. Some as bought from 'im got pies from one pile; others, like me, got from another."

"Ah... so you ate a pie and listened for gossip and scandal?"

"As you wished," Arthur protested, as if, unbidden, he would do no such thing.

"So I did. And you must have overheard some tale or I would not be hearing of these pies."

"Aye. Right after them gentlemen near came to blows, a fellow told the pieman his brothers was gone to London. Brothers is carters. They was takin' a chest to Westminster, to the abbey."

"That is your news?"

"Not all of it," Arthur replied defensively. "Told you it might have naught to do with books. You said..."

"I know. Tell me what else you heard."

"The chest was locked and not to be opened. And 'twas not to get wet. A linen shroud, waxed stiff, was to cover the box."

Arthur's tale became more interesting. "Did the man say who it was hired his brothers for this work?"

"Some scholar. Wore a scholar's robe, an' was tonsured."

This identification was of no help. Near half the men of Oxford might fit such a description.

"When were they to take this chest to Westminster?"

"Said as they left a week and more past. Told the pieman as how 'e wouldn't be seein' 'em for a fortnight."

"Seems about right, to travel to London with a cart and horse and return. These carters might be finished with their work and on their way home by now, I think."

"Aye, so I thought. An' the fellow spoke the same."

"You talked to him?"

"Aye. Told 'im I heard 'im say 'is brothers was carters

an' how my lord might be needin' some sturdy lads for a bit o' work."

"You learned their names?"

"Aye. Their place, too."

"Good man. Perhaps there is nothing to this, but it will be worth seeing to."

"Thought as much. Roger an' Henry Carter. Live on Kybald Street. Got a stable behind for horse and cart."

"You went there?"

"Aye. I'll show you the place."

I trudged off with Arthur into Oxford streets crowded with late-afternoon business. It was but a short way down St John's Street to Grope Lane, then right on Kybald Street to the carters' house. The building housed two families, with entrance doors at either end.

One of these doors was open to the mild autumn afternoon; I rapped my knuckles upon the door-post and awaited a response.

A well-fed matron answered my knock, glanced at my scholar's robe, and said, "You'll be wantin' 'Enry. Ain't back from London yet. You can pay what's due then."

The woman thought I was the scholar who had hired her husband. Perhaps, was anything to be learned from the woman's error, I might make the most of it.

"I thought as how the roads be dry, he might have returned sooner than expected," I explained. Arthur stood a respectful distance behind me and nodded agreement. If the woman thought it strange that a scholar-monk should have a burly companion garbed in a noble's livery, she gave no sign.

"Nay. Expect 'im Monday, maybe, an' 'e travels on Sunday. 'E don't like to, y'unnerstand, but 'tis a long way, London an' back. 'Im an' Roger done it once before, an' that was two… three years past."

"You will send word when he returns? I wish to be certain of the safe delivery of my chest."

"Aye. Soon as 'e's home."

"You know where to find me?"

"Aye. The Abbey of St Mary at Eynsham…ask

for Brother Michael."

"Just so. I will await a word from your husband."

Arthur grinned broadly at me as I turned from the door. I could not help myself and smiled in return. Perhaps the shipment to Westminster had nothing to do with stolen books. But perhaps it did. It was worth considering, anyway.

"This puzzle of stolen books seems soon to be solved," Arthur remarked cheerfully as we returned to Canterbury Hall.

"Perhaps. Who can tell what might have been in the chest, and if it was books, whose they might be. And if they were Master John's books, how did a monk of Eynsham come to have them?"

"Might be 'e knows a scholar at Canterbury Hall," Arthur suggested.

"Likely. Most scholars and monks here know one another, especially do they come to Oxford from the same house."

"The monks what study at Canterbury Hall is Benedictines?" Arthur asked.

"Aye, as are those at Eynsham."

"Then we have but to wait 'til the carters return an' from Brother Michael or the carters discover what was in the chest an' where it was took."

"There may be more required than that. If the chest did hold books, the monk would say they belonged to the order and were being returned to Westminster. Such might be truth, and was it not, who could gainsay him?"

"Oh. But would a monk lie... a man in holy orders?"

"I would not like to think so. But would a scholar steal another man's books? Never! Yet it surely happened at Canterbury Hall, and some of the scholars there are monks. A lie to cover a theft might not be wrenching even to a monk."

"'Tis easier to lie than to steal," Arthur concluded.

"Aye. And I have other work for you while we await the carters' return. Tomorrow you will go to the inn, mount your horse, and return to Bampton. Tell Father Thomas he is to read the banns at the Church of St Beornwald this Sunday and those following for Hugh de Singleton and Katherine Caxton. And tell Lord Gilbert and Lady Petronilla also. Lord Gilbert charged me this day to tell him how my suit progressed. You may return Monday. Perhaps the carters will have arrived and we may gain information upon which we may act."

Arthur grinned at me. "Always liked to bear good news."

Chapter 7

When I awoke on Saturday – All-Saints Day – my chauces were dry and my cotehardie nearly so. I was pleased to be seen once again as different from the horde of black-gowned youths and men who swarm Oxford's streets. Benedict thought such a desire sinful, so his rule prescribed a uniform habit for monks of his house. I did not feel impious as I drew my fur coat over my shoulders. I felt warm. Perhaps the sainted monk might have thought that sinful also.

But Master John's gown had proven useful. When I donned the garment I did not know it might assist my purpose. Perhaps God knew. Had I not been tossed into Oxford Castle's malodorous gaol, I would have felt no need to scrub the stink from my clothes. There would have been no reason to approach Henry Carter's wife in the guise of a scholar-monk. Then surely I would have left the woman without the knowledge of a monk of Eynsham and his hire. Did God then set Simon Trillowe against me, so that from his evil intent, was I shrewd enough to see how, good might come? I must ask this of Master John – does God send evil so that it might be turned to good, or does He but permit evil, and allow us to use it for good, have we the stomach and wit to do so? And what of the world's evils which remain so terrible that no good seems ever likely to come from such calamity? I found myself wading in waters too deep for me. I will allow the bishops to consider the point. But perhaps I will some day ask Master John his thoughts on the matter.

I walked with Arthur to the Stag and Hounds and saw him off to Bampton and the delivery of his happy announcement. I then set my feet to Holywell Street and was nearly there when from an alley off St Mildred's Lane the thatcher appeared whose broken collarbone I had set. His left arm rested in the sling I made for him. He raised his right in greeting and bowed. I asked the fellow how he did.

"Not so well," he replied.

"How so?"

"Can't sleep… least not layin' in me bed."

"The injury is painful, then?"

"Aye. Do I lay on me back, the ache is fierce. 'Tis but little better do I turn to me right side. So I sleep as I can, sittin' in the straw upon the floor, me back against a wall."

"I have some potions which may help. Call upon me at Canterbury Hall after the ninth hour and I will give you herbs which you may mix with ale before you go to your rest. They will allay the pain, perhaps enough that you will sleep."

"'Twould be a Christian thing, are you able to help me so. The broken ladder near did for me afore I set foot on the roof. Never fell from a roof before."

"A break in the ladder?"

"Aye. 'Twas whole when we left it aside the yarn-spinner's 'ouse, but when I set it against the roof and went to climb, a rung dropped from under me and pitched me to the dirt."

"What was amiss?"

"When I made the ladder I notched the sides, then bound the rungs to 'em with thongs. One of the thongs was missin'."

"And the ladder was whole when you took it to the yarn-spinner's house?"

"Aye."

"Why did you not notice this when you began your climb?"

"Somebody bound the rung to the side with a cord of dirty yarn, so 'twould seem all was as should be."

"But the yarn would not hold a sturdy fellow like you?"

94

"Aye. Pitched me to the mud on me arse. No harm done. Not then."

"You repaired the ladder?"

"Aye. An' then got careless, like, on the roof."

The thatcher winced to think of his error, tugged a forelock in respect, and turned away to set off toward Canditch and the Northgate. I stopped him.

"There were three of you at work on the yarn-spinner's roof. Perhaps one of the others replaced a weakened thong and thought it would serve."

"Nay. Asked 'em. Knew nothin' of it."

"What is your thought on the matter?"

"Some fellow used me ladder, broke it, an' tried to mend it so's none would know. Could'a broke me neck."

"And this misuse occurred after you took the ladder to the yarn-spinner's cottage?"

"Must've. Me an' me lads went up an' down over an' again before, to see what must be done on the roof. Didn't give way then."

"Well, I am sorry for your hurt, but pleased it was no worse. Come to Canterbury Hall after the ninth hour and I will have herbs ready which may help you rest."

The man tugged his forelock again and left me to continue on my way to Kate. I had no special reason to call on her this day. A man pursuing a maid needs no reason to seek her presence. Indeed, reason might be an obstacle to love, not an aid. But I thought of a purpose for my visit as I approached Holywell Street.

Caxton smiled a greeting as I entered his shop and waved me through the door toward his workroom. I found Kate at the table, stitching a gathering of parchment to another. She peered up at me, then exclaimed, "Oh!"

She lifted her left thumb to her lips. My unannounced appearance had caused her to thrust the needle into her thumb. I wish it might be that she would always respond so to my presence. Not that she should stab thumb with needle, but that she might lose track of her occupation when I appear. Some day, and perhaps not long hence, my hair will cease growing and my belly may begin. Then my appearance will not be likely to cause her to grow careless of her work.

"I am sorry to startle you."

"I, uh, did not expect you this day. Father said we would meet at St Peter's-in-the-East on the morrow, there to pledge betrothal."

"Aye. But I have no obligation this morning to draw me from Holywell Street, so I'd enjoy your company, if I may do so without interrupting any labor."

"'Tis no interruption. I can stitch a gathering and speak to my love at the same time."

"Is there a word more pleasant?"

"Than what?" Kate asked.

"Love. You name me as your love. I think I will never hear so sweet a declaration."

Kate blushed and returned to her stitching.

"Since we spoke last I have learned two new things."

She looked up from her work, sucked again on her punctured thumb, and awaited news of recent discoveries.

"So, 'tis not true," I observed.

"What is not true?"

"That you can sew a gathering and listen to me as you do."

Kate lay her work on the table. "Perhaps not," she agreed. "Will this new knowledge help discover Master Wyclif's books?"

"Mayhap. It's too early in the search to know. But what I have learned bears further inquiry."

I told her of Arthur's discovery, and of the carters' task; of the monk who hired the work, and the precautions taken so the monk's chest would remain dry. I told her of meeting the injured thatcher, and of his mysteriously damaged ladder. Kate's brow furrowed as I concluded the tale.

"When we walked beside the Cherwell you told me you suspected the thieves went over the wall with a ladder."

"Aye."

"But you could find no mark at the base of the wall to tell if this was so."

"Aye."

She was silent for a moment. "Perhaps there was a sign at the wall which you did not see, because you sought another."

"How so?"

"You sought two cavities in the grass where a man might have stood a ladder."

"I did, and found nothing."

"Perhaps there may be, in the grass at the base of the wall, a bit of leather thong, snapped from the thatcher's ladder. You did not seek such a thing, so might have overlooked it, even was it before your eyes."

"'Tis near time for dinner at Canterbury Hall. So soon as my meal is done I will go again to search the wall."

The pottage at Canterbury Hall this day was not up to the usual standard. The lack of achievement startled me, as the usual standard was easily met. Perhaps it was bland because of the day. Saturday is, of course, a fast day, so no bits of pork hid in the bowl.

Master John peered at me from above his spoon throughout the meal. He is an impatient sort. Am I away from the Hall on his business, he will know what I may discover so soon as I pass the porter's gate. There was no reason to leave him in suspense, so I told him of the carters' work, Brother Michael of Eynsham, and the injured thatcher and his disjointed ladder.

"Brother Michael of Eynsham, you say?"

"Aye, so the carter's wife did say. You know this monk?"

"We were students together at Balliol College." Wyclif grimaced as he spoke.

"Your face," I commented, "says more than your words."

"We were not friends."

"How so?"

"I had no reason to dislike the fellow when we first met, nor he me, as I know. But we were flint against steel from the first. Did I take one point in a disputation, Michael of Longridge took the contrary."

"Did he do so with other scholars?"

'I cannot recall. It was twenty years and more past. Then, in our second year at Balliol another scholar noticed coins missing from his purse. There was reason to suspect Michael, 'though I don't now remember why. It was my idea to notch a penny, then see did it go missing. It did, and a few days later, when we were at an inn, Michael paid for his wine with the notched coin."

"He was dismissed from Balliol?"

"Nay. He pleaded poverty, which was true enough. Promised to repay all. When he learned 'twas my thought to notch the coin, he had more reason to dislike me, I think. 'Twas Nicholas Map he stole from. Nicholas said he would make no trouble was he repaid, but the theft became known. The tale has followed Brother Michael, I think. He sought preferment, but is at Eynsham – a poor house, I am told."

"Have you had discourse with him of late?"

"Nay. I've not seen the man for... ten years, perhaps."

"I am about to search at the wall again," I announced. "Will you come?"

"Nay. The scholars of Canterbury Hall await my wisdom. What do you seek at the wall?"

"Kate thought, did the thief use the thatcher's ladder and damage it, some part of the broken thong used to fix the rungs to the poles might have fallen in the grass. This would be a confirmation, I think, of what we suspect, if such a bit of leather strapping be found."

"Aye. I wish you success."

We parted, I to the porter's gate, Master John to the hall, where tables had been cleared and benches moved to turn the space into a place of learning.

I stepped into Schidyard Street and was surprised to see Kate awaiting me there. She smiled when I appeared.

I wish it may always be, that her fair face will reflect joy when her eyes fall upon me. It will be my duty as husband, I think, to make it so.

"You are about to search the wall for a broken cord of leather?" she asked.

"Aye."

"I was hopeful I might search with you. Four eyes are better than two, and seeking the solution to a mystery appeals more than stitching gatherings."

"Your father can spare you from the work?"

"He must do so soon. He is seeking an apprentice to replace me."

"Come. I will show you the place where the thieves, be that how they entered Canterbury Hall, must have come over the wall."

Two thatchers were busy at the yarn-spinner's cottage, their work protracted due to the loss of one of their number. They looked up from their work as we skirted the wall. As I think back on the moment, it was probably not "we" they observed so intently. Being in Kate's company brings a man more attention than he might otherwise receive. And perhaps, more than he might want. I considered this and made note to myself that, was there a time I wished to be incognito, I must not be in Kate's company. Or would she be a successful distraction? What man, beholding Kate, would remember her unremarkable companion?

While I considered this we reached the place where, if a ladder was used to scale the enclosure, it would have been placed.

The thatchers got little work done for the next half-hour. Each time I looked from the grass to the yarn-spinner's roof, I found them studying me. Or studying Kate, which was more likely. I found occasion to study her myself. Had I been more alert to my business I might have found the leather thong. But it was Kate who did so.

The leather strip was far back from the wall, five paces or so, well away from where any ladder might have stood. As if, in a fury, whoso had broken the thong then flung it away in anger.

Kate held the slender strip of leather above her head and laughed in satisfaction. It is not often a woman is allowed triumph over a man. I smiled at her sport, and thought as how a bailiff might be well served to have an observant wife.

Kate held the thong out to me. There was but one more thing to do with it. I carried it to the yarn-spinner's home, where the ladder stood propped against the north wall. The thatchers watched me approach, then one recognized me as the surgeon who had treated their companion. He shouted a greeting from the roof, loosened his rope harness, and slid to the top of the ladder. Kate and I met him as his feet struck the ground.

"You be the leech what set Aymer's shoulder to rights," he declared.

"Aye. I saw him this day. The injury troubles him."

"It does. He'll be more careful, like, on a roof, next job."

"He is to come to Canterbury Hall this afternoon for some herbs which will dull the ache and perhaps grant sleep."

"'E'll be grateful, can you do that."

"He told me also that he was pitched from this ladder when you first set to work here."

"'E was," the thatcher laughed. "On 'is arse in the mud. Splutterin' curses, 'e was."

"A thong was missing, he said, and the rung fastened with but a length of yarn, dirtied so it would appear to be a strip of leather."

"'At's right."

My eyes traveled to the ladder. A new thong, lighter in color than the others, marked the repair. I held out the broken thong found in the grass. The thatcher peered at it, then at his ladder.

"The lass found this in the grass between here and the wall about Canterbury Hall. A match for the others, would you agree... but for the new repair."

"Aye, 'tis. But why was it there?"

"Someone may have used your ladder to go over the wall and commit theft."

"Must've torn the thong on the way down," the thatcher mused.

Aymer Thatcher appeared around the corner where Canterbury Hall meets St John's Street. I turned to greet him, showed him the broken thong, and bid him follow Kate and me to the porter's gate. I have had good result in treating the pain of injuries with a potion of wild lettuce and hemp seeds and root. Mixed with ale, these herbs bring sleep and allay much affliction. I might have included seeds of columbine, but I mistrust the use, for too much is poison. A man in great pain might be tempted to take more than he was advised. Then all pain, and his life, would be ended.

I left Kate and the thatcher at the gate, found my pouch in the guest chamber, and poured generous portions of the herbs into a bottle, which I sealed with a wooden plug. In my pouch was also a small vial of flax-seed oil mixed with the oil of monk's hood. The concoction is potent in relieving aches when rubbed on the afflicted joint, but deadly if consumed.

I found the thatcher leaning against the wall, and Kate also, pressed close to the stones. Her brow was furrowed, her face pale. My first thought was that this thatcher had made free with his tongue while I was seeing to his relief. I was about to speak sharply to the fellow when, following Kate's gaze, I saw two men sauntering down St John's Street toward Canterbury Hall: Sir Simon Trillowe and a youth I took to be his squire.

I handed the bottle of herbs and vial of oil to Aymer and was about to instruct him in their use when Sir Simon's path brought him before us. He stopped, stared at me, then Kate, then back to me. He smiled. No, he smirked, and finally spoke.

"We meet again... Hugh, is it?"

"Master Hugh," Kate replied.

"Do maids speak for you?" he jibed.

"Perhaps those who would not speak to you would willingly speak for Master Hugh," Kate rejoined. Her cheeks were flushed red.

"Ah, but Mistress Kate, you have just spoken to me."

"'Twas of need, not pleasure, be sure." Kate turned from Sir Simon and found something engrossing beyond the Canterbury Hall gate which demanded her attention.

"Perhaps we will meet again, Master Hugh." He emphasized "Master". "Indeed, I am certain of it." He walked on. The youth turned to me and laughed.

What was I to do? Seek Lord Gilbert and complain? Of what? Had I been threatened? Probably. Could I prove it? No. Did I want Lord Gilbert to think me incapable of winning my own battles? I resolved that, for so long as I remained in Oxford, I would wear my dagger under my cotehardie. I was sure Sir Simon spoke true. We would meet again. He would see to it. His injured pride demanded balm.

I instructed the thatcher to mix a portion of the lettuce and hemp into a pint of ale an hour before he wished to sleep, and told him of the caution he must take in applying the oil to his skin; that no trace of the liquid must touch his lips. He tugged his forelock in gratitude and respect and asked what was owed for this relief. I collected a ha'penny and the thatcher set off clutching the flask and vial to his chest with his good hand. Kate and I followed.

We were walking on Catte Street when Kate finally spoke. "Sir Simon is angry with me, I think."

"At us. Had I hoped to win you, and lost, I would be as cross as he."

"But you would not threaten another."

"Would I not?"

"Nay. I would not wed such a man, and you are not."

"Aye," I agreed. "I would endure my loss in silence."

I had not thought of the Lady Joan Talbot, now the

Lady de Burgh, for many months. As I spoke her comely face came to mind. But only briefly. Kate is quite capable of banishing thoughts of other females from my mind.

I left Kate at her father's shop with the promise that we would meet on the morrow for troth plight and hear the banns first read. I do not remember what the Canterbury Hall cook served that evening for supper. It was surely another pottage with maslin loaves, else I would remember. Stolen books and a comely maid possessed my thoughts.

Master Wyclif accompanied me to St Peter's Church next morning. With Master John and her father as witnesses, Kate vowed before a priest to become my wife, and I pledged to make her so.

Before the mass a curate stood and announced to the congregation our intention to wed. He asked was there any who knew of reason we might not. I half expected Sir Simon to appear from behind a pillar and denounce our purpose. But he did not, nor did any other, and so the banns were announced. Twice more the priest would do so, then Kate might become my wife.

I thought as we left the church that day that I detected envious glances from other young men directed to me. Perhaps it was my imagination.

Arthur arrived next day in time for dinner. I was not surprised. Arthur dislikes missing a meal. He was rewarded for his alacrity. Dinner this day at Canterbury Hall was a pease pottage with coney and onions.

When the meal was done I drew Arthur to the guest chamber to question him regarding Bampton and how the reading of the banns was received. He sat upon a bench, belched with contentment, and conveyed the congratulations of Lord Gilbert and Lady Petronilla.

"The lady sent servants to Galen House this morning, early, as I was settin' out for Oxford. Told Lord Gilbert it must be made fit for a bride. Knowin' Lady Petronilla, 'twill be so, an' soon."

"I hope it will be soon needed. But I cannot take a bride to Bampton and leave her there while I return to

Oxford to seek stolen books. Come, we'll seek the carters' house and see have they returned from London yet."

They had not. No horse peered out from the tiny barn, and there was no cart in the toft. I left Arthur on Kybald Street and told him to loiter about the place. Should the carters return he would find me at Canterbury Hall, but not before supper. I told him I intended to retrieve Bruce from the stable behind the Stag and Hounds and visit the Abbey of St Mary at Eynsham.

From Oxford to Eynsham is near five miles. Bruce is not a beast to be hurried, so I heard the abbey bells ring for nones as we splashed across the Thames at Swinford.

The abbey hosteller was pleased, I think, to learn that I did not require the abbey's hospitality for the evening. I told the fellow that I wished to see the abbot, on Lord Gilbert Talbot's business. This was not so much a falsehood. Lord Gilbert had set me to find Master John's books, so the commission made the work Lord Gilbert's business, would you not agree?

The hosteller turned Bruce over to a servant and instructed him to see the old horse to the abbey stables. This servant was the largest man I had ever seen. I am taller than most men, but this fellow was a head taller than me. He could look Bruce in the eyes as he led the old horse away. The arms which took the reins were as thick through as my neck.

The hosteller led me to the western range of the cloister, where it is common among Benedictines for the abbot to enjoy private quarters. I am sure I could not have entered this chamber had I announced my presence as an obligation to Master Wyclif. The service of a powerful lord will open many doors barred to those whose service is to lesser folk.

The abbot answered the hosteller's knock upon his door with a rasping invitation to enter. Abbot Thurstan was a small man. His wizened body was shrunken in a habit which once might have fit, but he was now lost in its folds. His head no longer needed a razor. The fringe of white hair circling his skull was nature's work. My father, no monk, wore such a tonsure, as will I, no doubt, some years hence.

The sun, now low in the western sky, illuminated the abbot's lodging with a brassy glow. He was a dark outline in the light pouring through the windows behind him. Dust floated and flickered, golden motes in the air. The abbot's head was rimmed in a gilded fringe as the sun tinted his silver locks.

Abbot Thurstan had been seated at a large table upon which an open book indicated his interrupted pursuit. As he stood he plucked spectacles from his nose. To think that in the last century there were some who thought these small bits of brass and glass were the devil's work. How could this be so, when they are such a boon to those whose eyes are weary with years?

The hosteller announced me as Master Hugh de Singleton, about Lord Gilbert Talbot's interests. Abbot Thurstan bid me be seated in one of three chairs which occupied a corner of his chamber, and set himself in another.

"How does Lord Gilbert?" he asked in a thin, cracking voice.

"Very well, as does the Lady Petronilla."

"Good." A distant look came to the old man's eyes and he stared as if drawn to some image beyond my shoulder. "I knew his father, Lord Richard. An estimable knight... but I forget myself."

The abbot reached for a small bell upon his table and rang it. A lay brother appeared at the door nearly as soon as he placed the bell back upon the table.

"Wine for our guest, Jerome, please."

Jerome scurried off about this task and Abbot Thurstan turned again his attention to me. "How may I serve Lord Gilbert?"

I was about to tell him when Jerome reappeared with an ewer of Rhenish wine and two silver goblets. Lord Gilbert's name did indeed command respect.

Jerome filled the goblets and silently left the chamber. Abbot Thurstan motioned for me to take one of the goblets and lifted the other with a trembling hand. The wine was excellent, sweet and clear. We sipped in silence for some time, until the old monk seemed to remember himself, and put the question to me again.

"Ah, how may we serve Lord Gilbert?"

"A friend of m'lord has been robbed."

The abbot's brow furrowed and he drew his lips thin across yellowing teeth. "I am sorry to learn of any theft, but what has this to do with the abbey? And what has been stolen?"

"The stolen items are such as an abbey might wish to purchase," I replied.

"Hah," the abbot chuckled. "Not this abbey. We are forty monks and seventy lay brothers and can but feed ourselves and do no other. Our debts," he waved a feeble, veined hand, "mount each year. Since the great death our tenants are few and income much reduced. No, we will not purchase stolen goods, be they ever so desirable, for we can purchase few goods at all."

"Would the abbey be asked to serve another in such a matter... that is, to act as broker for another purchaser?"

The old man stroked his chin, much as Lord Gilbert might do. "I might answer that more honestly did I know what has been stolen."

"You have been asked to act as agent?"

"Did I say that? I have not. But did I know what is taken, I could tell you if it be likely I, or Prior Warin, would even be asked."

"Books."

"Lord Gilbert sent you to find stolen books? Whose books?"

"A friend."

"Never mind." The old monk took another swallow of his wine. "I think I know. 'Tis Master Wyclif's books you seek, is this not so?"

"Aye. Has this news come to Eynsham already?"

"We learned of it some days past. What has Lord Gilbert to do with this theft?"

"I am Lord Gilbert's bailiff at Bampton. Master

Wyclif is a friend. When I told Lord Gilbert that Master John asked my help in recovering his stolen books, Lord Gilbert released me from my duties at Bampton to do so. Master Wyclif is a favorite of Duke John, as you may know."

"So 'tis said. I wonder," the old monk mused, "if the thief knew his act might set two great lords against him?"

"Some do not consider their deeds until the consequences are upon them."

"Aye. Well, no thief will sell his taking here. Does any seek to do so, I will send for you... Where do you lodge?"

"Canterbury Hall."

I left Eynsham convinced that the abbot knew nothing of Master John's books. It was too soon to seek Brother Michael. To do so would give warning if he had to do with the theft, and did he not I would learn nothing of value from him. But I had planted a seed in the abbey ground. Now to be patient and see would it grow.

The sun rested in tree-tops to the west when Bruce splashed across the Thames at Swinford. I dislike traveling alone at night since the evening Henry atte Bridge attempted to deal me a mortal blow on the road from Witney, so I prodded Bruce with my heels. To little effect.

No miscreant accosted me this night. I left Bruce at the Stag and Hounds and stumbled through dark streets to Canterbury Hall. The porter was not pleased to be roused from slumber to open the gate to me.

I found Arthur fidgeting on the bench in the guest chamber. "'Bout to set out an' seek you," he chastised. "Thought you might've met up with the thief, or maybe Sir Simon again."

"Nay. Bruce will not be hurried. Have the carters returned?"

"Not yet."

A cresset lighted the chamber. I saw in its glow a loaf and a cup. Arthur followed my gaze. "Brought a loaf an' some ale from the kitchen," he explained.

I would not need to seek my bed hungry. I thought this the only laudable result of the day. I was wrong. The seed was sprouting.

Chapter 8

The carters returned to Oxford on Tuesday. I had sent Arthur that morning to prowl Kybald Street and the neighboring lanes. He returned to Canterbury Hall for his dinner with no news, but an hour after eating his fill of another pottage he hastened breathlessly across the enclosure from the porter's lodge to advise me that the carters were at that moment unharnessing their horse.

Arthur followed close behind as I hurried from St John's Street to Grope Lane. The carters lived but a few paces east of Grope Lane, on the north side of Kybald Street. We found the brothers in the yard behind the house, tending to horse and cart. After such a journey both would need care.

Henry Carter and his brother were twins. Most men must peer into a well or catch their image in a glass window to see how they appear to another. Not these brothers. They had but to glance at each other to know their features. This duplication seems to me to prove false the notion that, should a woman bear twins, she has lain with two men.

"Henry?" I asked.

One of the carters looked up from considering wear to the axle of his cart and answered, "Aye?"

"You have just returned from a long journey, I am told."

"Aye. To London, to the abbey at Westminster," he replied quizzically.

The brother had just hung the harness on a peg in the barn. He stood in the open door, peering suspiciously at me. Most men, I think, are leery of those who pry into their business. I drew two pence from my purse and offered the coins to the carter. I watched his eyes soften.

"What were you commissioned to take to Westminster? It was a chest, I am told."

"If you know what it was we was hired to take, why need to ask?"

"Do you know what was in the chest?"

"Nay. 'Twas sealed an' locked an' we was told 'twas not to be opened."

"And this chest was to be covered and kept dry... is this so?"

"Aye."

"A monk from Eynsham hired this work?"

"Why do you ask when you know the answers? An' why concern yourself with my work?"

"Forgive me. I am Hugh de Singleton, bailiff to Lord Gilbert Talbot at his manor at Bampton."

This revelation did not seem to impress either Henry or his brother. They stared impassively, awaiting any further information I might care to impart.

"Did you deliver the chest to the abbot?"

"Nay. We was to take it to a monk there name of..." Henry turned to his brother, who stood yet in the open barn door. "Who was it we was to give the chest to?"

"The librarian, Brother Giles."

"Was he expecting this chest? Or was he surprised when it was delivered?"

"He was expectin' it, alright."

"What was your pay for this work?"

"A shillin' an' eight pence. Half when we took the job, half now we're back an' job's done."

"You are to collect from Brother Michael at Eynsham?"

"Aye. Time enough today. I'll walk there an' collect what's due."

A thought came to me. I drew another ha'penny from my purse and offered it to the carter. "When you speak to Brother Michael tell him a wheel came loose from your cart as you neared Westminster and pitched the chest to the verge. He will surely ask was the chest damaged. Tell him, 'Yes, 'twas split at the end.' If he then asks were the contents damaged, tell him, 'No, the books were not harmed.'"

"Books? The chest was full o' books, then? Figured 'twas so, bein' we delivered 'em to a librarian."

"Aye, I believe so. I will return tomorrow. Report all he may say about the chest and its contents."

Wednesday morning, as the bells of St Frideswide's Priory announced terce, I set out for Kybald Street with Arthur close behind. The carters were at work behind the house, Henry splicing the whiffletree where a crack showed, and his brother greasing the harness he'd hung on the barn wall the day before. Or was it Henry greasing the harness? The brother at work on the cart peered up under frowning brows as I approached.

"Did as you asked," he muttered. "Cost me tuppence. Monk said as how we'd damaged 'is chest 'e wasn't due to pay all."

I fished two pence from my pouch and held the coins to the man. His face brightened considerably. "Hoped you'd be good for it," he said as he reached for the coins.

"What else did the monk say, besides reducing what he owed?"

"Asked did anything spill from the chest to the mud of the road. I did as you said an' told 'im the split in the chest was small an' no harm come to the books what was in it."

"Was the monk relieved to learn this?"

"Aye. Then, when he turned to leave me he thought better of it, come back, an' said, was any to ask what was in the chest, I was to tell 'em I knew not. In truth I did not see what was in the chest, an' have but your word on it. So wouldn't be like a lie."

I thanked the carter for his service and set off toward St John's Street with Arthur trailing. The carter's words stung me. I had paid a man to deceive another. Doing so had discovered, perhaps, the location of Master John's stolen books. But was it acceptable in God's sight to discover one sin only by committing another? This worry did not trouble Arthur. He spoke gleefully as we turned the corner from Grope Lane to St John's Street.

"Reckon we know where Master Wyclif's books has gone to an' who stole 'em, eh?"

"It does seem so. Although how to prove it so is another matter. Monasteries often trade and sell books, so they may be copied and libraries enlarged."

"Oh," Arthur replied thoughtfully, and walked on in silence. As we approached Canterbury Hall he spoke again. "So, 'less you could prove the books was Master Wyclif's, the monks would say they was tradin' an' you couldn't say otherwise?"

"Aye. And perhaps they were. We do not know that the books in the chest were Master John's."

"Was it not so," Arthur mused, "why did that monk in Eynsham tell the carter to say nothin' of what was in the chest?"

"It is suspicious, but I must be sure before I make any charge."

"How will you do so?"

"I know not. But I will tell Master John what has been learned. He is a wise man. Perhaps he may suggest a path to follow."

Master John Wyclif is indeed a wise man, but not well-versed in the ways of felons. He was attentive to my tale of books in a chest taken to Westminster, but was at as much a loss as I as to how to discover if the volumes were his or not, and if his, who had stolen them and how they came into the possession of a monk at Eynsham. We three sat, silently considering the issue, when the cook's bell called us to our dinner. Another pottage. I had two good reasons to solve this puzzle. When I found Master John's books I could wed Kate, and I could return to Bampton and escape the pottages of Canterbury Hall.

I was not yet finished with my dinner when I heard excited voices approach the hall. The door banged open, bringing a frown to Master John's face, and the porter entered, accompanied by another man, unknown to me.

The porter cast about, found me in the dim autumn

light which managed to penetrate the windows, and pointed my way. His companion nodded and strode vigorously toward where I sat with Master John. The man who approached was a solid, bull-necked fellow, dressed well, and clearly accustomed to dining from a full trencher.

"Master Hugh de Singleton?" he asked when he stood before me.

"Aye."

"I am Sir Walter Benyt, come from Bampton at Lord Gilbert's urgent request."

"Urgent?" I replied stupidly.

"His lad, the young Richard, has broken his leg... playing on the castle parapet and tumbled off. As I am on my way to London, Lord Gilbert asked me to seek you and beg your speedy return to treat the lad."

"I will do so," I announced, and pushed back my bench so abruptly it tumbled over on the flags. Arthur was up from his place at the same instant, for he had overheard the plea. I had not before heard of this knight, but Lord Gilbert often entertains new guests.

"Young Master Richard is a good lad," Arthur observed, "but of strong will. I heard the nurse screechin' at him some time past to stay off the parapet."

Master John sat near and heard the exchange. I promised him I would return so soon as I might, sent Arthur to the Stag and Hounds to ready the horses, and announced that I was off to the Holywell Street to speak to Kate and would join Arthur at the inn.

I went first to the guest chamber where lay the sack of herbs and instruments I had brought to Oxford. This I threw over a shoulder and hastened to the porter's gate, which I reached as Sir Walter mounted his horse and with his squire clattered across the cobbles toward Schidyard Street.

I wondered briefly that Sir Walter's beast seemed so fresh and willing, prancing about, eager to be off. The horse appeared to be young and strong. His sprint from Bampton seemed to do the animal no harm. Concern for the horse was no concern of mine.

I delayed at Caxton's shop only long enough to speak briefly to Kate and explain my mission. She kissed me lightly on the cheek and bid me farewell and good success in the task before me.

Arthur had Bruce and the old palfrey saddled and waiting when I arrived, breathless, at the Stag and Hounds. Streets were crowded but we urged our mounts through the throng as best we might. Once we were past the castle, the mob thinned and we pushed the horses to a trot as we approached Oseney Abbey.

Riding Bruce at a trot is not an experience I would wish for any. Well, perhaps for Sir Simon Trillowe. The old dexter was not bred for such travel and I was severely jostled while trying to maintain my place upon his broad back. Arthur had much the easier time of it upon the old palfrey, but it soon became clear that his ancient beast could not keep up the pace and would fail long before we reached Bampton. I signaled Arthur to slow his mount. We continued at a fast walk, a gait more suited to both horse and rider.

The road west toward Eynsham and Bampton passes Oseney Abbey, crosses the Thames on Oseney Bridge, then leads through fields for the first two or three miles. It then enters a dense wood before a gentle decline to the river crossing at Swinford. My mind was occupied with the treatment I would undertake when young Richard was in my care, so I gave no notice to the two men, one large, one small, who walked before us on the road.

We were nearly upon the fellows when they turned, having heard our approach, and I saw that the smaller man held a sword close to his leg, so as to disguise that he had it unsheathed and in his hand. Arthur saw the weapon at the same instant, and frowning, turned to me. The larger man carried a cudgel.

As I turned in the saddle to Arthur I caught movement from the corner of my eye. Three horsemen broke from thick cover some hundred paces behind us. These three carried short swords which they waved over their heads as they charged down upon us.

The choice was plain: two men afoot in one direction, one with a sword, or three mounted men in the other, all armed.

"To the river!" I shouted to Arthur, and jabbed my heels into Bruce's elderly, tender flanks. The old horse lumbered into a gallop and bore down upon the men before us who, I think, had thought to block the way. A second glance at Bruce's ponderous approach convinced them of the impractical nature of the task and I caught a glimpse of them diving into the shrubbery beside the road as Bruce thundered past at full gallop.

I turned to see if Arthur followed. He did, urging the old palfrey to greater speed with a swat of his hand upon the beast's rump. Behind Arthur the swordsmen careered in pursuit.

These fellows were mounted upon fleet coursers. Already they had halved the distance at which I had first seen them. Ahead lay the Thames and Swinford. It became my goal to reach the river before these attackers were upon us. Why hope of the river was confused in my mind with safety I cannot say. But it was certain the three who charged after us had evil intent, and Arthur and I were the object.

It was my purse they sought. So I believed. But I gave no thought to halting Bruce and surrendering my coins. Too many times I had heard of men waylaid upon the road, robbed, then put to the sword, their corpses tossed aside into the forest. Dead men cannot identify those who have despoiled them.

We won the race. Bruce galloped into the Thames with a mighty splash. Arthur on his palfrey was but a few strides behind. Bruce seemed to understand the urgency of the matter. He plunged into the current, creating a wash in which Arthur and the palfrey followed. A few paces behind Arthur the first of our pursuers, a red-bearded fellow wearing a green surcoat, also splashed into the stream.

Bruce's great strength and longer legs caused him

to leave the palfrey farther behind as together we plunged through the deepest part of the ford. I turned to urge Arthur to haste, as if such admonition was necessary, and saw him do a strange thing.

He leaped from the palfrey's back into the current. A log, which I had not before seen, drifted nearby. Arthur splashed, waist deep, to the log and lifted the water-soaked timber above his head. This was a feat of which I, or any normal man, would have been incapable. But Arthur is a sturdy fellow.

Arthur crouched in the frigid stream, turned to the first of our pursuers and, when he judged the distance reduced enough, threw the log over his head with both hands toward the man's horse.

Arthur's aim was remarkable. The log struck the beast squarely between the eyes. The horse staggered for a moment, then plunged and reared on the slippery stones of the ford. The rider yanked mightily on the reins, trying to control the frightened animal. Instead, he persuaded the horse to rise on hind legs, forefeet flailing the air little more than an arm's length from Arthur's chin.

The beast danced thus in the ford for a moment, then lost his balance and with a great splash toppled over backward into the river. His sword-wielding rider disappeared beneath the struggling animal into the waist-deep water.

Without its rider the palfrey had slowed its progress through the river to a near standstill. Arthur forced his way through the current to the horse, found a stirrup, and raised himself, dripping, to the saddle. With a kick of his heels he put the old horse again into motion and was soon up to Bruce. I had become so captured by the events unfolding behind me that I had neglected to continue prodding Bruce across the stream.

Together Arthur and I and the two old horses emerged dripping from the Thames. Behind us, midway across the river, the upturned horse continued to struggle, belly up, hooves flailing the air, nostrils blowing gouts of water. Of the animal's rider all that was visible were his boots. What remained of him was in the Thames, under the struggling horse, for he had not thrown himself free before the beast pitched over backward upon him.

His companions pulled their mounts to a halt in the midst of the ford and went to work extricating the drowning man from under his frightened horse. To remain and observe this work would have been entertaining. Perhaps a similar event may occur when I will have leisure to enjoy the spectacle.

Bruce and the palfrey clawed their way up the west bank of the river and together Arthur and I prodded the beasts to a gallop. It was but a mile, or little more, to the abbey at Eynsham. I thought our mounts might travel that distance before they collapsed, and thus bring us to safety.

A few moments later our wheezing beasts drew up before the monastery gatehouse. The hosteller was within, discussing some matter with the porter. He remembered me, but peered disapprovingly at men who would misuse their horses so.

Arthur was drenched through and shivering from the cold. I asked the hosteller was there a fire where we could warm ourselves and poor Arthur might dry his dripping clothes.

I thought some explanation for our state in order, and so told of our close escape. The hosteller's expression softened and he sent for a lay brother to care for Bruce and the palfrey while Arthur and I sought the calefactory and the fire which Benedictines keep burning in winter months, unlike Cistercians, who seem to believe that one grows closer to God as the temperature falls and chilblains increase.

We were eager to continue our journey. Arthur was dry and warmed on one side, and nearly so on the other, when Abbot Thurstan entered the calefactory.

"Master Hugh; we meet again. Brother Jacob has told me of the circumstance. I am pleased our house may offer respite."

"We are in your debt," I acknowledged. "Do thieves

often prowl the forest between here and Oxford?"

"Nay. Years ago a band of young knights, finding no employment to their liking, for England was at peace then, would sometimes venture south from their lair near the King's hunting lodge at Woodstock. But not for many years have they made an appearance. I am sorry to learn they may have returned. Even the monastery was not safe from their pillaging, and villagers suffered often their looting and rapine."

Arthur, steaming by the fire, growled a response to this information. "They wasn't no common brigands. They had fine coursers under 'em, an' their tunics an' cotehardies wasn't such as folk livin' hard in a forest is likely to wear."

I thought back to the attack and found myself in agreement with this assertion. "This is so. Their garments were more suited to an Oxford street than a forest glen."

The old abbot seemed glum. Our observations did not bring him joy. "It will be a time of trial, should it be that free companies have returned to the shire."

"Surely the sheriff will see them harried out of his bailiwick?" I protested.

"If he had a mind to do so. But even so, they strike and are gone before the sheriff can be summoned. So it was when they tormented us in past times."

"Perhaps Lord Gilbert may take a hand in the matter," I suggested.

"It would be a great mercy did he do so," the abbot sighed. "But some gentlefolk turn away from free companies, do they leave their manors untouched. If a lord choose to drive them from his lands, they will then turn a special visitation upon his tenants and villeins. So some lords think 'tis best to leave them to their thievery, if they practice it against others."

"Are they likely to prowl the road to the west? Toward Witney and Bampton? We are called to Bampton on an urgent matter. Lord Gilbert's son has broken his leg. I am a surgeon, and am summoned to deal with the injury. This delay will cost us the light of day as it is."

"In earlier times they did not strike much in that direction. There are few forests there to hide them, 'til one is past Burford, I am told."

"Aye," I agreed. "Lands between here and Bampton are flat and fertile and many prosperous manors are there. But since the plague the forest now encroaches. Much assarting will be needed before these lands may be again put to the plow."

"After the swim one of their fellows took," Arthur chuckled, "perhaps they will think better of attacking us again."

"Or," I mused, "they may wish revenge upon us and lay in wait beyond Eynsham."

"This eve?" Arthur asked. "They will think us secure and well bedded for the night in the abbey's guest chambers. Better we be on our way now. Tomorrow they might well set upon us."

Arthur's argument made sense. The abbot insisted we visit the kitchen for a loaf and ale to refresh us for the journey, and sent a lay brother to the stable for Bruce and the palfrey. They had been fed, the lay brother announced. Bruce seemed to observe me with an accusing eye, removed as he was from a comfortable stall to set off again on a muddy road into the setting sun.

We entered Bampton on the High Street well after dark. No brigands sought our coin on the road from Eynsham. We saw no living soul until at the marketplace we came upon John Prudhomme attending upon watch and warn. The beadle challenged us, for it was dark and he could not see who rode upon the village streets after curfew. I asked of news of Richard Talbot, but John had none, being unaware of the child's hurt.

Bruce knew he was home. He turned without guidance into the castle forecourt and halted obediently before the darkened gatehouse.

Wilfred the porter is no light sleeper, nor is his assistant. I banged away on the gate with the pommel of my dagger until finally a sleepy challenge penetrated gate and portcullis. I shouted that I was returned as Lord

Gilbert required, and shortly I heard the wheel creaking to lift the portcullis, then the bar was lifted and the gate swung open.

All was dark in the castle yard. I thought there might be a light from the windows of the solar, but even that chamber was dark.

"Where is the lad?" I demanded of Wilfred.

"Lad?" he blinked.

"Aye… Richard. Arthur, take the horses to the marshalsea and wake a groom to see to them. I will find John Chamberlain and be about my business."

Wilfred watched as Arthur and I set about our tasks. It seemed a night for rousing sleeping folk. The chamberlain was also slow to answer the pounding upon his chamber door. I heard him shout that whoso thumped upon his door should cease, and that he would attend directly. His word was true. The door soon opened and John stood, cresset in hand and bare feet upon the cold flags of his chamber.

The light from his cresset told him who it was who had awakened him. "Master Hugh… you have returned late from Oxford. Are Master Wyclif's books found?"

"Nay. I am come to treat Richard, as Lord Gilbert requested."

"Richard?"

"Aye. Sir Walter delivered Lord Gilbert's summons."

"Sir Walter?" John replied sleepily.

"Sir Walter Benyt. He rode to Oxford at Lord Gilbert's request to seek my return."

"Lord Gilbert said nothing to me of this charge."

"I am to attend Richard. The lad fell from the parapet, so Sir Walter said, and broke a leg. I was to hasten to deal with the injury. Is the child with his nurse?"

"I, uh, suppose so. But he has no broken leg. Least not since I saw him chase a duck near the mill pond after terce this day. And who is Sir Walter Benyt?"

"You have no knowledge of this knight? He claimed to come from Lord Gilbert."

"He may have claimed so, Hugh, but no knight of that name has dined at Lord Gilbert's table. Do you wish me to wake Lord Gilbert so you may report this tale to him?"

"Nay... so long as you are certain no injury has befallen Master Richard."

"Of that I am certain."

"Then I bid you good-night, and apologize for troubling your slumber."

I found Arthur and released him to go to Cicily, his wife, and a warm bed, then felt my way along the dark wall of the hall until I reached the door to my chamber. Enough pale moonlight penetrated my window that I was able to find my bed without lighting a cresset. The bed was cold, but the hope that it would not long be so warmed me. This agreeable meditation I thought would bring sleep upon me, but not so.

Who was Sir Walter Benyt, was that his true name, and why did he call me from Oxford? Had his false account to do with the brigands who attacked near Swinford? Was it my purse they sought, or a thing more valuable to me? Did they seek my life? If so, there could be but two reasons for their mission: to prevent me finding stolen books, or to prevent my marriage to Kate Caxton. I knew of no other reason men might wish to do me harm.

Such thoughts pursued each other through my mind. I found little rest that night. I was yet awake when the Angelus Bell rang from the tower of St Beornwald's Church and roused a rooster to his duty in the poulterer's yard.

No one in Bampton Castle knew of my presence but for Wilfred the porter and John Chamberlain. So there was no ewer of warm water with which to fill my basin and wash hands and face, and no ale nor maslin loaf with which to break my fast. I sought John's chamber but found it vacant. As I turned from his door he appeared at the foot of the stairs which led to the solar and Lord Gilbert's and Lady Petronilla's chambers.

"Ah," he exclaimed. "You are well met. I have told

m'lord of your return, and the circumstance. He would see you in the solar straightaway."

A blaze in the fireplace warmed the solar against the chill November morning. Lord Gilbert was licking his fingers after devouring a morning loaf as John ushered me into the room. Lady Petronilla was not present. I thought she might be in attendance upon her injured child, and that John Chamberlain was somehow mistaken in his declaration that there was nothing amiss with Richard. But not so.

"Master Hugh," Lord Gilbert roared as he stood to greet me. Most lords would remain seated to address their bailiff. I recognized the honor. "John has told me of your presence, and that some fellow has passed himself as a knight, requesting your return to Bampton on my command. What did the scoundrel say his name was?"

"Sir Walter Benyt, m'lord."

"Bah… never heard of such a knight. And he told you Richard had broken a leg falling from the parapet?"

"Aye, he did."

"The child may do so yet, for all the screeching from Lady Petronilla and his nurse when he steals away from their notice. But to my knowledge the lad was yet unmarred when the nurse put him to bed last night."

"Arthur and I were attacked while on the road yesterday, near Swinford."

"Attacked, you say?" Lord Gilbert's face blackened and his brows drew together in a great scowl. "There is treachery here! Some knight lies when he says he comes from me. His tale puts you on the road, where knaves waylay you. How did you escape them?"

I told Lord Gilbert of the floating log and Arthur's use of it. He laughed heartily when I described the horse toppling over into the river, its rider pinned beneath it.

"God's eyes," he roared, "I'd like to have seen that. His fellows did not pursue you then to Eynsham?"

"Nay. Or if so, we reached the abbey before them."

Lord Gilbert's laughter subsided and he went to pulling at his beard, a sure sign that his thoughts grew serious. "Whoever this Sir Walter Benyt may be, he and those who sent him to you with this tale will know that when you arrived here you would know the truth of the matter. They will expect you to return to Oxford. We must be certain they can do you no harm when you do. You do intend to return, do you not?"

"Aye. I have learned some things which may lead to recovering Master Wyclif's books, but that is uncertain. They are not recovered yet."

"Why," he puzzled, "would someone invent a tale to put you on the road where you could be assailed?"

"I thought at first, when the rogues were charging down upon us, that they sought my purse. But now, I think not."

"'Twas not your purse they wanted," Lord Gilbert agreed. "It was you, I think. How have you angered men so that they seek to do you harm?"

"I have thought on this. I seek stolen books. There are surely men who wish me no success. If they guess I may be close to a discovery, perhaps closer even than I know, they might wish to do me ill."

"And you are to wed a lass who had once a proud suitor who wished to do you mischief. I am told the banns were read in St Beornwald's Church upon Sunday. I congratulate you, Hugh. We must keep you alive and whole until you are wed. After that, the lass... Kate, is it? Aye, Kate... she may take responsibility then.

"You must be more cautious, Hugh," Lord Gilbert continued. "After dinner I will accompany you back to Oxford myself. We will travel with half a dozen grooms. I think three men lurking in a wood near Swinford will allow us to pass."

My appetite was better this day than when I last dined at Bampton Castle. For the first remove there was pork in pepper sauce, roasted partridge, and parsley bread with herbed butter. For the second remove there was a fruit-and-salmon pie and dates in syrup. For the third remove the cook presented roasted capon, an egg leach, spiced apples, and pear-and-herb fritters.

Returning to the pottages at Canterbury Hall would be a trial. But in Oxford I would be near to Kate. For her presence I will gladly bear the dietary afflictions of Canterbury Hall.

As the subtlety was brought to Lord Gilbert after the third remove, he gave order that horses be readied for the journey to Oxford. Bruce, and Arthur's old palfrey were weary from travel the day before, so Lord Gilbert did not press the beasts to much speed. I worried that the day would be far gone before he and the grooms attending us could return to Bampton. Even a powerful lord and his retainers might not wish to be on the road after dark. A noble's ransom will fetch more shillings than his purse will carry.

My concern was answered at Eynsham. Lord Gilbert drew our party to a halt before the abbey and asked – no, demanded – the porter to fetch Brother Giles, for so the hosteller was named. When he appeared he was told that Lord Gilbert and six grooms would require shelter that evening. The hosteller bowed and promised all would be ready when Lord Gilbert returned.

At Swinford Lord Gilbert raised a hand to halt our party and asked to be again told of Arthur's feat with the floating log. He chuckled anew at the tale and when Arthur urged the palfrey up to his side Lord Gilbert playfully swatted his groom upon the shoulder.

"I told you when I sent Arthur to accompany you to Oxford he was a useful fellow, did I not?"

"You did, and I have found him so more than once this past fortnight."

Lord Gilbert urged his courser into the river and our party splashed across the ford. When we had crossed he raised a hand again and asked whereabouts it was that the three horsemen had set out after Arthur and me the day before. I told him that observing the landscape had been low on my priorities when I saw men wielding swords emerge from the forest, but he charged me to take the lead and see could I not discover the place where the knaves lay in wait. We might, he asserted, learn something of the fellows did we find where they set their ambush. I thought this unlikely. I was wrong.

I prodded Bruce forward while attempting to recognize landmarks I had seen earlier going in the opposite direction on a galloping horse. This was not a successful endeavor until, some five hundred paces from the river, I saw an opening in the wood. A narrow path led to the north, which was the direction from which the three horsemen had appeared. This trail was near to overgrown with brambles, but it seemed possible that horses in single file might traverse it. I pulled Bruce to a halt and examined the forest through the aperture. Lord Gilbert reined his mount to a stop beside Bruce and studied the narrow opening.

"Was it here they lay in wait?" he asked.

"I am unsure. Does the path pierce the forest deeply enough that three horses may be hid from whoso may pass on the road? Fallen leaves obscure the ground. I see no hoofprints."

"We shall soon know," Lord Gilbert announced, and swung down from his saddle. I dismounted also, as did Arthur. Lord Gilbert instructed the others to wait with the horses, then plunged into the narrow, thorn-bordered path. Arthur and I followed.

Where this trail verged upon the road there was grass, but a few paces into the forest the track turned to mud. Too little sunlight penetrated the canopy for any but the hardiest brambles to prosper. The earth here was covered with a yellow overlay of fallen leaves, so that the bare ground was concealed until Lord Gilbert swept leaves from the track with the toe of a boot.

"Hah," he shouted triumphantly. "See here, Hugh."

He pointed to the damp earth at his feet. The prints of several horses were clearly impressed into the mud.

"Here is where the scoundrels lay in wait for you, Hugh."

I agreed that this was likely, as there was no other reason for horses to be upon this hidden forest track. This was the wrong season to seek blackberries, and the path was too shaded, and no man would do so from horseback even was it midsummer.

The low afternoon sun penetrated to the path in mottled patches of golden light. In June this might be so only at mid-day, but now, in November, many leaves had fallen so that even a slanting sun could partially illuminate the thorns and nettles which lined the trail.

Lord Gilbert, Arthur, and I gazed about this dent in the forest, seeking nothing in particular and finding just that.

"There were horsemen here," Lord Gilbert scoffed, "but the hoofprints of their beasts will not lead us to them."

Several times as we entered the forest thorns had fixed themselves to my chauces and coat. Another did so when I turned to follow Arthur to the road. I bent to release my coat from the bramble and against the dark twigs a tendril of green, illuminated in a tiny pool of sunlight, caught my eye. Lord Gilbert, now behind me, saw me pluck the object from a thorn and hold it to my eye.

"What have you there?"

I turned and held a wisp of green wool out to his inspection.

"Ah," he exclaimed. "The knaves did not leave this track whole after all."

"No. It seems they have abandoned a clue."

Some months earlier I had discovered a tuft of black wool in a bramble patch in a grove north of Bampton. The find led to a blackmailer and a murderer. I wondered if the green threads in my hand would lead to stolen books or a disappointed suitor.

Chapter 9

*L*ord Gilbert and his six grooms halted at the Castle Mill Stream and bade Arthur and me farewell. The streets of Oxford were crowded with folk completing the day's business. No man was likely to accost me in such a public place, and Lord Gilbert was eager to return to Eynsham.

Arthur and I again left our horses at the Stag and Hounds. Bruce seemed pleased to enter the yard behind the inn. Perhaps he considered the place a second home. We entered Canterbury Hall in time for supper, a pease pottage with maslin loaf and cheese. I was not much hungry.

Master John was surprised at my early return. After supper he called me to his chamber to learn of the journey and the treatment he supposed I had given to Lord Gilbert's son. Master John seems always ready to hear of surgeries I have done.

I explained that Sir Walter Benyt, was that his true name, had misled me, and told of my brush with felons on the road. Master John was of the same opinion as Lord Gilbert.

"There is villainy in this," he spluttered. "'Twas not only your purse they sought!"

"I have angered some who now wish to do me harm," I agreed.

"On my account, perhaps. I will be a wretched man should evil befall you as you seek my books. See to your safety, Hugh."

"Perhaps I was attacked by men in league with Sir Simon Trillowe?"

"Hmm. The sheriff's son who would have pursued Kate Caxton."

"Aye. We met a few days past outside the gate to Canterbury Hall. He is not content, I think, to let the matter rest."

"Young knights are a vain and vexatious lot. Well, he must be content, like it or not, in a month, will he not?"

"Aye. Kate will be my wife, we will dwell in Bampton, and I need see the fellow no more. If I find your books."

The Angelus Bell rang from the Priory Church of St Frideswide and I could not stifle a yawn. Master John grinned. "I thought 'twas only we aged who must go to our beds with the Angelus Bell," he jested.

"You? Aged?"

"A figure of speech. Older than you, Master Hugh. Although there be mornings my bones seem to creak more when I rise from my bed than they once did. In holy writ a man's years are three score and ten... but few there be who see that many seasons. So wed your Kate and make the most of the years God will grant you."

"I will do so. I did not sleep well last night for weighing who might have misled me and sent me to Bampton, and why they did so."

"Then be off to your bed, and leave the matter with God for the night. Thinking on it when you might be sleeping will bring no solution, and on the morrow, when you might be rested and have your wits about you, you will be doltish for loss of rest."

I did as Master John advised. But it was not so easy to fall to sleep as he suggested. Arthur had gone to the guest chamber before me and was snoring contentedly upon his pallet when I opened the door. Worry did not keep me awake, but Arthur's spluttering did. I know not how long I lay wakeful in my bed, but must have fallen to sleep before midnight, for I do not remember hearing the sacrist ring the priory bell for vigils.

I was awake, considering whether or not to rise from my bed, when a knock upon the guest chamber door announced the arrival of a kitchen servant with an ewer of warm water. Arthur peered up at me from his pallet as I poured the water into a basin and washed my hands and face. He considers such activity unnecessary. It is quite enough, in Arthur's view, to wash one's hands before eating.

I had no plan for this new day to seek enlightenment about Master John's stolen books. I thought rather to seek Kate and walk with her again along the Cherwell, did the gray clouds which obscured the sun this morning not produce a cold rain.

I told Arthur what I intended, set him free to his own devices for the day, and was about to walk through the gate to St John's Street when the porter stepped from the gatehouse. He made to set off toward the guest chamber, then saw me approach and halted.

"Master Hugh," he greeted as I approached. "There is a fellow here who seeks you." The porter turned and nodded toward the gatehouse.

The man who awaited me was no Oxford scholar. He wore no gown, but was dressed fashionably in parti-colored chauces and a deep-brown cotehardie of fine wool. Over this he wore a surcoat also of brown wool. He was of middle age, with a paunch the result of prosperous business. I had seen the fellow before, but could not remember where or when.

"Master Hugh?" the man bowed slightly in greeting. "Good day to you, sir."

"And good day to you. How may I serve you?"

"Nay. 'Tis I who will serve you. I am John Colyn, stationer of Northgate Street. You visited my shop some days past with a list of stolen books."

"I did. Have you news?"

"I do. A ragged young scholar visited me late yesterday. He wished to sell a volume, one of those on your list: *Sentences.*"

Peter Lombard's work is well known and much used in the colleges. There are surely many copies of the book in Oxford. I was convinced that Master Wyclif's books had traveled by cart to Westminster, so was not prepared to think the stationer's announcement of any importance. A hungry student might well wish to sell a book if its price would keep him fed for another term.

"Did you purchase the book?"

"Nay. The lad was not pleased with my offer. Said he would seek another who might pay more."

"What did you offer?"

"Fourteen shillings. He had not the volume with him. I told the lad I would promise no more unless I saw the book and might judge its condition."

"Think you another will offer more?"

"May be. If the book has not been ill used it might fetch twenty shillings."

Over the stationer's reply I heard excited voices from the gatehouse. The sound did not at first register with me. The porter was in feverish conversation with a female. Or rather, a lass was in feverish conversation with the porter, for it was a feminine voice which eventually seized my attention. Kate's voice.

I turned from the well-fed stationer and hastened to the gatehouse as the porter left his post and came toward me.

"Ah, Master Hugh, there is a maid here seeks you. I told her you were in discourse with another, but she will not be quieted 'til you see her. 'Twill be no hardship for you, sir. She be a pert lass."

I hastened through the gate, John Colyn striding behind, and found Kate waiting impatiently on Schidyard Street.

"Hugh... we must hurry," she exclaimed as she took my arm and drew me toward the High Street. "A young scholar wishes to sell a book from the list you gave to father. I am sent to fetch you. Father is bargaining with the lad to detain him 'til you arrive."

I suspected Robert Caxton's customer must be the same youth who offered *Sentences* to John Colyn. I needed no further urging to haste, although I was yet convinced that Master Wyclif's books were in the abbey at Westminster and my task now was to see how they might be recovered from that place.

John Colyn's description of the young scholar as

"ragged" was accurate. The youth who stood before Robert Caxton was pale and haggard. He was too young to grow a proper beard, and evidently too poor to afford a visit to a barber. A few feathery whiskers curled unmolested from his chin. His gown was near to threadbare. Had he no sturdy cloak he would endure a cold winter in the months to come.

The youth had brought the book with him on his visit to Caxton's shop, perhaps learning from John Colyn that its presence, was it not ill used, might generate a more liberal offer. Caxton was peering at the volume open upon his table as Kate and I breathlessly entered the shop.

It is difficult to pretend indifference when one has so obviously arrived in haste. Surely the scholar had seen Kate hurry away. Now she abruptly reappeared with a companion.

Caxton looked up briefly from the book as Kate and I tumbled through the door, but quickly resumed his examination of the volume. The youth snapped his head to follow Caxton's gaze when we darkened the open door, but when Caxton returned to the book, seemingly paying little notice to me or to Kate, the scholar also dismissed us and turned his attention back to the stationer. In a few steps I was close enough to overhear their conversation.

"*Sentences* is a book much in demand," the youth claimed. "'Tis a set book all scholars must know, and most do own."

"Aye. You speak true," Caxton replied. "Most, I think, do already own this work. So I am not persuaded I could readily sell it."

"'Tis in fine condition," the lad rejoined. "You will find few like it."

"It is, but for notes some scholar has penned in the margins. Are these your comments I see written here?" Caxton pointed to the page open before him.

"Nay. The monk who owned it before me so wrote."

"I wonder why he chose to sell it?" Caxton mused.

"Said he was to enter a house which had already a copy in its library. An' monks may own nothing of their own, so he was minded to sell the work to provide a small dowry for his sister, who had little to offer a suitor since the great death took away their parents."

This tale seemed plausible. But I knew also that Master John enjoyed writing remarks of approval or criticism in the margins of his books. The young scholar suddenly realized that my hurried entrance likely had to do with his book. I had moved behind Caxton to peer over his shoulder at the volume as it lay open upon the table. He assumed I was a possible buyer. His next words were addressed to me.

"Worth twenty shillings, sir, would you not agree?"

Perhaps the youth hoped I might bid against Caxton.

"It is well bound," I replied. But before I could comment further a margin note caught my eye. I bent over Caxton's shoulder for a closer look, for the light on such a gloomy day was poor. A previous owner had written a phrase in Latin and below the comment signed with his initials, "JW". My theory that Master John's books were now lodged in the abbey at Westminster shattered and fell in pieces at my feet.

I reached over the stationer's shoulder and with a finger silently touched the place on the parchment where Wyclif had marked the page.

"The sheriff's man has visited the shop," Caxton said, "with a list of books recently stolen. I will make offer of eighteen shillings for the work, but first I must know of the monk who sold it to you, so I may be sure I do not purchase stolen property."

I watched the young scholar as Caxton spoke, to see did he recoil at the words. He did. His eyes grew wide and a corner of his mouth twitched.

"The... the sheriff?" he stuttered.

"Aye," Caxton replied calmly. "All who deal in books have received notice to be alert. This volume is on the list of missing books, so I must be sure you came by it lawfully before..."

Caxton could not finish. The youth looked wildly

from me to Kate to Caxton, then in a flash he swept up the book from the table and bolted for the door. I leaped to stop him, but caught my foot as I attempted to vault the table. I tumbled to the floor at Kate's feet while the ragged scholar disappeared through the door. By the time I untangled my limbs and followed, the youth had taken to his heels and was fast disappearing down the Holywell Street.

Regardless of his gaunt appearance, short rations did not slow his feet. I pursued him, but to no avail. He ducked through the throng at the Northgate, but by the time I could manage to push through the crowd there he had disappeared among those who had business on Northgate Street. I gave up the chase and returned to Caxton's shop.

Kate and her father pressed me with excited questions when I returned. For most of these I had no answers. I did not know where he had gone, I did not know how to find him, and I did not know what he would next do about Master John's book. But I had a fair idea. A penniless scholar who would sell a stolen book is not likely to abandon the attempt if to do so will leave his stomach empty. I told Kate and her father that I intended to visit Oxford's stationers again so soon as I finished my dinner, to see had any others been offered the book. If so, did they know where the seller might be found; if not, to be aware an offer was likely.

I met Arthur on St John's Street as we both approached Canterbury Hall. I told him of the appearance of one of Master John's books. He was as surprised as I had been, assuming, like me, that the carters had hauled them off to Westminster.

Once past the gatehouse I went straight to Master John's door. He was not within. We found him in the hall in conversation with two scholars, while others prepared the room for dinner.

Master John is a good reader of men. One glance at my face told him I had news and was eager to share it. He dismissed his companions and turned expectantly to me.

I told him of the book, the poor scholar, and the initialed note in the margin.

"'Tis my book, Master Hugh. Well done, well done." He nearly danced with glee. "I congratulate you."

"But I lost both thief and book."

"You will find the fellow again. I am sure of it. So my books are yet in Oxford. This is good news indeed."

It did seem so at the time.

I was eager to visit Oxford's stationers, so bolted my meal. It was but another pottage, with maslin loaf. What more may a man wish than the companionship of a virtuous and comely wife and a belly well filled with a savory repast? I might have both of these so soon as I found the pillaged volumes. I told Arthur the reason for my haste and set off for the gatehouse and Schidyard Street. I left him chewing the last of his loaf, with instructions to catch up when he might.

I included Oxford's bookbinders in the search this day, though it was unlikely the youth would seek to sell there. But one other stationer had been offered *Sentences*. He had offered twelve shillings and the youth did not accept. This was surely the same ragged scholar. The stationer described him, to the meager whiskers upon his chin.

I thought the youth might now become cautious, and delay some days before again attempting to find a buyer. Nevertheless, I warned the stationers he had not yet visited to be wary, and promised to visit their shops each day to see did the scholar appear. I did, but he did not.

On the third day – it was Martinmas – I sent Arthur to enquire of the stationers in my stead and went to Holywell Street to seek Kate. It was a bright day. The sun only occasionally was lost behind clouds which scudded in from the north, driven by a brisk breeze. A good morning to walk the Cherwell, I thought. Kate agreed.

I spoke to her of my frustration. She did not immediately reply, but after we reached the stream and had walked silently for many paces she asked where it was I had last seen the youth when my pursuit failed.

"Just inside the Northgate. I saw him disappear before St Michael's at the Northgate as I tried to push through the throng which gathers at that place."

"If you were in danger of being apprehended for theft," she asked, "where would you go?"

"Some streets I knew well," I replied, "where I might dodge into some alley or press myself into a hidden doorway."

"Perhaps if we watched by the Church of St Michael the thief might travel past. Three days have passed. He may think he is safe, and so venture upon the streets. If that he lives near the church we might see and follow."

"We?"

"Four eyes are better than two," she laughed, "and 'twas me who found the broken thong in the grass."

This I could not gainsay. We walked the river to Trill Mill Bow, then returned through the Southgate to Holywell Street. I promised to call for her after dinner, and returned to Canterbury Hall with more sense of purpose than in many days.

None of the other stationers, Arthur reported, had been offered *Sentences*. I did not expect otherwise. I told Arthur of Kate's plan, and told him he would accompany us. Arthur had not seen the youth, but I had other work for him.

We finished our pottage and set off for Holywell Street as the bells of St Frideswide Priory rang for sext. Kate awaited me with sparkling eye, a courser ready for the chase.

A great, ancient tower stands before the Church of St Michael at the Northgate. Kate and I positioned ourselves against the north wall of this tower, just by the corner, where in conversation I might look past her toward the Northgate, and she might peer around my shoulder in the opposite direction down the Northgate Street. Arthur I sent to High Street, with instructions to watch for our approach. Did he see us appear from the north, he was to watch for the poor scholar we would follow and join the pursuit.

The youth appeared shortly after the bells of the Carmelite Friars rang for nones. I watched the Northgate while in conversation with Kate, but the youth did not appear there. He came from a cordwainer's shop across the street from where we stood.

Kate knew before she turned that I had seen our quarry, for I hesitated in the midst of conversation and she saw my eyes fix upon some distant prospect.

Together we watched the youth stand before the shop and peer in both directions before he set off toward the High Street. I did not think at the time to wonder why an impoverished scholar would visit a shop which sought the custom of the wealthy.

Kate and I walked behind the youth as he strode south on Northgate Street. We were able to lose ourselves among the passers-by, so the lad gave no sign he saw us.

I saw Arthur ahead, leaning against the corner of a goldsmith's shop. His location reminded me that I need make a purchase at some such place. Shortly after I spied Arthur he stood erect from the wall and nodded. I pointed toward the scholar, now but a few paces before us. I was some concerned that he might turn, see us in the throng, and take flight. But he did not.

Arthur fell into step behind Kate and I, and we followed as our prey passed Carfax and turned down Great Bailey Street toward the castle, then made his way down Little Bailey Street. There were fewer folk about on the street here. We dropped farther behind our quarry so as not to give notice of our presence.

The ragged scholar took no notice of us, or of any other upon the street. A few paces past St Ebbe's Church, but a short way from the Littlegate, he turned and disappeared into a tavern.

The Red Dragon is much like other taverns liberally sprinkled about Oxford. It is of timber, wattle and daub, two stories, with a thatched roof above. Did the youth enter the place for a cup of wine to quench his thirst, I wondered, or did he reside in the rooms under the roof? There was but one way to answer these questions.

I bid Arthur return to St Ebbe's Churchyard and make his way to the alley which ran behind the Red Dragon and the structures on either side of the tavern. I assumed there was a rear door from the Red Dragon opening to the alley, and assumed further that if the youth saw me enter the front door he might make for this alley and escape.

I gave Arthur time to place himself in the lane behind the tavern, told Kate to wait across the street before a taylor's shop, and entered the dim tavern. Several patrons sat upon benches, elbows on table, evidently enjoying both the wine and conversation. Most of the customers were students, but the scholar I sought was not among them.

The proprietor of the Red Dragon is a scrawny fellow. When he saw me enter he stood behind his table and reached for an ewer and cup, assuming I wished to quench a thirst. I had to disappoint him.

"The youth who just now entered, has he gone up to his lodging?" I asked, nodding toward the stairs which occupied a rear corner of the tavern. Such an assertion was a risk, but I thought it slight, and believed I would have more success with the master of the place did he assume I owned some acquaintance with the scholar I sought.

"Aye," he bowed, and placed the ewer back upon the table.

The tavern's upper storey held a dark, narrow passageway which ran the length of the rear wall of the building. Six openings opposite the wall indicated chambers of lodgers at the tavern. These openings were draped with cheap hempen fabric to close each room from those who passed in the corridor.

I moved silently from one curtained portal to the next, listening for sounds of occupation. At the third opening I heard footsteps, and a bench being drawn across the planks of the floor. I swept the hempen screen aside and found myself staring into the wide, frightened eyes of the lad I sought. I opened my mouth to challenge the youth about Master John's book, but he acted before I could speak.

There was a window in the wall of this cell, opposite its entrance, which gave opening to the street. It was but a simple frame, hinged upon one side, and covered with an oiled skin. The scholar leaped from his bench, flung open the window, and before I could speak climbed through it and dropped to the street. I ran to the open window in time to see him dash toward the Littlegate. Kate watched him run, then looked up at me. I shrugged in answer to the question in her eyes. I had found and lost my quarry.

There was little hope of catching the fleeing youth. For one who appeared ill fed, he showed remarkable heels when pressed. Light bathed the tiny chamber now the window was open. I examined the place, hoping to find Master John's book among the few objects in the place. I was disappointed.

The chamber was hardly wider than I am tall, and no more than five paces from window to hempen drape. In this space there was a bench, a small table, a bed, and a mean chest of shabby construction.

No book lay upon the table, nor upon the bed. I drew the straw mattress from the bed to see was the book hidden there. It was not. The chest had no lock. I opened it and found only clothing – a spare kirtle and braes and a gown more tattered than the one the youth wore.

What had become of *Sentences*? The lad had no book in his hands when he dove through the window. And what of the other books stolen from Master John?

I left the barren cell and returned to the tavern. Its occupants were as they had been when I entered, the proprietor sitting with his ewer, idly drumming fingers upon a stained table while he awaited custom.

"The youth who lives above," I began, "does he carry a book with him when he comes in and goes out?"

"Ask 'im," the man rumbled. It was surprising that such a deep voice came from such a lean, boney frame. "'E went up to 'is lodgin' just before you."

"He is not there."

"'E ain't?" The fellow frowned. "I seen 'im go up, but not come down."

"He departed through his window."

"You be no friend of 'is, then."

"I do not know the lad."

"Why d'you seek 'im... an' why ask of books?"

The tavern keeper seemed a plain and honest sort. I decided to speak frankly to him and trust my judgment was not flawed.

"The youth has tried to sell a book not long since stolen from another."

"From you?"

"From a friend. What is the lad's name?"

"Robert... Robert Salley."

"Has he lodged with you long?"

"Since Michaelmas term last year."

"He seems ill fed."

"Aye. An' often short on 'is rent, too."

"Have you seen him with a book?"

"Aye, but that's expected of scholars, ain't it?"

"Surely. But in his room there are no books now. And he took no book with him when he went through the window."

"Prob'ly sold it... to feed himself another term."

"'Tis likely."

It seemed likely also that one of Oxford's stationers or bookbinders had seen an opportunity to make a profit from stolen goods, and purchased Master John's book. It would be no trouble to send another, unknown to the stationers, to enquire was a copy of *Sentences* offered. The stationers of Oxford knew me and Arthur and knew why we sought *Sentences*. An unprincipled stationer might hide the book from us but offer to sell to another. But where were Wyclif's other books? Had perhaps some other unscrupulous bookseller acquired them? Then why not *Sentences*? Would a dishonest merchant buy twenty-one books but not one more? This made no sense.

I opened the tavern's rear door and called to Arthur, who stood but a few paces away in the lane behind the tavern. Together we left the place and joined Kate, who was twitching with curiosity to learn what had happened in the tavern. I told them both.

I directed Arthur to loiter on Little Bailey Street and Littlegate Street. Should the youth return to the Red Dragon, he was to apprehend him and take him to Canterbury Hall. Arthur could not catch the lad in a foot-race, but one so puny as this scholar would never break free of a man like Arthur, once he had a hand upon the lad's shoulder. And Robert Salley had never seen Arthur, so could be approached without being frightened. I told Arthur to return to Canterbury Hall with the Angelus Bell did the youth not return to the tavern.

I walked with Kate to the Holywell Street, then returned to Canterbury Hall. Master John greeted me expectantly but I was required to disappoint him with the unsatisfactory outcome of the day's quest.

"Take heart, Hugh. You learn more each day."

"But what I learn serves but to confuse me."

"That youthful scholar will surely return to his lodgings," Wyclif concluded. "Then Arthur will have him. His chamber might be meanly furnished, but for a poor man even little is too much to lose."

"I believe he has sold *Sentences* to some unprincipled stationer. It was not in his room, and he did not have it in hand when he went through his window. Tomorrow, early, I would like to send another to call upon the stationers of Oxford, seeking a copy of *Sentences*. A scholar new to Oxford, and not well known, would suit. Have you a scholar here at Canterbury Hall who could undertake this commission?"

"Aye. I have such a man. Roger Gaddesden is new to Oxford and the Hall this term."

"Is he a monk or secular?"

"A secular. But why… ah, I see. If a Benedictine from Eynsham has to do with this, it might be best to exclude other Benedictines from the duty."

I heard the Angelus Bell ring from St Frideswide's Priory Church. Darkness was upon the town. Arthur soon stalked through the gatehouse and reported no success. Robert Salley had not returned to the tavern.

Master John and Arthur and I plotted the next day while we consumed a supper of pottage and maslin loaf. When the meal was done Wyclif called Roger Gaddesden to his chamber and I explained what was needed of him on the morrow. The man was near my own age, but seemed as exuberant as a child when told what was required of him. He was as much in awe of Master John as I had been when a student at Balliol College.

Chapter 10

Next day at dawn Arthur and I set out for the Red Dragon while Roger Gaddesden prepared to visit stationers in search of Master John's stolen book. Clothed in Lord Gilbert's livery of blue and black, Arthur was a memorable sight. I bid him discard this uniform temporarily and don a laborer's garb. He was not pleased at the reduction in station, but agreed with the necessity when I explained what was needed of him.

I thought it best that Arthur and I not be seen together near the Red Dragon, so bid him wait in Pennyfarthing Lane while I went first to the tavern to see had Robert Salley returned in the night. The proprietor had not yet opened his door for customers. I thumped upon it until my knuckles grew tender before the fellow opened to me.

No, Salley had not returned. Yes, I might inspect his lodging myself did I desire. I did. The bare room was as I left it the day before. I departed the tavern, found Arthur wandering Pennyfarthing Lane, and told him to spend the morning watching Little Bailey Street and Littlegate Street for Salley's return.

The poor scholar did not return to his lodging that day, nor any other so far as I know. His trail was cold. Roger Gaddesden found no copy of *Sentences* offered, nor did any stationer know where such a volume might be had. One was willing to take an order, advising Gaddesden that a scribe in his employ could produce a copy in three months. Master John's book, like Robert Salley, had disappeared.

I sent Arthur to prowl Little Bailey Street next day also, knowing not that the ragged scholar would never again be seen near the Red Dragon. But another was seen there, and this appearance served to deepen my confusion.

On the days when I assigned Arthur the boring task of pacing up and down the lanes near the Red Dragon, the fellow had only a maslin loaf for his dinner, washed down with a cup of ale from the tavern. So he was eager and punctual when the bell at St Fridewide's rang for vespers and thereby warned that supper was about to be served at Canterbury Hall.

Between spoonfuls of pottage Arthur told me of a visitor this day to the Red Dragon. Shortly after the sixth hour, while he was within the tavern concluding his sparse dinner with a cup of ale, Sir Simon Trillowe entered the place. At first Arthur thought it was me entering the shadowy tavern.

"You an' Sir Simon be much alike, since you began growin' a beard. An' he was wearin' a fur coat much like yours."

Sir Simon bought no wine or ale, but strode directly to the stairway. His entry, Arthur reported, seemed not to interest the proprietor, who but glanced at Sir Simon as he entered, then showed no further interest in his presence.

Sir Simon mounted the stairs to the upper floor of the tavern, spent but a few moments there, then clattered hurriedly back down to the ground floor. He walked straight to the tavern-keeper and addressed the fellow in whispered conversation. Arthur had seated himself by a far wall so as to be inconspicuous did Robert Salley return. He was too far distant from the parley to hear, but he saw the proprietor shake his head to answer several questions from Sir Simon.

Sir Simon, Arthur added, left the tavern in a black mood. His brow was furrowed, his chin thrust forward, his visage foul.

This information was near as hard to digest as the Canterbury Hall pottage. Who, or what, had Sir Simon sought at the Red Dragon? And why did failure cause the man such discontent? Did he seek Robert Salley also? If so, why? I had accepted Master John's commission to seek a thief and stolen books, but rather than solve the riddle, my efforts had only found new mysteries. There was nothing to do but scratch my head in bewilderment, so I did.

If I found Robert Salley I might press the youth about Master Wyclif's book: how he came by it, and where may be the others. But I could hold no threat over Sir Simon Trillowe, to demand why he visited the Red Dragon and what he sought there. Perhaps it was not Salley Sir Simon pursued, but from Arthur's description of the event Sir Simon did not find what he wished, and Salley was gone from the place.

I walked alone – I did not wish any who frequented the Red Dragon to see Arthur in my presence – next morning to the tavern. The place was newly opened for business but had not yet attracted custom. I ordered a cup of wine and settled myself at a bench. The wine was well watered and I wondered that the mayor and sheriff did not fine the fellow. Just such practice caused the terrible St Scholastica Day riots that took so many lives when I was new come to Oxford.

Perhaps the sheriff or the mayor had taken note of the business and sent Sir Simon to collect a fee which would turn the law from the Red Dragon's door? But Arthur had seen no coin change hands, else he would have said, and had seen the tavern-keeper shake his head, "No." I dismissed the thought.

The low morning sun did little to illuminate the interior of the tavern. The proprietor gave no sign that he recognized me as the man who sought Robert Salley three days past. He was bored, drumming fingers upon his wine-stained table, and eventually began a conversation about the weather. November in England. Is there no other thing in November to complain of, the weather will always suit.

I wore my fur coat this day, for the morning was chill. So it was clear to the fellow that I was no college scholar, and of some means; a man whose custom he would like to keep. It would have been easier for him to do so had he been less liberal with water in his wine.

When he saw that my cup was near empty the tavern-keeper rose, ewer in hand, and approached my bench. I waved him away and as I did so I saw recognition flash across his face.

"Ah… you was seekin' Robert Salley yesterday," he said in his gravelly voice.

"Nay. 'Twas three days past I sought him. Has he returned?"

I thought I knew the answer to that question, but thought it could do no harm to ask.

"Pardon… a gentleman lookin' much like you was 'ere seekin' the lad yesterday. He's not been back. Never seen 'im before, but 'e knew what 'e was about. Went straight up to Salley's lodgin's, an' when 'e saw 'e wasn't there come straight down an' asked when 'e was like to return. Told 'im I hadn't seen the fellow since Wednesday."

"Did you tell him how it was when Salley disappeared? How another sought him, and he went through the window to escape?"

"Aye."

"How did the gentleman take the news?"

"Right black about it, 'e was."

"Did he ask to be told when Salley returns, if he returns?"

"Nay."

I wondered why that could be. I was about to offer the man tuppence would he promise to send word to the porter at Canterbury Hall did Robert Salley appear. Why would Sir Simon not do likewise? Perhaps he knew where the poor scholar might be was he not at the tavern.

I opened my purse and gave the tavern-keeper tuppence; for the wine and for his eyes, which I asked he keep open for either Robert Salley or Sir Simon. Did the poor scholar return, he agreed to send his wife to Canterbury Hall with the news. Did Sir Simon, whose name I did not let fall, call again, he would report the event and conversation to me when I next called. I did not tell the fellow that Arthur would also be watching for

Salley and Sir Simon. Perhaps I did not fully trust the tavern-keeper. He was willing to take silver from me. Might he accept coin from another to ignore or mislead me? Perhaps I am become too suspicious of other men.

I found Arthur where I left him, on Fish Street, before St Frideswide's Priory, and told him of Sir Simon's search for Robert Salley.

"Why would 'e be seekin' the likes of a poor scholar?"

"Could be coincidence," I replied, "or it could be that Salley has something which Sir Simon wants."

"Or knows somethin' Sir Simon wants to know," Arthur added. "An' if 'e wants somethin', might be the same thing we want of 'im."

"Aye. Perhaps both, for the scholar has little else another man might want, but for Master John's book."

"Why would Sir Simon want that?"

"'Tis worth twenty shillings. Even a young knight would not despise such a sum."

"But 'ow would 'e know Salley had it, an' 'ow did the lad come by it anyway?"

This conversation occupied us as we walked through a misting rain to Canterbury Hall and our dinner. I was much pleased with my fur coat and felt some guilt that Arthur, striding beside me, was not so warm or dry. The difference in our situations did not seem to trouble him. Perhaps he had lived cold and wet so long that the conditions were of no consequence to him.

Being chilled and damp did not spoil Arthur's appetite. He plunged into his bowl of pottage with his usual enthusiasm. And, in truth, the meal was some better than common. This was a fast day, so no pork flavored the peas and beans, but there were lentils and scraps of capon to season the mix. The cook, however, seemed to enjoy a balance. The ale was stale.

The sun was beginning to appear through breaks in the clouds when dinner was done. Arthur was surely pleased with this development, for I sent him to watch over the Red Dragon again. He would stay dry for the afternoon.

As for myself, I thought to get my feet wet, walking the path by the Cherwell with Kate. The banns had been read twice now from St Peter's Church. Once more, two days hence, and we might wed. I was eager for that day, and might have thought to hasten it by continuing a search for books and thieves. But Kate's company was a strong lure. I yielded to her attraction and set out for Holywell Street. It was well I did so, else finding Master John's books might have taken longer. Indeed, I might not have found them yet. Was it Kate who drew me to Holywell Street and the path along the Cherwell, or was it a push from the Lord Christ?

Robert Caxton smiled as I entered his shop and called to Kate, who was employed again in the workroom. I wonder that he could smile at a man who was about to take daughter and assistant from him, and cost him the income from a house as well. Mayhap he remembered days past, when he courted Kate's mother. A man must find it difficult to view his daughter so, as from another, younger man's eyes. Perhaps the same sentiment will comfort me twenty years hence.

I was correct about damp feet, although Kate seemed not to mind. The grass was wet with the morning's mist and soaked our shoes, already muddy from Oxford's streets. I was engrossed in Kate and our conversation so did not notice the clot of black gowns before us on the river bank until we were nearly upon them. Four youths gazed at something in the river, taking no heed of our approach. It was a normal reaction to peer also into the river, to learn what held their attention. It was a corpse.

A body floated face down but a short way from the river bank. It was prevented from following the current downstream by a leg entangled in a branch broken from some upstream tree which had lodged against the bank. Water weeds waved in the gentle current 'round the dead man's head, like unshorn green locks.

The four who stood studying the corpse were young scholars. They babbled excitedly among themselves but took no measures to draw the unfortunate fellow from the water. My feet were already wet, and the corpse lay in water barely knee deep. I gave my coat to Kate, drew off my shoes, pushed my way past the students, and waded into the Cherwell. In a few moments I freed the lifeless form from the broken bough and hauled the corpse upon the river bank.

I do not recommend wading in the Cherwell in November. Although I had only gone into the water to my knees, I was chilled and shivering when I dragged my burden to the path. While I resumed my coat two of the young scholars turned the drowned man to his back. There was silence for a moment, then one exclaimed, "'Tis Robert."

Robert is a common name. My future father-in-law bears it. So I did not consider that the drowned man I had pulled from the Cherwell might be Robert Salley even though the youth had gone missing.

I turned while donning my coat to view the pale, bloated face which now gazed whitely at the sky. It was indeed Robert Salley. I recognized his tattered gown, now soaked and clinging to his spare frame, and the sparse whiskers which ornamented his chin.

I saw another thing as well. I knelt beside the corpse for a closer look at the dead scholar. A faint purple bruise, nearly invisible, circled his neck.

Kate and the four who had discovered Salley in the river followed my gaze. Kate saw where my eyes fell and spoke first. "What has caused such a mark?" she whispered.

"Thick fingers, pressed tight, would make such a bruise."

"Fingers?" one of the scholars exclaimed. "But surely Robert has drowned... he was in the river."

"He may be drowned," I agreed. "There is a way to tell."

"How so?" the youth asked.

"If his lungs are filled with water, he drowned. But if his lungs are not full of water, he died before he went into the river."

"How can this be known?"

"We will lift him by his feet. If water pours from his lips, he died in the river. If no water, or very little comes forth, he died upon land."

I motioned to a scholar to take one sodden leg, and I grasped the other. Together we lifted Robert Salley until his corpse was near vertical. Kate held her hand to her lips as we all watched the dead man's mouth. Little water came from the waxen lips; perhaps a drop or two.

"What does this mean?" another of the students asked when we had dropped poor Salley to the river bank.

"It means," I replied, "that he was murdered. Strangled, then placed in the Cherwell so that, was he found dead, all would assume he was drowned."

"We must send for the sheriff," another said.

I agreed. Two of the scholars set off for the castle while Kate, I, and the other two kept watch over the mortal remains of Robert Salley. I wondered if, in the depths of the Cherwell, ink might be soaking from Master John's *Sentences*.

Our place on the banks of the Cherwell was across the town from the castle. It was half an hour and more before I saw the scholars return, followed by two sergeants. These officers had surely been chosen for brawn, not wit. They studied the corpse, debated calling the hue and cry, poked poor Robert in the ribs with a toe as if he might be roused from slumber, then cast about for evidence that a crime might have been committed.

It was with some difficulty that I convinced them that this was so. Their lives would be simplified was Salley's death but mischance. Scholars have perished in Oxford rivers before, usually when drunk, falling from bridges or river banks. The sergeants, after much persuading, reluctantly agreed that the indistinct purple bruise about Salley's neck suggested strangulation.

One sergeant left us to seek castle servants and a litter, the other remained to watch the corpse. He made no effort to question me or the four students. So far as he was concerned Salley was but another penniless youth, come to Oxford, far from home, who had the misfortune to die unknown and unmourned. He would be buried on the morrow in a pauper's grave in his parish churchyard.

I was not satisfied with this conclusion to Salley's brief life. There was much coincidence in the matter. A youth who possessed and wished to sell a stolen book is found strangled in the river. This same scholar was sought by Sir Simon Trillowe for reasons I knew not. Might these events be tied? If so, it was no neat bundle.

The sheriff's man showed no curiosity about the corpse at his feet. He chewed upon a fingernail and stared impassively across the water meadow toward the spire of St Frideswide's Priory Church.

The four young scholars began to drift away in a knot toward the East Bridge. I drew Kate after me and caught up with them.

"You recognized the dead man," I reminded them. "Did he make enemies readily?"

"Nay," one replied. "Was a quiet fellow, was Robert."

"How did you know of him?"

"He was of Balliol College, like us. But not this term."

"Not this term?"

"Robert had little coin. No patron, and his parents both dead of plague when he was but a babe."

"An orphan? Who took him in? Did he speak of this?"

"Aye, a lay brother at the abbey was cousin to his mother."

"The abbey? What abbey is that?"

"Salley, in the West Riding of Yorkshire."

I knew of this abbey. It is but a few miles from Clitheroe. Salley Abbey is a Cistercian House, and by repute is not wealthy, being found on poor, undrained land beside the river Ribble. A lay brother there would have few resources to spare for an orphan lad. But the abbey would provide an education for a boy who showed a quick wit. So Robert Salley had gained enough education to admit him to Balliol College, but had not the means to keep him there.

"You are of Balliol College also?" I asked.

"Aye, like I said."

"As was I," I told them. "Some years past, now."

The four youthful scholars peered at me, at my warm fur coat, and at my comely companion, then exchanged glances which seemed to say, "Perhaps much study is of value."

"Robert had made no enemies?"

"He was not one to best another in dispute," one remarked. "Quiet, like."

"Not likely some felon killed him for his purse," another added. "No reason to murder someone like Robert."

"Did you see him frequently? Was he much about in the past few days?"

The four scholars were silent for a moment, then one spoke. "Haven't seen 'im for three, four days. Doesn't live with us now. Did, once, but took cheaper lodgings at some tavern over near St Ebbe's Church."

"When you last saw him did he seek your aid? Was he troubled?"

Three of the black-gowned youths shrugged and peered at the other, who had reported seeing Salley earlier in the week.

"Owed me four pence. Said as he'd have it for me soon. Didn't seem troubled; seemed content. I'll not see my loan repaid now."

"And this was four days past?"

"Aye... Monday."

This news was of interest. Robert Salley thought on Monday he might soon come in to money; from the sale of Master John's book, I had no doubt.

"Did Salley own many books?" I asked.

"Nay," they chorused, and laughed grimly, as one. "Had to borrow or rent when a book was needed."

"I wonder how he thought to come by money to pay

a debt? Did he say aught about that? Perhaps he received the coins and another knew of his gain and murdered him for it."

The four exchanged glances, then the youth who last saw Salley replied. "Didn't say where he was to find the money. Strange you should speak of books. He did ask if I knew of any who might wish to buy Lombard's work, *Sentences*. Didn't think he sought a buyer for himself. How could he afford such a work? Thought he asked for another."

As we spoke the sergeant returned with two castle servants and a litter. We watched silently as Robert Salley was rolled onto the frame and carried off toward the East Bridge and the High Street. The servants dealt roughly with the corpse, but Robert Salley would mind little.

I was wet from knees down and chilled, and wished to return to Canterbury Hall and seek dry chauces. But there was more to learn this day.

"Salley wished to find a buyer for *Sentences*, you say? Where did he keep this book?"

"At his lodgings, I suppose. Didn't say."

I decided to be frank with these Balliol scholars. "It was not found there. It was a book stolen from Master John Wyclif many weeks past."

"Master Wyclif's book?" one exclaimed. "How would Robert come by that? He was no thief."

"A man hungry enough might become what he was not," another of the scholars suggested softly. "You are sure," he continued, "that this was Master Wyclif's book that Robert wished to sell?"

"Aye. I saw the book when Salley tried to sell it to a stationer on the Holywell Street. It is Master Wyclif's book, there can be no doubt. I saw Master John's mark by a note he made on a page."

The scholars peered at one another with furrowed brows. "We've heard of Master Wyclif's loss," one said. "Twenty books stolen, 'tis said."

"Twenty-two."

"Did Robert take them," another puzzled, "why did

he seek to sell but one?"

"And where are the others?"

"There are no books where he lodges," I told them. "I found the place... a tavern on Little Bailey Street. Salley eluded me when I sought him there. Had I caught him, he might yet be alive. Master Wyclif has commissioned me to seek his books. I searched the place where Salley slept. There were no books there."

"And little else, I'd wager," a scholar remarked through pursed lips.

"Aye. A bed, a table, a bench, and a small chest with little in it. Did Salley have other friends where he might have left the book 'til he found a buyer?"

The young scholars exchanged glances again, this time with a wary cast to their eyes. I had asked a tender question. I did not press the matter, but waited until one might find his voice and explain. This did not happen readily. I was about to speak again when one found his tongue.

"Robert has... had... kin nearby. Not as he ever won much aid from him. Couldn't, really, as monks are to own nothing."

"A monk, in a house near Oxford?"

"Aye. Another cousin to his mother, Robert said."

"Which house is it?"

"Eynsham."

"Did Robert travel there often?"

"At first. But not much in the last year. Got nothing when he did seek his cousin, so gave up, I think."

"Did he name this monk?"

"May have. Don't remember." The speaker peered at his companions. They all shook their heads to acknowledge ignorance, but one finally spoke.

"He was from Longridge, or some such place. Robert said as 'twas not far from Salley and the abbey. He's librarian at Eynsham Abbey."

Unless another monk from Longridge had place at Eynsham Abbey, Robert Salley was cousin to Michael Longridge. My assumptions regarding the monk were in

153

tatters. If he hired the carters to transport Master John's stolen books to Westminster, how did Robert Salley come by one of them? Perhaps Longridge took pity on his impoverished relative and gave him a book, knowing well he would sell it to feed himself.

If such a thing occurred it showed a lack of thought on the monk's part. A stolen book offered for sale in Oxford must soon be identified. Perhaps Longridge had, after all, nothing to do with Master John's missing books. Perhaps he sent books to Westminster in sale or simple exchange, one abbey to another. Perhaps Robert Salley was in league with other penniless scholars. Perhaps with others who knew the worth of Master John's books, he conspired to steal, then sell the volumes. Perhaps the other missing books were with Salley's companions in mischief. There were too many "perhapses" to the business.

I had no more questions for the scholars. What use were more questions when I found no answers for the questions already asked? Kate took my arm and we walked north to the East Bridge. The youths watched us depart enviously. Their wistful expressions caused me to stride with head high and shoulders back. Pride is a sin, but it is difficult to walk with Kate and remain humble.

Chapter 11

We walked silently, absorbed in our own thoughts of death and murder. Who would mourn Robert Salley? Is there a greater loss than to die unlamented? Kate must have contemplated similar notions. She broke the silence.

"I wonder will any seek St Ebbe's Church tomorrow to see Robert Salley buried?"

"There will be few who know he's dead," I replied.

"The one who did murder will know. And the Balliol scholars will tell others before this day is done."

"So among those who will grieve at St Ebbe's Church tomorrow will be a few of Salley's friends and, perhaps, a murderer. I will join the mourners."

I left Kate at Holywell Street. Arthur I found stalking the lanes about the Red Dragon. I told him of Robert Salley's death and together we made for St Frideswide's Lane and Canterbury Hall.

After supper that evening I sought Master John and told him of Robert Salley. His eyes gleamed in the light from a cresset as I explained that the dead scholar was a cousin to Michael of Longridge.

"This may be of significance," he declared, when told of the relationship. "Would you agree?"

"It so may be, but how or why eludes me," I admitted.

"Me also, but there is a tie between the two and my stolen books or I am much mistaken."

Master John is seldom mistaken.

Most men, when they die, are borne to church by family and set down in the lych gate. Robert Salley was taken to St Ebbe's Church by two castle servants. I suspect he spent little time in the lych gate and no priest met him there to escort his corpse to the church.

Arthur and I arrived next day at St Ebbe's Church as the sacrist at St Frideswide's Priory rang the bell for terce. Dark days of winter approached, so this was but a short while after dawn. I thought it unlikely that any priest would rise early from his bed to say mass for Robert Salley, and likewise thought it doubtful that any funeral for the poor scholar would last long.

My timing was excellent. A few black-gowned scholars milled about the church porch. Among these I saw the youths who had found Salley in the Cherwell. Some townsmen mingled with the students. With one of these burghers was a maid of perhaps eighteen years. I looked also for a tonsure, but no hooded monk was present. If Salley's cousin from Eynsham knew of his death, he chose not to travel to Oxford. Or perhaps Abbot Thurstan refused him permission to leave the abbey.

A priest opened the porch door and bid us enter. There were but twelve souls present to follow him. If the love and respect a man earns in his life is reflected in the multitude who mourn at his funeral, it must be written that Robert Salley died in small repute.

The priest hurried through the mass, the Lord's Prayer, and the absolutions, then concluded with a brief sermon:

"Good men, ye see here a mirror to us all. A corpse brought to the church. May God have mercy upon him, and bring him to his bliss that shall last forever. Wherefore each man that is wise, make him ready, for we all shall die, and we know not how soon."

The priest spoke these words with little conviction, as if he, at least, expected to live yet many more years. But his observation gripped me, as if the giant I had seen at Eynsham had wrapped a fist about my heart and squeezed it still. Not for the first time I prayed silently that the Lord Christ would grant me enough days that I might wed my Kate and see children play about my feet.

Robert Salley's four friends took up his coffin when

the priest was done. We mourners followed them from the echoing nave into a churchyard now bright with sunlight. A morning fog had burned away. It was near pleasant enough to dispel grief for those who knew Robert Salley, but not for all. The lass was overcome and sobbed noisily into the shoulder of the older man who accompanied and steadied her. I learned later this was her father.

The priest blessed the ground and grave-diggers bent to their task in a far corner of St Ebbe's Churchyard. When their work was done the four who bore Salley to the place slipped short ropes under his coffin and lowered him into his grave. I was some surprised to see the coffin go into the hole. Most poor families will rent a coffin from a carpenter, then draw the corpse from it at the grave and bury the dead only in a shroud. Someone thought enough of Robert Salley to pay for a coffin. I wondered who, and if that person knew Salley well enough to know where he might conceal a book.

Sir Simon Trillowe may have sought Robert Salley when he was alive, but he had no interest in him dead. Or did not know that he now slept in St Ebbe's Churchyard. News of the corpse pulled from the Cherwell had surely been spoken of in Oxford Castle. The sheriff's officers knew Salley's name and certainly reported it. I decided that Robert Salley dead was of no importance to Sir Simon. In this I was but partly correct.

Although Sir Simon made no appearance at Robert Salley's funeral, I wished to be sure that he had no more interest in the youth. I sent Arthur to prowl about the Red Dragon. Someone might visit the tavern to claim Salley's possessions. I did not think it would be Sir Simon, but I had been wrong about so many things that I was no longer willing to consider any event unlikely.

As with other days, when I could think of no other task, my mind and feet strayed to the Holywell Street. Arthur walked south from St Ebbe's Church, toward the tavern, and I went north. I was nearly to the Northgate before I realized that I was following the maid whose tears had flowed so abundantly in St Ebbe's Churchyard.

She walked with the man upon whose shoulder she had wept. I was curious about the two, so slowed my steps and followed.

A few paces from the Northgate they entered a cordwainer's shop near straight across from the ancient tower of St Michael's Church. This was the shop where Robert Salley had appeared while Kate and I stood watching the Northgate. I decided to enter and learn what I might. I did not expect to be recognized as a mourner at Robert Salley's interment. I had kept to the fringe of the small assembly, the better to observe those who attended. And the lass and her escort were too much involved with the burial. I did not think they noticed much of their companions in sorrow.

A sign above the door announced that the shop was the place of business of John Stelle, dealer in finest cordovan leather and shoes. Here was no ordinary cobbler. Here was the shop of a man who could well afford to pay for a coffin, did a weeping daughter ask.

I was leaping to conclusions as I walked through the door. Sometimes the leap to a conclusion over a chasm of ignorance may land a man in error and affliction. I have known it so often enough that I try to avoid such a vault. But there are occasions when such a jump results in benefit and wisdom. This day was such a time.

It was John Stelle who attended Robert Salley's funeral. The man who now stood behind a table of leather goods and shoes was the same who mourned at St Ebbe's Church. He greeted me politely, with no trace of recognition in his eyes.

"Good day, sir. May I interest you in any of these fine goods?" The fellow eyed my fur coat and decided I was a likely customer. As he spoke he swept a hand over a table of costly items from Cordova. There were sheaths of finest goatskin for daggers, and shoes of goatskin and horsehide. Yes, I thought, you may surely interest me in such wares, but not today.

The cordwainer's red-eyed daughter watched me from an open door at the rear of the room. The lass would have been no beauty when at her best. But now her cheeks were pale and swollen and her eyes red. Her nose was over large. So is mine, truth be told. But the grieving maid's nose ended in a bulbous appendage the size, if not the color, of a grape. Unkempt hair splayed from under her hood. A belt of her father's finest cordovan circled her cotehardie. Her father's prosperity was reflected in her ample waistline.

This shop was much like Robert Caxton's business. The front room held goods for sale and could be opened to the street with shutters which were lifted in clement weather.

Behind this room was another, entered through the door where the maid now stood. I imagined it to be, as with the stationer's shop, a workroom. In a rear corner of the front room a steep, narrow stairway led up to what was surely private quarters above. The shop and its goods spoke of success and prosperity. It is, no doubt, easier to live well selling to the rich than to the poor.

"You have just come from Robert Salley's funeral," I replied.

"Aye," the cordwainer agreed, somewhat startled at my assertion. The lass choked back a sob and stumbled away from the door. I heard her sit heavily upon a hidden bench in the workroom. She was a well-fed maiden who would sit heavily regardless of the time or season, but her collapse was, perhaps, more pronounced this day.

"Did you know him well?"

"Well enough," was the reluctant reply.

"Had you cause to see or visit with him since Monday?"

"Aye. Why do you ask? Who are you?"

"I am Hugh de Singleton, surgeon, and bailiff for Lord Gilbert Talbot at his Bampton estate."

I saw the fellow's nose wrinkle, as if I had tracked manure from the street into his shop. Such is a common reaction when men learn I am a bailiff. Most such officers are noted for their ability to cheat both their employer and his tenants and villeins.

"What does a bailiff from Bampton have to do with poor Salley? 'E wasn't from there."

"No. From the west riding of Yorkshire."

"Aye... and a scholar at Balliol College."

"When he could afford it, I am told."

"He was goin' to resume 'is studies next term," Stelle declared.

"He'd come in to money, then?"

"In a way."

"What way? His friends told me he was alone in the world but for a cousin at Salley Abbey and another who is a brother at Eynsham. He'd get no coin from a monk."

"Why do you care where 'is money come from?" The cordwainer spoke with some hostility.

"Because it may have been ill gotten."

"What? Robert Salley was an honest lad."

"Then why did he try but a few days past to sell a stolen book? One book will hardly finance a return to Balliol College. But the book he tried to sell was one of twenty-two stolen a month past."

"The books what was taken from Master Wyclif?" Stelle asked with incredulity. "Robert wouldn't steal another scholar's books."

So word of the theft at Canterbury Hall was now known even on Northgate Street.

"He may not have stolen it, but he had it in his possession and tried to sell it to a stationer on the Holywell Street a week past. I saw the book, and saw him with it. 'Twas Master Wyclif's book, there can be no doubt."

To this the cordwainer had no reply. His mouth worked, open and closed, like a fish in Shill Brook.

"I suspect that others know of this book, and his possession of it may have to do with his death," I concluded.

"His death? He drowned in the river. So the sheriff's men said."

Here was interesting news. The sheriff's men knew that Salley was likely murdered. I showed them the bruise upon his neck. They, or the sheriff, had no interest in seeking the murderer, so had apparently told Salley's friends that he was drowned in the Cherwell, and there would be an end to the matter.

"Robert Salley did not drown," I told him.

"What? He was found face down in the Cherwell near to St Clement's Church."

"I know where he was discovered. I happened upon the place shortly after his friends found him... although they did not know who was in the water when they saw him. 'Twas me who drew the corpse to the bank."

I heard another choking sob from the workroom in response to the word "corpse". The maiden who occupied the chamber was much stricken by this business. I decided to avoid the word in what remained of the conversation at Stelle's shop.

"If you pulled Robert from the water, then you'll know 'e drowned," Stelle countered.

"I am a surgeon, trained in Paris. When I see the print of fingers about a dead man's neck I know what has sent him to the next world."

The cordwainer's eyes opened wide and his mouth worked open and shut again before he managed to speak. "His neck? There was a mark upon Robert's neck?"

"Aye. And no water in his lungs. He was dead before he went into the river. You knew him well, you say. Did he speak of any who sought him harm? Was he troubled, or did he seem fearful of his safety?"

I caught movement from the corner of my eye. Stelle's daughter had reappeared in the doorway. We both turned to her when she spoke.

"He had something others wanted, he said. They was seekin' him so he could not go to his lodging. Asked to sleep in the workroom for a few days."

"Did he say what it was these men sought?"

"Are you one of those who sought Robert?"

"I am. You heard me tell your father that Robert Salley possessed a book stolen from Master John Wyclif. I know not who else may be seeking the volume, or if the book was their reason for pursuing him. Perhaps it was some other possession of his they sought?"

"Not likely," the cordwainer said softly. "The lad owned nought but the clothes upon his back."

"Yet he was to renew his studies next term?"

"We, ah, had an arrangement," Stelle replied. I heard the daughter sob softly again. I said nothing and waited to hear if this arrangement would be told me. It was.

"Robert was to wed Bess," Stelle said, with a nod toward his daughter. "Wanted to take up law."

"So you were to finance your future son-in-law's education?"

"Aye."

"The thing that others wanted," I said to the lass, "did Robert keep it with him?"

The lass hesitated and glanced at her father. From the corner of my eye I saw him shrug. He would leave this decision to his daughter.

"Kept it 'ere. Wrapped in a linen cloth," she replied.

"You've seen the parcel?"

"Aye," she sighed.

"Is it much like a book in size?"

"Aye... it is."

"Where is it now?"

Bess turned her head slightly toward the workroom. "On a shelf, with father's leather goods."

"If you will bring it here you will discover, I think, that the linen wrapper conceals a book. *Sentences*, writ by Peter Lombard. On some pages you will find notes written in the margins, and initialed by the maker 'JW'."

"John Wyclif," Stelle muttered.

The cordwainer looked to his daughter, nodded toward the workroom. The lass rubbed an eye with a knuckle, then turned and disappeared into the room. She appeared a moment later with a parcel wrapped in unbleached linen of rough weave. This she placed on the table before her father.

Stelle seemed reluctant to touch the package. I waited for him to do so, although it required great patience. I thought it best for him to discover the truth of my prediction than for me to produce the volume.

A slender hempen cord held the linen wrapping in place. Stelle began to struggle with the knot. His thick fingers were unsuited to the task, as he soon recognized. He drew a small dagger from his belt and sliced through the cord.

It was indeed *Sentences* which appeared when the cordwainer drew the linen from the book. He opened it at random and turned a few pages until he found a note written in the margin. "I have no Latin," Stelle said. "I cannot read what is writ here, but you speak truth. The comment is initialed."

He pointed to the page and Bess peered over his shoulder to see for herself. "This is one of Master Wyclif's stolen books?" the lass asked softly. "This is most unlike Robert. He once spoke of Master Wyclif. He had great admiration for his teaching."

The lass sniffed, and wiped her nose with the back of her hand. 'Twas most unappealing. "An' Robert, even so poor as he was, was not a man to take another's goods. I have heard him speak harshly of those who do so."

The cordwainer nodded solemnly in agreement with his daughter. "We who do business in the town," he added, "may not be scholars, but we are not fools. We know where Master Wyclif stands, and most approve. When news of his loss came to Northgate Street, near all who seek custom on the street were woeful for his loss."

I made to reach for the book, but Stelle placed a hand upon the open pages. "May be all is as you say, you seekin' Master Wyclif's books. But I don't know you. I'd be more content did Master Wyclif himself call for the book. I'll not hold what belongs to another, but I would see it go to its proper place."

This seemed to me a reasonable precaution on Stelle's part. There was a fleeting thought that, if I left to seek Master John, the cordwainer might hide the book and deny knowledge of it when I returned. I put the notion from my mind. Employment as a bailiff has created suspicion of all men in my mind. Perhaps a healthy skepticism is useful to my profession, but it is no pleasant way to live.

I told Stelle that I would return with Master John immediately and set off at a trot down the Northgate Street. I found Wyclif in his chamber, awaiting the cook's summons for dinner. I was breathless but managed to blurt out news of my discovery. Master John did not hesitate, but sprang from his bench. Together we set off for the cordwainer's shop, Master John's gown and beard flowing in the north breeze like that of an Old Testament patriarch.

Stelle stood in the same place as when I left him. The book had not been moved, not even a leaf was turned, for Master John's marginal note and initials were plain on the page.

Wyclif moved cautiously from the shop entrance to the cordwainer's table, as if he feared that his book might take fright and flee did he approach too hastily.

"Master Wyclif," Stelle greeted him with a bow. "You honor my shop. This fellow tells me he seeks your stolen books, which near all in the town know of, and that this volume is one of yours stolen some weeks past."

Master John moved around the table for a better view of the open book. He scanned a few pages, inspected the cover, then spoke: "Master Hugh speaks true. I asked him to find my stolen books and he has done so... one of them."

As he ended his claim Master John lifted his eyes from *Sentences* and gazed quizzically at me. I knew his thought.

"Did Robert Salley speak of other possessions kept elsewhere?" I asked Stelle.

"Not to me. Bess!" he called for his daughter. When the maid appeared he addressed her. "The book is indeed Master Wyclif's. You were near married to a thief. Did Robert speak of other goods he might have hidden elsewhere?"

The lass sniffed loudly and shook her head. The cordwainer turned first to Master John, then to me. "I am much grieved to know I have harbored a thief. Please accept my apology."

Wyclif nodded. "I hold no grudge against an honest man betrayed by another. Master Hugh, our dinner awaits."

"I will join you soon," I replied. "I would have more conversation here."

Wyclif shrugged, lifted his book, and turned to the door. "As you wish. I will tell cook to keep your meal hot 'til you appear."

Good, I thought. Even the warm pottage at Canterbury Hall holds few charms. Cold pottage does not own any appeal. Perhaps I have dined too often at Lord Gilbert's table in Bampton Castle. To a beggar or mendicant friar the pottage at Canterbury Hall might seem a feast, hot or cold.

Wyclif disappeared through the shop door with *Sentences* clutched tightly to his chest in both arms. He was unlikely to allow the book from his sight, I thought. Perhaps he might sleep with it under his pillow this night.

"There remain two questions," I said to Stelle. "How Robert Salley came by Master Wyclif's book, and who murdered the poor scholar."

"He was a thief," the man muttered. "Probably died at the hands of one of 'is band."

"I have doubts," I replied.

"What? That a friend did away with 'im?"

"Aye, that, and that he was a thief."

"He had a stolen book. He was a thief. An' I nearly wed my daughter to 'im."

"True, he possessed a stolen book, but was he one who would despoil another? You said he was not."

"So I thought. Been wrong before."

"Perhaps, but there is much about this business which rings a false note."

"How so?"

"There are yet twenty-one books missing. No man could carry off twenty-two books from Canterbury Hall by himself."

"So he made off with a book to sell to his own profit, an' his fellows learned of it an' slew him."

"That could be how it was," I agreed. "But I think it sure that possession of Master Wyclif's book caused Salley's death. You should take care. Those who took his life might trace the book here. They have killed once for it. They might be willing to do so again."

Stelle blanched at this thought and glanced to the workroom door. His daughter had disappeared but I could read his thoughts. Children are a great joy; also a great worry.

"How did Bess come to meet Robert Salley?"

Stelle was silent for a time, then spoke hesitantly. "Bess was comin' back from the baker with loaves for the day. A company of young scholars began to follow... an' taunt her. She's no beauty, I know that well enough. One of the lads took no part an' finally spoke up for her. Made the others stop, Bess said, and walked with her to the shop to see they didn't start in again."

"This was Robert Salley?"

"Aye."

"Would a lad so troubled by those who would hector a maid then commit an injustice himself? Stealing another's books does not fit the character of such a fellow."

I might have added that Robert Salley's appearance may have led to his also receiving mocking words. Perhaps he came to the maid's aid because he had been jeered in similar fashion.

"I was ready to think ill of a dead man who cannot defend himself. You think then he was no felon?"

"He possessed a stolen book, which he would have sold. Perhaps he knew the book was stolen, perhaps not. I think he knew... mayhap not at first, but when I pursued him from the stationer's shop on the Holywell Street he must soon after have known what he possessed."

"Then where did he come by the book?"

"The very question I asked. And did another want the book so badly they would do murder for it?"

"'Tis but a book," the cordwainer sighed. "Surely not

worth a man's life."

"The book? No. But the circumstances of Robert Salley's possession of it... that might be worth a life. To someone it was."

Two days past I had but to seek stolen books. Now a corpse lay across my way. I believed that solving Robert Salley's murder might set me on the path to Master John's books. I resolved to begin the work promptly. But first I would seek a belly full of pottage at Canterbury Hall.

Chapter 12

The scholars had finished their meal when I entered the hall. I had always imagined some disdain in their eyes. I was but a bailiff, and a surgeon, not a physician. But this day I felt a new respect. They knew I had recovered one of the stolen volumes. My new-found status might have been severely reduced had they known the part simple good fortune played in the discovery. Or perhaps it was God's doing. Master John would say so.

I saw no gain in sending Arthur back to prowl the streets about St Ebbe's Church and the Red Dragon. I bid him accompany me and after dinner we set off for the Canditch Street and Balliol College. I sought the four scholars who carried Robert to his grave. There was, I believed, more to learn from them than I had thought a few hours before.

Our arrival at Balliol College was fortuitous. As we drew near I saw the scholar to whom Salley had owed four pence departing the place. I hailed the youth and he paused to allow us to approach.

East of Balliol on the Canditch there is a tavern where scholars often gather. I invited the lad to enjoy a cup of wine with me. He was pleased to do so, as I knew he would be. I was once a Balliol scholar. I know how such fellows think.

The tavern was quiet. There were few patrons at such an hour. I motioned to a wine-stained table and, cups in hand, Arthur, I, and the scholar sat on benches about it.

"You have lost four pence," I began.

"Aye. Dead men pay no debts."

"I have learned some things about Robert Salley this

day, and about you."

"Me?"

"You and your friends. Robert Salley's friends. He did not seek other lodging only to preserve his meager funds, did he?"

The youth did not reply, but I said no more. I have learned that those who own a troubled conscience dislike an uneasy silence and may soon fill it with words. I was not mistaken.

"Robert was annoyed with us, 'tis true."

"You maligned his appearance and his poverty 'til he could bear no more, is this not so?"

"'Twas all in jest," the youth agreed softly. "He laughed with us."

"His heart did not laugh with his lips."

"Nay. We saw that when he left us to seek other lodging."

"But it was your belittling the lass that finally drove him away, was it not?"

The youth was silent again. He had not touched his wine. He looked from me to Arthur as if seeking comfort. He found none.

"We did not guess he fancied the maid."

"Would you have chosen your words with more care had you known?"

"Aye. We did not purpose to be cruel."

I made no reply. Perhaps this assertion was true, perhaps not. I had other concerns. "Have you and your friends thought about who might have wished to murder Salley?"

"We spoke much about this long into the night. He was not the kind to make enemies. He would challenge us only when we made sport of the lass. He moved to other lodgings rather than dispute with us."

"He was in possession of one of Master John Wyclif's stolen books."

"Robert?" the scholar exclaimed.

"The book was returned to its owner this day. There can be no doubt. Before your words drove Salley away, did he speak of fear for his safety?"

"Nay." The youth finally took a swallow from his cup. "'Twas the opposite. Seemed sure of his future. Was to renew his studies next term. And spoke to me but a few days past of paying what he owed."

"When death came upon him he was unprepared?"

"Aye, so we believe."

I learned nothing from the conversation but that the young can be cruel and thoughtless. I knew that already. I was once young. I drank the last of my wine, bid the youth good day, and motioned for Arthur to follow. We left the scholar staring over his half-empty cup.

My mind turned to the small chest I had seen in Robert Salley's chamber. Rather than return to Canterbury Hall, I told Arthur we would once again seek the Red Dragon. The place was as bereft of custom as the tavern on the Canditch we had recently visited.

The scrawny proprietor sat where I had last seen him, his elbows on a crude table. He peered from me to Arthur with curiosity. He had seen both of us in his tavern, but not together. He croaked a greeting and asked did we seek wine.

"Nay. The young scholar who lodged with you, Robert Salley, is dead. Have you been told?"

"Aye. The young gentleman who sought 'im two days past was here 'bout the sixth hour. Told me the lad was murdered an' the sheriff would have his goods, to see could anything be learned from what 'e owned."

"There was little in his chamber but an old chest."

"That was all the fellow took. Just the chest."

I thanked the man for his time. I needed no more wine this day, a thing which the tavern keeper's expression indicated was a disappointment to him. It was also to Arthur, I think.

So the sheriff knew that Robert Salley was murdered and Sir Simon used the knowledge to claim Salley's chest. Yet other of the sheriff's men told John Stelle that the poor scholar drowned in the Cherwell. There was much amiss here.

I had seen nothing in the decaying chest but worn and tattered clothing, so could not say if some other thing might have lain below the garments. Sir Simon Trillowe thought so, else why claim the old chest. But it was sure twenty-one books were not hid beneath the clothing in the chest.

Arthur and I stood in the muddy street before the Red Dragon and exchanged puzzled expressions. Was Lord Gilbert Talbot present he would have lifted one eyebrow to show perplexity. I had tried to master the expression, but failed. I could no more raise one brow at a time than I could discover a murderer or twenty-one missing books. I had succeeded in but two endeavors since beginning the quest for Master John's books: I had found *Sentences*, and I was soon to wed a comely and agreeable lass.

Why, I wonder, must it be that my failures so occupy my mind that I spare little thought for my successes? I resolved to think upon more cheerful things. This would have been less difficult had events of the next hours chanced differently.

The sun was low in the southwest when Arthur and I approached the gate to Canterbury Hall. Few townsmen or scholars were about. Streets were near empty. Was our return earlier in the day, when folk were about their business, I might not have noticed the giant from Eynsham Abbey. Indeed, the fellow was a hundred paces and more behind us. The light was poor, and he trod the shaded side of the street, so that his face was obscure. His size was not. He walked with another of normal stature. Had he been alone, at that distance I might not have noted his bulk. But aside a man of ordinary height his size was obvious. That I noticed him at all was but a matter of a random glance up the street before I passed through the gate.

Even so I might have given the man no more notice. But when he saw that I studied him from before the gate of Canterbury Hall, he and his companion seemed to exchange words and turned quickly into an alley off St John's Street.

Arthur had paid no attention to me or those I observed, but strode on through the gatehouse. When he saw I lingered on the street he returned, a puzzled expression upon his face. Perhaps he worried that we might miss our supper of warmed-over pottage did we not hasten to the hall. I thought an explanation due him.

"Two men have followed us, I think."

Arthur peered up St John's Street in the direction of my gaze.

"They have ducked into an alley, or perhaps set off up Grope Lane."

"You think they sought your purse? 'Tis not yet dark enough for thieves to be abroad. Perhaps they were about some business."

"Perhaps, but I think not. When they saw I paid them notice they turned aside. And one I have seen before. At Eynsham Abbey, when I went there to consult the abbot, I saw a servant there larger than any man I ever saw. This was the same fellow. I have never seen in Oxford a man of such size."

Arthur stared thoughtfully down the darkening street, then spoke. "Odo Grindecobbe."

"You know the fellow?"

"Heard of 'im. 'Tis said he bested Hamo the Tanner when Hamo and 'is troupe passed through Eynsham."

This was troubling news. Hamo the Tanner challenged all to wrestle when the jugglers and contortionist in his troupe were done with their performances. His neck was as thick around as my thigh. I had never seen him lose. It was the tanner's daughter who was found in Bampton Castle cesspit two years past, murdered and hid there by Sir Robert Mallory.

Arthur and I turned from the empty street and went to our supper. I was not much pleased to think that a man like Odo Grindecobbe might have an interest in me, and his appearance this day was not but coincidence.

I fell to sleep a short time later to the music of Arthur's snores, lulled to my slumber by the pleasant thought that on the morrow at the Church of St Peter-in-the-East, and at St Beornwald's Church in Bampton, the banns would be read for the third time. I might then wed Kate Caxton.

I had become accustomed to Arthur's snores, so it was not the nocturnal din which awakened me, but the lack of it. His rumbling was muffled, then ceased. A heartbeat later I heard a scrambling and tossing about from Arthur's pallet, as if a hog was rooting for acorns in the straw. I had no time to contemplate this curiosity. At the same moment a hand clamped over my mouth and another went about my throat.

The uproar from Arthur's side of the chamber increased, but I was too much absorbed in my own struggle to take notice of it. Two men were upon me, perhaps three, for I felt hands, arms, and legs pinioning me from all sides.

I attempted to yell for help, but as soon as I opened my mouth a woolen rag was stuffed in to muffle my cry. It might have been linen. The flavor was indistinct.

The tumult caused me to fall from my bed to the stones of the floor, but this did not gain me any escape from my assailants. I was turned to my stomach and my arms were bound tight behind me. A cloth was wrapped about my head to keep me from spitting out the fabric stuffed in my mouth, and another was tied about my eyes. My legs were then seized and a cord tightened about my ankles. I was trussed up like a Christmas goose.

Arthur received similar treatment, but he is a brawnier fellow than me, and battled our captors more vigorously, if the noise from his pallet was any indication. As I lay bound upon the flags, with a man sitting upon my rump, I heard the sound of a fist or club delivering a blow. I did not identify the thump then, but learned later what it was that silenced Arthur. After this blow I heard nothing but the heavy breathing of men who had exerted themselves, and the thumping of my own heart.

My mouth and vision were stopped, but not my ears. I heard the chamber door swing open and a moment later a hushed voice spoke that the way was clear. Two men lifted me at feet and shoulders and carried me from the chamber.

I was taken to the Canterbury Hall yard, so attempted to signal my plight by shouting through the gag in my mouth. I produced little sound, but a great response. Someone striding near struck me a great blow across the ear and though I was blindfolded, I saw the stars of the heavens in all their glory.

After twenty paces or so one of my captors slung me over a shoulder and I was carried up a ladder. I did not understand the motion at the time, addled as I was from the blow across my skull, but did a moment later when I was pitched over the wall and felt the world drop from me until my head and shoulders met the sod at the base of the wall.

I was briefly stunned, but the ground was soft and did me no great injury. And when my face met the grass the cloth tied about my eyes was brushed up against my forehead. I found that I could see under the veil, though enough yet covered my eyes that my captors would assume I was yet blind.

I lay in the wet grass, considering my plight, and heard another body strike the sod beside me. Arthur grunted as the breath left his lungs, but I heard no more from him. He was insensible from the blow delivered in the chamber.

Our captors began to speak in low tones, careless of being heard. "Don't know why we didn't just kill 'em."

"We're not to leave bodies where they might be found, as Salley was. And this one," I felt a boot in my ribs, "has questions to answer."

I was once again lifted by ankles and shoulders and carried off. But not far. I felt myself lifted to the air, then dropped, belly first, across a smooth, hard, rounded surface. The object under me moved. I was splayed across a saddle. In the silence of the night I heard horses blowing and shifting their hooves. I heard another speak softly to his horse and we began to move. I could see little from the slit between my cheek and the cloth over my eyes, but saw enough to observe the mud of town streets under the hooves of the beast which bore me. I assumed that Arthur was likewise transported, for the sound of many horses mingled with the squeak of harness leather.

We had traveled this way but a short while when I heard hooves striking stone rather than mud. I turned my head and could see a bridge beneath me. We were leaving the city, but by which bridge? Did we travel east, across the Cherwell and Eastbridge? Or perhaps south, across the Folly Bridge? Or west, across the Castle Mill Stream Bridge to Oseney Island?

Our progress was not challenged by any who manned a city gate. I pondered this. Coins had changed hands, or someone of influence authorized our passage. In a short time I heard a horse ahead of my own strike stone again. Another bridge. Did we travel west, across the Thames, or south? Both roads required two bridges to leave the town. While I thought on this a bell sounded from nearby. It was a bell hung from the tower of Oseney Abbey. We went west.

It was not yet dawn; the sacrist did not sound the bell for lauds, but for vigils. I had been dragged from my bed in the middle of the night.

I am not a skilled horseman. Long hours in the saddle bring me a tender rump and no joy. In the next hour I learned that sitting in a saddle is a benign way to travel when compared to being tossed across a horse on one's belly.

I heard a voice call for a halt, for which I was grateful. Rough hands dragged me from the saddle and dropped me to the mud of a road. In the moonlight I could see shoes and boots under the chink in my blindfold.

Occasionally while we traveled our captors exchanged low words. I could not identify voices, but came to recognize five different speakers. Three, it seemed, were coarse, unlettered men, and two spoke as gentlemen. One of these gave the orders and answered questions.

Two of my captors picked me from the mud, a hand under each shoulder, and I was dragged to the verge, my heels making streaks in the mire. They did not stop, however, when away from the road. I felt myself dragged through the sodden autumn leaves of a forest floor. Occasional strands of ground ivy clutched at my shoes and broken twigs and fallen branches clawed at my chauces.

We journeyed this way for some distance. The men who hauled me through the wood were winded by the time I heard another command them to halt. They did, and dropped me to the leaves. I then overheard a muted discussion as two of my assailants discussed the location of a thing they wished to find. The forest was quite dark.

I heard a mumbled oath to my left, assumed it was Arthur who tried to communicate with me, and grunted a reply with dry tongue. For this I received a kick in the ribs.

I heard feet pushing through the fallen leaves, the sound diminishing as the makers distanced themselves from their comrades. Silence descended upon the forest, but not for long. I heard a distant shout, and moments later was hoisted again by the shoulders and dragged farther into the wood.

"We're to leave 'em here," a voice said. "Sir Simon will learn what they know, then be rid of 'em as he will. Our task is done."

I felt myself hauled onto bare dirt. No foliage grasped at my heels. Here I was dropped, and Arthur also. I next heard a sound as if brush was being swept across the earth. When our captors again spoke their words were muffled. The conversation seemed to involve a dispute and quickly grew loud enough to hear clearly. One of the gentlemen ordered another to remain until Sir Simon arrived, to insure Arthur and I would not escape our bonds. The man so instructed loudly announced his displeasure at spending the remainder of the night in a cold, damp wood. The exchange ended with a sharp sound which I took to be a palm across a cheek. Another voice said, "We'll take your horse. Sir Simon will bring another." The argument seemed ended.

I next heard footsteps, which rapidly grew faint and

soon vanished. We were alone, somewhere in a wood, where Sir Simon Trillowe would seek us. I thought I knew what his questions might be, although what interest he might have in Master John's books or Robert Salley was a puzzle to me.

A soft curse broke the silence of the forest. I heard next a sigh, and what seemed a body falling to rest among the leaves of the wood. Arthur and I were not alone.

I rubbed my head quietly against the dirt where I lay and after several attempts managed to scrape the blindfold from my eyes. We had been deposited in a crude hut, probably used by swineherds. I saw Arthur's dark form to my left. His shadow moved and occasionally groaned in discomfort.

Whatever Sir Simon wished to learn, it was clear what he intended when he had no further use for me. He would "be rid of 'em as he will." And our attackers had been instructed not to leave corpses about where they might be found. Sir Simon intended me soon to be a corpse. Might a man's wounded pride lead him to kill?

I believe I am like most men. I call upon the Lord Christ when in need, but forget to speak to Him when my life is smooth and pleasant. I treat the Savior like a lawyer; I call upon Him only when I am in trouble. I vowed to amend my ways and prayed that some escape might appear before Arthur and I were made food for worms. I told Him of my plight, and pointed out that, unless He intervened, I was likely to die soon. I concluded this prayer with the thought that, although He was surely occupied dealing with all the troubles men bring upon themselves and others, it would require of Him little effort to see us set free.

I do not know what I expected from this petition. Perhaps I thought my bonds would miraculously loosen. That did not happen. I lay shivering upon the cold dirt, as firmly trussed as ever. My fur coat would have been welcome, but it lay in the guest chamber at Canterbury Hall. Unless one of our captors now wore it, assuming I would have no future need of it.

Arthur's struggles soon ended. Whatever he had tried to do to free himself had failed and he abandoned the effort. His dark form seemed more visible. Moonlight was beginning to penetrate the chinks in the brushy walls and roof of the hut, filtered through the leafless branches of the forest. How early would Sir Simon leave his bed and seek me? This was Sunday. Perhaps he would attend mass and consume a leisurely dinner before he sought the hut. I decided I must not assume this would be so.

Arthur was soon dimly visible. I saw his hands tied at the wrists behind his back, for he lay on his side facing away from me. I saw his fingers twitch, and it came to me what I might do. My work must be silent, for our guard was present, sleeping, near the door of the hut. I could hear his regular breathing, and occasional snore.

I rolled and writhed until I lay with my back to Arthur and reached for his bonds with numb fingers. He understood readily what I intended, and held his bound wrists away from his back so my fingers might find better purchase upon the knots fastening his arms.

My fingers felt stiff as twigs from the cold and the bonds pressing tight about my wrists. I tried to get a fingernail under the knotted cords. All the while I heard or imagined noises in the forest which my mind construed as footsteps approaching. Haste did not improve the effort. Defeated, I released Arthur's bonds and forced myself to breathe more slowly; to search the hempen cord with my fingers until I might find a likely twist in the rope where I could undo the knot.

Arthur waited patiently while I explored his bonds and tugged at the knot. Gradually, after teasing it for what seemed an hour, I felt the knot loosen. Arthur felt it also. I heard him grunt approval through the gag. His joy was premature. The cord around his wrists was knotted three times or more. I had succeeded in loosening but one of these. Arthur was as securely bound as before this minor success. Failure was not to be contemplated. I resumed work on the tangle at my back.

I lay upon my right shoulder while I tried Arthur's

fetters. My right arm soon grew numb from its constricted place under my body. I was forced to roll to my stomach so to restore feeling to my arm and fingers. Arthur believed my movement a signal that I had given up the struggle. He became much agitated, grunting and groaning and attempting to speak softly through his gag. I feared he would awaken our sleeping sentinel. Arthur had surely heard our captors speak of our fate, and was unwilling to resign himself to such an end. No more so was I. I rolled back to my side and reached again for the knots. Arthur quieted when he felt me do so.

The knot refused to yield. If we were to free ourselves from this hut before Sir Simon and doom approached, another path to release must be found.

I left my place in the dirt and writhed forward until my hands found the knots behind Arthur's head which held his gag in place. These would not need to be untied. Tight as they were, with a steady pull the blindfold and gag might be pulled over his head. So I hoped.

And so it was. Both gag and blindfold came loose with but a few moments' tugging. I heard Arthur spit out the sodden rag from his mouth with a quiet oath.

I wormed my way back until my head was even with Arthur's bound hands and turned so my knotted gag was at his fingers.

"Ah," he whispered with a thick tongue, "I see what you're about."

I felt his fingers grasp the fabric of the blindfold and work it loose. Next came the gag. Like Arthur, I spat the soggy woolen remnant from my mouth. But not with an oath. I thought it unseemly for one who but a short time before had beseeched God for aid to speak now with an imprecation. And with a drowsing guard but a few paces away, this was no time for unnecessary words.

"I felt the tie loosen," Arthur whispered. "You must be at it again. My fingers be too thick to deal with knots, or I'd 'ave a go with yours." I felt him push his bound wrists against me, offering them for my struggle. Our efforts could not be completely silent, but I heard a rising breeze sighing through the bare forest boughs which served to cover the sound of our work.

"I've another plan," I replied. "Are your teeth strong, or rotted?"

"Strong. I've lost but one, an' another's a bit loose for the blow I took when we was set upon."

"Then turn to me. I will place my bonds before your mouth. See can you chew through the cord."

I heard Arthur shift his place. A moment later I felt his teeth at work on the rope about my wrists.

It took Arthur less time to gnaw through the hempen cord than I have taken to write of the business. My dinner knife and dagger lay on the table in Canterbury Hall's guest chamber, did our captors leave them unmolested, else I might then have quickly freed Arthur. His knots were easier to undo with free hands, but required time and effort. When Arthur's hands were free we set to work on the ropes about our ankles and were soon loosed from our bonds.

"Let's have at the fellow they've left behind, then conceal ourselves in the forest and take Sir Simon when he approaches," Arthur whispered through clenched teeth. He was angry and ready for battle. But I thought such a course unwise.

We were free, but unable to leave our cell for the guard stationed beyond the bushy door. During our struggle to free ourselves I had heard him snort and change his position several times, but he seemed to remain aslumber.

"My dagger and dinner knife are in the cell at Canterbury Hall. Sir Simon will not seek this place alone. And he and his companions will come armed."

Arthur's countenance fell as reality nudged thoughts of vengeance from his mind. "We might hide ourselves to see does he come alone," he hissed. "Alone, even armed, we might take 'im." Arthur was unwilling to abandon retaliation.

"He will not do so. He will have companions. When they find this hut empty they will scour the forest seeking us... with swords in hand. We must be away when Sir Simon arrives."

Arthur frowned and wrinkled his brow, but said no more of retribution. I went to the door, which was but a collection of sticks bound together with ground ivy and tied on one side with more ivy as a hinge. I gently pushed at this crude barrier and through a thin crack studied the forest.

Our snoring guard lay with his back against a tree three or four paces from the hut. I motioned to Arthur to take my place to see what must be soon done.

"I will open this door slowly," I whispered, "so as to make no sound. When it is wide enough to pass, follow me. We may fall upon the fellow before he gathers his wits. If he awakens while I move the door, abandon caution and have at him."

He did not awaken. In silence Arthur and I crept from the hut and stood over the snoring guard. The leaves of the forest floor were wet and made no sound to betray our advance. His dagger he carried in a sheath attached to a belt, and the fellow was so senseless that he did not awaken when I drew it carefully from its place.

Nearby lay a dead branch, fallen from the oak against which the guard slumbered. Arthur pointed to it and motioned as if to bring it down upon the guard's head. I nodded, and so he did.

The blow was not so hard as to kill the miscreant, but his sleep would be protracted. We hauled the fellow to the hut, found the cords which had bound us, and trussed the guard securely. When we were done Arthur glanced about and found the woolen scrap which had been stuffed into his mouth. This he rubbed enthusiastically in the dirt, then wadded it into a ball and crammed it into the fellow's mouth. The Lord Christ commanded us to do good to those who use us badly, so this was surely a sin. I pray Christ will forgive Arthur for this, and me, for I did not remove the filthy rag, but was pleased to see it done.

I wished to return to Oxford, but knew not which way to find the road which would take us there. I glanced about until I saw in the pale light of early dawn what seemed to be leaves stirred by footsteps and the track of heels dragged through the mould of the forest floor, then motioned Arthur to follow.

"Keep silence," I whispered. "Any other man about in this wood will mean us harm. We must hear them before they hear us."

Arthur nodded understanding, although I believe he would yet have wished a fight, and set off behind me as quietly as a man of his bulk might permit. I followed the leafy trail for near five hundred paces before a narrow clearing appeared. It was the place in the forest where, near a fortnight earlier, three mounted men had waited for Arthur and me to pass on the road, and where one of the fellows had left a tuft of green wool upon a thorn.

I approached the road cautiously. I did not wish to meet Sir Simon coming from Oxford as we attempted to return. The sheriff's son and his party would be mounted. We should hear them approach around any bend in the road before they would hear or see us afoot. So I hoped.

And so it was. Near the third hour, when we had walked two miles or more, I heard several horses approaching beyond a wooded turn in the road. I looked to Arthur and as one we leaped from the road to clamber through an overgrown hedgerow. Beyond this pile of stones and brush was a meadow now grown up in weeds and thistles. The lord of this place had not enough tenants since the plague to see all his lands cultivated. Bad for the lord; good for me and Arthur. We were well able to hide ourselves before the riders came into view.

From our place of concealment we peered through the bare branches of the hedgerow to see who came our way. It was indeed Sir Simon Trillowe, with two armed men riding on either side, one leading a riderless horse. These fellows did not appear pleased to leave a warm fireside this chill day, and Sir Simon's mouth was drawn tight and a scowl rested upon his brow. Did he blame me for the necessity of his journey?

I recognized Sir Simon's companions. One was Sir

William, who had accused me of stealing my own coat, the other wore a red beard.

The red-bearded rider accompanying Sir Simon wore a green surcoat. It is possible to make many shades of green by mixing the blue of woad and the yellow of weld. The green this fellow wore was dark, like a new oak leaf in June. Much like the thread in my pouch. Arthur muttered a wrathful oath. "Thought that log did for 'im when 'e went into the river under 'is horse."

We watched the riders pass. They looked neither to the left nor to the right, and had they done so, Arthur and I would have been unnoticed. We wore brown and grey, filthy with the mud of the road and the dirt of the swineherd's hut, and blended well with the rocks and vegetation of our place of concealment. When Sir Simon was well past and his horse no longer heard, I motioned to Arthur to follow and clambered over rocks and through underbrush to regain the road.

"We must make haste," I explained. "When Sir Simon finds the swineherd's hut and his man bound there, he will cast about in the forest seeking us. But not for long. When we are not found he will hurry back to Oxford. We must be in the town before then. He will not attack us where others will see."

I hoped this prophecy to be true. Arthur seemed content with the prediction. We walked east with rapid steps and soon the bell tower of Oseney Abbey was in view.

We hurried across Oseney Bridge and the Castle Mill Stream. I thought to seek Kate and explain my absence at mass this day and the final reading of the banns, but decided rather to return to Canterbury Hall. I wished to brush my garments, wash filth from my face, and seek evidence of our captors in the guest chamber while the event was fresh in my mind.

Chapter 13

Perhaps the Lord Christ guided my steps. As we turned from St Frideswide's Lane I saw Kate, her father, and Master John standing before the gate to Canterbury Hall.

Robert Caxton seemed agitated. He gestured vigorously as he spoke. Caxton and his daughter stood with their backs to our approach. It was Master John who saw us first.

He pointed our way. Kate and her father turned, and immediately Kate took to her heels and fell upon me there in the street. I was some embarrassed, but her embrace drove discomfort from me.

Much hurried conversation followed. Kate told me that she was at first angry that I had neglected attending mass. But her father convinced her I was not a one to do so without good reason. So after the mass they sought Master John. He went to the guest chamber and discovered that we were absent and the place left in much disarray. He had just told Kate of this, and his fear that something was amiss, when Arthur and I appeared around the corner from where they stood.

I told them of our capture and escape, and the part Sir Simon Trillowe had played in the affair.

"We must speak more of this," Master John declared, "but not here in the street. Women are not welcome at Canterbury Hall, for monks reside here, but 'tis in my power to make exception. We will withdraw to my chamber and discuss this matter."

The cook rang the bell for dinner as Master John shut his chamber door behind us. I saw Arthur's eyes widen in alarm. I suspect he worried that our discourse was so important that we must not interrupt it even for a meal. Not so.

Master John looked up from his table when he heard the bell. "An empty stomach," he opined, "will not help to resolve this matter." Then, looking to Kate, he added, "None but the porter saw your entrance here, I think, but it would be unwise to set you at table in the hall. You must remain here while we go to our meal. I will bring a loaf and a bowl for you when we return."

Kate did not seem pleased with this announcement but knew better than to challenge convention. Those who do may occasionally succeed, but often bear scars for the achievement.

The pottage this day was thick with peas and beans, flavored with an occasional bit of pork. I was fortunate in finding a sizeable chunk of meat in my bowl. Arthur saw this, and gazed reproachfully at me. His bowl, I think, did not reward him with much flesh.

The bread was warm, a maslin loaf of wheat and rye, and the ale was near fresh. It was good to be alive – dirty but alive. Especially as there were men about who plotted it would not be so.

After the meal Master John commanded the cook to take a bowl of pottage, a loaf, and a cup of ale to his chamber. If this order surprised the cook he gave no sign. He was prompt. We had but closed the door to Master John's chamber behind us when the cook rapped upon it with Kate's dinner in hand. Master John set Kate at his table and she began to eat while we sat facing one another upon benches to begin discussion of the matter at hand.

"Think you Sir Simon was behind this abduction?" Master John began.

"There can be no doubt," I agreed.

"Would a man kill another for a maid?" Caxton wondered aloud.

"'Twas not for Kate he did this... not for Kate alone," I replied. "He is a vain man, and his pride is sorely wounded for Kate's dismissing his suit. But there is another matter which drives him as well, I think. He wishes information of me, so our captors said. And they spoke of Robert Salley's corpse discovered. Salley had naught to do with Kate, nor would Sir Simon need instruction from me to court a lass."

"This business is to do with my books, then," Master John declared. "I little thought when I asked your help in the matter that the undertaking might risk your life."

"But what can Sir Simon have to do with your books?" Kate asked between bites of maslin loaf.

"'Tis a mystery," I agreed. "Robert Salley was not known to Sir Simon, else Salley's friends would have mentioned it. And how did he come by one of the stolen books? Did Sir Simon have to do with the theft? And what did Sir Simon and our assailants have to do with Salley's death? They were certainly involved, else why speak of his discovered corpse as a troublesome thing?"

"Think carefully, Master Hugh," Wyclif urged. "Is there no other reason Sir Simon might wish you ill? Have you never encountered him before this business? Perhaps when a student at Balliol College you ran afoul of him."

"Or a companion?" Caxton added.

"May hap, but I think not. I was not a contentious sort. I remember no great disagreements. When the St Scholastica Day riots erupted in the town, I fled. Some scholars thought me a coward," I confessed.

"We will receive no assistance at the castle, this is sure," Wyclif asserted.

"Aye. It would be foolish to complain to the sheriff of his son. And what proof of his crimes have I but seeing him on the road and hearing our captors speak of his wishes?"

"Perhaps Lord Gilbert might confront the sheriff," Caxton suggested. "He spoke severely to Sir Simon when you were falsely accused of stealing your own coat."

"He would do so," I agreed, "but how could his intercession find stolen books or tell us who took poor Salley's life?"

"There may be one whose authority could do what even Lord Gilbert's may not," Master John suggested.

Silence followed this remark. Kate looked up from her pottage, spoon midway between bowl and lips. None who heard his words could imagine who Master John thought of greater authority than a peer of the realm. He enlightened us.

"Duke John thinks well of me. I was born on his lands in Yorkshire. Does the sheriff protect his son, Duke John would intervene, I think. 'Twould be best to know first, however, before confronting the sheriff."

"How can we know this?" I asked.

"You might take a letter."

"To the Duke?"

"Aye. He has been my patron since I came to Oxford as a youth. He will not turn away a man who brings to him a supplication from me."

"Where may he be found? He has lands and castles in the north and in France."

"He will not be at Pontefract in November," Wyclif advised. "No man would reside there for the winter when he might enjoy the Savoy."

"The sheriff will not be pleased to know we have brought Duke John against his son," Caxton observed. "He is a spiteful man, 'tis said."

"We can hardly make of him more an enemy than he is already... or soon will be when he learns what his son has been about and how he's been thwarted."

"He is not popular in the town," Kate added. "He is likely to levy a fine upon a shopkeeper for the smallest offence. Father heard from a silversmith of Fish Street that there are plans to complain of Sir John to the King."

"Travelling to Westminster might serve two ends," Master John advised. "You may seek Duke John's service, and you will be well away from Sir Simon, who may not wish to abandon his pursuit of you."

So the conclusion of our discussion: on the morrow Arthur and I would set off for Westminster. Master John would write a letter this night which I would carry to John of Gaunt, Duke of Lancaster, third son of King Edward III. I was apprehensive of this journey. I had never met a Duke.

Monday dawn brought news; some good, some bad. Flakes of snow blew across the Canterbury Hall yard. I clutched my fur coat – our assailants had not stolen it – tight about me and made for the kitchen where I hoped to find loaves warm from the oven to fortify me and Arthur for our journey.

I saw the porter leave his post at the gatehouse as I crossed to the kitchen. He walked hurriedly to Master John's chamber and thumped firmly upon the door. I gave this event no thought and entered the kitchen.

The kitchen was warm and I was tempted to linger. But this would not get me to Wallingford, where I proposed that Arthur and I would seek an inn for the night. I tucked two loaves under an arm and departed the kitchen in time to see Master John turn from the porter, with whom he had evidently been in conversation. The scholar did not glance my way. He walked swiftly across the yard, approached the guest chamber, and was about to pound upon the door when I greeted him.

Master John spun on his heels. When he saw it was me who spoke his countenance broke into a smile.

"Ah, Master Hugh... there is good news this day."

"What?" I grumbled, glancing at the sky and the occasional flake of snow dropping from low clouds. "Arthur and I will begin our journey with a snowy wind at our backs rather than in our faces?" I am occasionally given to sarcasm. This a flaw I recognize but have not yet mastered. And the wind was indeed from the northwest.

"Nay, Hugh. You need not set out today. Perhaps not tomorrow or next day, either." Master John noted my puzzled expression and quickly continued. "Sir John Trillowe is replaced as sheriff. Roger de Elmerugg has been appointed the post. The town is abuzz with the news."

I remembered Sir Roger. He was sheriff for a time some years before. I could recall no complaints against him; no more so than any man assigned to keep the peace and enforce the King's law. Sir Roger is not, I think, a man of great wealth. When Roger de Cottesford replaced him three years past all suspected it was because de Cottesford offered King Edward more for the post. If de Elmerugg was now again ensconced in the castle, it was unlikely he outbid Sir John for the office. Perhaps the burghers of Oxford had made good their threat to complain to the King of Trillowe's high-handed and pecuniary governance.

I understood Master John's smile. "Sir Simon no longer has the castle to protect him should an investigation of these matters come close to him."

"Just so," Wyclif agreed. "He is yet a danger to you, I think, but not so worrisome as before."

"Indeed," I smiled. "'Tis he who has cause to fret now. I have heard Lord Gilbert speak well of Sir Roger. They fought side by side at Poitiers."

"There will be less trouble to dig to the truth now," Wyclif agreed. "How will you be about it?"

"I must give the matter some thought. This is too great an opportunity to spoil with foolish measures."

"Aye. Prudence and forethought. Virtues Oxford scholars generally neglect. How did you acquire them, Hugh?"

"You will recall when hasty judgment nearly led me to see Thomas Shilton hanged for a murder neither he nor any man committed?"

"Aye, I remember well... the lass all thought was dead was a wench in a tavern just off the Canditch.

"Very well," he continued. "I will abide your caution. But set yourself in my place. There now seems a door open for measures which may see my books returned to me. Can you grasp my impatience?"

I could. Many scholars did not accumulate twenty books in a lifetime of study and collection. Even while he spoke, thoughts jostled about in my mind of deeds which might resolve the matter to Master John's satisfaction. Since our escape from the swineherd's hut and our encounter with Sir Simon and his cohorts, an image of a horseman wearing a green surcoat had much engaged my mind. Perhaps, could the fellow be discovered, he might be persuaded to tell what he knew of Sir Simon's business. Yesterday this would not have been so, but now Sir Simon could not demand loyalty from others and threaten the castle dungeon did he not receive it. I spoke of this to Master John.

"Will you seek aid of Sir Roger?" Wyclif asked. "He is no friend of Sir John, 'tis said."

"He may be minded to help us, but I think today he will be visited by many supplicants. By evening he will be pleased to be rid of them, and will likely recall little of their petitions. Better to wait a day or two to call on him. Arthur and I will observe Oxford's streets, seeking a man with a reddish beard who fends off the cold with a green surcoat."

Arthur was privy to this conversation. I gave him one of the cooling loaves and we discussed this new state of affairs while we broke our fast.

Arthur munched thoughtfully for a moment, then said, "What if the fellow owns two surcoats? One for ridin', like, an' another for town?"

Arthur may be no scholar, but neither is he a fool. "We will search for a red beard. We must hope the fellow has not both shaved and changed his coat. We will divide the town, I think. You walk about the castle, up to Rewley Abbey and the Carmelite Friars, then back to St Ebbe's. I will go about from St Frideswide's to the Canditch, then east to the Cherwell."

"Best stop at Caxton's shop," Arthur grinned, "and see that the fellow has not called there for ink or parchment."

"I will do so," I laughed, and slapped Arthur across the back. We had been through much in the last fortnight and I was grown fond of the man.

I walked with Arthur down St Frideswide's Lane, then left him at Fish Street, where he continued west on Pennyfarthing Street toward the castle. Folk were just beginning to venture out upon their business and shopkeepers were opening shutters. I saw more than one cast a frowning glance to the clouds. The occasional snowflake fell on upturned cheeks.

Any man who could might wish to keep to his bed on such a morning. Certainly a young gentleman, did his father leave him sufficient funds, would look with disfavor upon any venture which called him out of doors early this day. I did not expect to see many young knights on the streets, wearing green surcoat or otherwise. I did not.

I walked a circle, from the Northgate to Holywell Street, thence to Longwall Street and the Trinitarian Friars. From there I turned right and strolled west on St John's Street until I was once again before the gate to Canterbury Hall.

The sacrist of St Frideswide's Priory rang the bell for terce as I stood before the gate, contemplating which way I might next go. There are streets and alleys in Oxford where searching for a gentleman would be like seeking salmon in a well. I set off for the High Street, then circled north on School Street and once again back to the Northgate. I found nothing but a blister upon my heel for the morning's stroll.

Arthur was prompt for dinner. Some things in this life are unchangeable. After bowls of pottage, this day flavored with fragments of mutton do I not mistake me, we set off again to search for our quarry.

But first I sought Kate. She was employed in the workroom when I entered the shop, and was eager to learn more of Sir John Trillowe's dismissal. I told her what I knew, which was little more than her father had already learned from gossip among the merchants who sought custom on the Holywell Street and Canditch.

"A red-bearded gentleman wearing a green surcoat accompanied Sir Simon yesterday. A fellow much like that was pitched into the Thames when Arthur tossed the log a fortnight past."

"I remember you speaking of the man and his swim," Caxton frowned. "He carries a grudge, I think."

"So do I. Arthur and I are exploring the town this day to see can we find the fellow. He is in some service to Sir Simon, I think, but now that Sir John is dismissed he may wish to trim his sails to the new breeze."

"You sought the gentleman this morning?" Kate asked.

"Aye. Few gentlemen wearing any color were about."

Caxton grimaced. "True enough; nor scholars. We saw little trade."

"Custom seems unlikely to improve, father, so I will find my cloak and accompany Hugh. Four eyes will serve better than two." Where had I heard this before?

That may be so, but if a thing is invisible to two eyes it will also be to four. The afternoon was not a total loss. No time spent in Kate's company could be so. Indeed, I found myself gazing upon her more than upon those we met on the streets. But I think I had yet enough wit about me that a green surcoat or red beard trimmed short would have arrested my attention.

I delivered Kate to her father's shop as the grey day darkened to night. Snow no longer drifted from the sky, but the snow had brought cold with it. Or had the cold brought the snow? I decided to ignore the question. I had enough on my mind.

Arthur was at the guest chamber before me. "Lots of folk about the castle forecourt this day," he said by way of greeting. "None of 'em with red beard or green surcoat."

"If the fellow we seek is a companion of Sir Simon, as seems so, he'll not venture where he no longer has friends."

"So I should pay no heed to doin's at the castle tomorrow?"

"Do not ignore the place, but spend your time in the town and across the Castle Mill Stream. I think we must do more than watch. Visit some taverns. Give the landlord a ha'penny and ask has he a customer who resembles this wayward knight."

I did not linger over a supper of warmed pottage but sought my bed. I fell to sleep with thoughts of Kate. I was become accustomed to Arthur's snores, and visions of Kate can drive other cares far from me.

Kate had bid me call for her next day so she might seek our green-clad prey with me. I crawled from my bed as a bell rang for matins from the tower of St Frideswide's

Priory. This was not a thing I was eager to do. This day was colder than the day before. But no snowflakes appeared to remind me of the chill.

Kate was not pleased when I told her she might not accompany me this morning. I intended to visit taverns and did not want Kate either to stand on the street before such places or to enter and suffer the ogling and comments her appearance was sure to produce.

So I circled Oxford from Northgate and Fish Streets east to Longwall Street, and spent three pence at five taverns and an inn. All for naught. Perhaps the fellow wore another cloak when he sought wine. I was eager for dinner, to learn if Arthur had been more successful than me. He had.

I saw Arthur striding around the corner of St Fridewide's Lane as I approached Canterbury Hall. I knew from forty paces he had found success. There was joy in his step and in the grin which split his face when he saw me.

"What news?" I asked when he drew near.

"Our friend frequents an inn across the Castle Mill Stream, on a lane just off the road to Oseney Abbey. We have passed it by often. 'Tis called the Fox's Lair."

I knew the place; I had spent some nights there in years past. Its guests ranked above those who frequented the Stag and Hounds. When I became bailiff for Lord Gilbert I thought my new station entitled me to a softer bed and better wine when duties called me to Oxford. But the inn was not so conveniently located as the Stag and Hounds.

"Did you learn a name?"

"Aye; Sir Jocelin Hawkwode."

I had not before heard of this knight. "Did you discover where he lives?"

"Nay. Innkeeper knew not. Thought the man new to Oxford. Only been a customer since Lammas Day or thereabouts."

Sir John Trillowe had taken office in July. Sir Simon might have gathered friends about him soon after. I wondered if Sir Jocelin might soon leave Oxford if Sir Simon's position – now dissolved – was the reason he had come. If so, it was important to find the fellow soon.

We ate our pottage and maslin loaf hastily and set out for the Castle Mill Stream Bridge. It was my plan that Arthur and I would alternate visiting the Fox's Lair and circling about the place. I was some worried that Sir Jocelin might recognize us, so told Arthur that when he entered the inn he should take his wine to some dark corner of the place where a new patron, his eyes accustomed to daylight, would not see him.

The precaution was unnecessary. Hawkwode did not appear at the inn. I was annoyed at the failure, but Arthur seemed pleased that we might perform the same duty on the morrow. He spoke several times of the quality of the claret while we made our return to Canterbury Hall.

I was surprised to see Robert Caxton standing before the gatehouse. When he saw us appear he immediately hurried to meet us.

"Good evening," I greeted my future father-in-law. "What news?" It was clear from his pace and expression that he had tidings to relate.

"The man you seek… Kate has found him."

"Kate?"

"Aye. You did not return after dinner, so Kate thought to venture out and watch for the fellow you seek."

"She found him? The red-bearded knight wearing a green surcoat?"

"Aye, she did."

"Where?"

"You sought the man in taverns and inns. Kate thought of another place a young gentleman might frequent."

My wit was slow. Caxton saw and when I made no reply he continued. "She went off to the Church of St Mary the Virgin, an' sat where she might see those who pass up an' down Grope Lane."

Then I understood. Kate had risked her reputation to aid my search. Most of the whores of Oxford reside in and work their trade on Grope Lane.

"The man I seek is Sir Jocelin Hawkwode," I replied. "Arthur learned his name this day, and we watched for him this afternoon at an inn he is known to frequent."

"He sought his pleasures elsewhere this day," Caxton chuckled. "Kate saw the man you seek leave a house on Grope Lane just before the ninth hour. She followed him."

"To a house? Was she seen?"

"Yes… and no, she thinks not."

"She can take me to the house where Hawkwode resides?"

"Aye. You are to call in the morning and she will take you there. 'Tis a grand house on Great Bailey Street."

I ate my pottage that evening in silence, pondering how best to approach a man who had tried twice to do me harm. Would he seek a third opportunity did he know I pursued him? Master John noted my pensive demeanor and when the meal was done invited me to his chamber.

"Have you sought Sir Roger yet?" he asked.

"Not yet. I have been seeking a man who has some part in the matter."

"The knight of the green surcoat?"

"Aye. His name is Sir Jocelin Hawkwode. He lives, I am told, in a house on Great Bailey Street."

"Hawkwode?"

"Aye. You know the name?"

"There was a youth by that name some years past at Queen's College. I think it was Jocelin. I have told students that when I see them some years in the future, if I remember them well, they may assume 'tis because they were excellent scholars, or poor ones. I will allow them to decide which they might have been. The mediocrities I am unlikely to remember many years hence."

When I called upon him two years past Master John remembered me well, or said he did. I did not wish to pursue the matter further.

"You have little memory of a Jocelin Hawkwode?"

"The name is familiar, but nothing more."

"I wonder what interest the fellow can have in your books?"

"Perhaps none," Wyclif mused. "He is a companion of Sir Simon. You saw them together on the road. 'Tis Sir Simon's interest in books and your search which must be the key to this mystery."

"I think time has come to seek Sir Roger's mind on this business," I said. "It was Kate who found where Hawkwode resides. She has promised to show me the place on the morrow. I will leave Arthur to watch the house while I seek the sheriff. I would like to know more of Sir Jocelin Hawkwode. Perhaps Sir Roger knows him well enough to know how he might respond when pressed."

Next morning was not so cold, for which small blessing I remembered to thank the Lord Christ before Arthur and I set out for Holywell Street. I was eager to learn of Sir Jocelin Hawkwode and his residence. Robert Caxton had not opened his shop for business when we arrived, but Kate was prompt at the door when I knocked upon it.

"Father told you of the house on Great Bailey Street where... what is his name?"

"Hawkwode... Sir Jocelin Hawkwode. Arthur learned his name yesterday and you found his abode."

"Shall I take you there?"

"Aye. 'Tis early, but we may catch the fellow before he goes about for the day."

Terce had not yet rung and the streets were near empty, so nothing impeded our progress to Great Bailey Street. The house Kate pointed out was a substantial dwelling, typical of an Oxford town house of a prosperous gentleman. It was two stories tall, and four chimneys indicated plenty of warmth available for cold winter days. A few tendrils of smoke rose from one chimney. Perhaps the cook was out of bed and at the day's business, but few others were, it seemed.

I wished to confront Sir Jocelin on the street, where he might be alone, rather than in his lair. The house was large enough to accommodate a dozen knights and squires. It would be folly to impeach the man where he might call companions for aid.

I required of Arthur that he escort Kate back to her father. She was not pleased. The banns were read and we might soon be wed, if I did not raise her choler too often. I was uneasy, for it seemed in the past days I had chosen to displease Kate more than once.

Across Great Bailey Street from Sir Jocelin's residence was the ancient moat and the castle. Shops around the corner on Pennyfarthing Lane were yet closed, so no customers walked the muddy streets. A man may lose himself in a crowd. Alone he cannot. I did not see a face peer from a window, but someone surely did. They saw me saunter up and down the road and plotted, while I awaited Arthur's return.

Perhaps the third time I traveled the street the door burst open as I passed the place and three young men charged silently from the house. They stumbled over each other briefly, then came running straight for me. One wore a green surcoat and a short red beard sprouted from his chin.

This was not the plan I had envisioned when I considered a confrontation with Sir Jocelin. Some day, when I greet the Lord Christ in heaven, I must ask why my schemes so seldom unfold as contrived.

My fur coat is warm, but not suited to flight. The heavy garment caught at my legs as I turned from my pursuers and ran. I am not sturdily made. In a fight with one of these knights I would be hard pressed. Against three I would find myself pummeled into the mud of the street, or worse. But an advantage of a slender form is a good turn of speed when I take to my heels. And most men find unknown reserves when pursued by those who intend them harm. My flapping coat slowed me but little.

The castle gate stood open little more than two hundred paces from me. Was Sir John Trillowe yet sheriff I would have passed the castle and fled toward Canterbury Hall. Was Sir Simon yet in residence the castle would have provided no refuge.

A few men about business in the castle walked to and fro through the gatehouse. Some heard my feet pounding through the mud and glanced up from their passage to see what provoked such haste. I threaded my way past these fellows and glanced over my shoulder to see what distance I had put between myself and my pursuers. I was pleased to see them skidding to a halt in the castle forecourt, unwilling to continue the chase and surely startled that I would seek refuge in the castle. I slowed my pace, turned to Hawkwode, bowed, and swept my arm in invitation to follow. He glared, shook his fist, and turned away.

Chapter 14

I had intended to call upon the new sheriff, mention my employer, and learn could Lord Gilbert's name bring me Sir Roger's aid. Sir Jocelin Hawkwode and his companions hastened this visit. Perhaps God chose to contrive my call upon Sir Roger this day, and devised this method to get me to the castle. If so be, it succeeded remarkably well.

This was my third visit to the castle. I was learning my way about the place. I knew well where to find the sheriff's chamber and set off for the hall with resolute steps. None challenged my passage. I gave appearance of knowing where I was going and seemed to have reason for going there. And a man wearing a fur coat on a cold day is thought to be of some means and therefore worthy of a warder's deference.

The anteroom before Sir Roger's chamber was already crowded with supplicants. I heard the hum of conversation while I was yet in the passage leading to the chamber. A dozen or more men and two women crowded the room. Many held documents in hand or rolled under an arm. A clerk, unknown to me, looked up from a table which guarded the door to the sheriff's chamber. His visage spoke; words were unnecessary: "Another who seeks a post or favor from Sir Roger."

The place before the clerk's table was empty. Those in the hall had presented their petitions and now awaited Sir Roger's will. The wait, I thought, might be long. I decided to see what Lord Gilbert Talbot's name might do to speed my appeal.

"I am Hugh de Singleton, bailiff to Lord Gilbert Talbot at his manor of Bampton. Lord Gilbert and Sir Roger fought side by side at Poitiers."

This information did not seem to impress the clerk. He shifted his gaze to admire his fingernails.

"Lord Gilbert has sent me to Oxford on a matter of some urgency," I continued. This was not exactly true, but was not untrue, either. "Lord Gilbert would be much pleased should Sir Roger find occasion to assist in the difficulty. Perhaps you might inform Sir Roger of my presence and Lord Gilbert's request."

The clerk rolled his eyes but did as I asked. As bailiff to Lord Gilbert I have much authority in Bampton, and some even in Oxford. Though it is true in Oxford I must occasionally flee from miscreants who respect neither me nor my employer.

The clerk pushed open the heavy oaken door and I heard voices through the aperture. Sir Roger had a guest already. The clerk stood in the doorway and repeated my words nearly as I had spoken them. The fellow was practiced at relaying messages to his master.

When the clerk was silent I heard a chair scrape across the flags and a heartbeat later a round, florid face appeared beyond the clerk, peering at me through the open door from under a pair of the shaggiest eyebrows I have ever seen. On a bright day Sir Roger carries with him his own shade.

"Bailiff for Lord Gilbert, eh," Sir Roger exclaimed, and pressed past his clerk through the doorway. "How does he? Is well, I hope. Enter... enter. How may I assist him?"

I did not hesitate. As I passed into the inner chamber I caught sight of envious glances from those who were before me seeking audience with Sir Roger. I felt guilty, but the emotion soon passed.

The sheriff's previous caller stood before a table which occupied the center of the chamber. A chair rested upon the flags behind him, and another where Sir Roger must have sat, was placed across the table from the visitor.

I did not know the supplicant I had displaced, but it was clear from his behavior that he was unwilling to leave Sir Roger's presence. The sheriff, however, seemed pleased for the interruption as opportunity to chase the fellow away.

"Be assured, Sir Thomas, that I will give the matter scrutiny." This the sheriff said while placing a meaty hand upon the small of Sir Thomas' back and firmly thrusting him toward the door. Sir Roger then nodded to his clerk, and the fellow pulled the door shut firmly before Sir Thomas could turn to protest his expulsion.

"Your name again?" Sir Roger asked.

"Hugh de Singleton."

"And in Gilbert Talbot's service at Bampton?"

"Aye."

Sir Roger motioned to the empty chair, and when I sat he drew up the other chair across the table.

"Is Lord Gilbert well? And Lady Petronilla? I've not seen m'lord since…" Sir Roger went to stroking his graying beard, then continued. "Since Whitsuntide four years past. He was at Pembroke. When plague returned he thought it was well to be in a barren place. Offered sanctuary to me and Anne until the pestilence passed and 'twas safe to return to Oxford."

"He is well, and Lady Petronilla and Master Richard, also."

"Excellent. Well, how may I serve Lord Gilbert?"

I told Sir Roger of Master John's stolen books, my arrest for stealing my own coat, and the attack on the road to Eynsham. I spoke of the death of Robert Salley and the recovery of *Sentences*. I related how assailants had come over the Canterbury Hall wall and carried me and Arthur to the forest. I told of Sir Simon Trillowe's name spoken, and Robert Salley's corpse mentioned, and recounted our escape and watching from a hedgerow as Sir Simon passed by. And then I spoke of a red-bearded knight who wore a green surcoat, and who but moments before had chased me to the castle – Sir Jocelin Hawkwode.

I saw Sir Roger's lip curl in distaste, as if he had taken a sip of costly Rhenish wine and found it gone to vinegar. I thought this a signal that he knew Sir Jocelin and, was I patient, I might discover his opinion of the knight.

"A hyena who will follow any lion," Sir Roger scoffed.

"I have hopes this is so," I replied. "What Sir Simon may have to do with Master John's stolen books I cannot guess. But I hope that Sir Jocelin might know, and be willing to say if pressed. Sir Simon and his father have no longer the authority to control or protect him. Why then would he protect them at his own peril?"

"Sir Jocelin will bluster like a champion when he feels power behind him," Sir Roger agreed, "but when the wind turns he'll bend, I think. Let us see."

Sir Roger lifted his surcoat from a hook on the wall and motioned me toward the door. When it opened all eyes in the clerk's anteroom turned to us, and several there who were seated stood to their feet. The sheriff turned to his harried clerk. "Urgent matters demand attention," he said loudly, so all could hear. "My return is uncertain."

A warder stood guard in the passage outside the clerk's chamber. Sir Roger directed the fellow to collect six sergeants and report to the gatehouse immediately. This command the sheriff barked in a tone which sent the man scurrying without a backward glance.

I followed Sir Roger down a stairway and thence to the castle forecourt. The warder and six armed men were but moments behind us in reaching the gatehouse. It would be unwise, the warder surely realized, to displease the new sheriff.

Two of the men who followed the warder were those who had appeared along the Cherwell five days past when I pulled poor Salley from the river. If they recognized me they made no sign. It is surely useful for a man to appear enigmatic when his overlord is supplanted.

It is but a few paces from the castle to Hawkwode's house. Sir Roger sent three men to the small toft behind the place to apprehend any who might depart the house there; the others accompanied us to the door, where Sir Roger, without hesitation, banged loudly with the pommel of his dagger.

Someone saw us approach, for the door swung open but a heartbeat after Sir Roger ceased pounding upon it. A servant, quite ragged in appearance, stood at the open door. Sir Roger did not wait for his greeting.

"Sir Jocelin Hawkwode," he bellowed. "Inform him his presence is required."

"Uh, Sir Jocelin is not within, m'lord."

"Oh? Where has he gone?"

"I know not, m'lord."

"When did he leave?"

"Yestere'en, m'lord."

"You lie," Sir Roger bawled, and pushed past the quaking servant. I and the warder and three sergeants followed.

"Search the place," Sir Roger directed. He then turned to the servant, who gave every appearance of a man whose knees were about to fail him. The man had backed against a wall for support, else I think he must surely have collapsed.

"Where is he? Speak, man, or there will be a cell for you in yon castle."

I am uncertain if the man did not wish to speak, or could not. His mouth worked, but no sound came forth. Sir Roger stepped closer to the servant, his arms akimbo, those great eyebrows furrowed to trenches plowed across his forehead. In similar place I might have shuddered a bit myself.

"Well?" Sir Roger spoke softly now, but there was menace in his voice. The silent servant swallowed and pointed to the stairs.

Sir Roger turned abruptly from the shaken man and strode to the stairway. I followed, and drew my dagger from its sheath. Preparation could do no harm.

A passage led the length of the dwelling from the top of the stairs. The sheriff had just set a thundering boot in this corridor when much shouting came from the toft behind the house. I ducked through a nearby door and crossed the room to a window which opened to the rear of the house. Ten paces or so behind the house was a small stable. Between house and stable was a yard of bare, muddy earth. A tangle of arms and legs were intertwined there in the muck. It was not readily apparent how many cursing, shouting men were engaged in the conflict, but it was sure that the sheriff's men there had apprehended some who wished to depart the precinct unobserved.

Sir Roger crashed back down the stairway. I thought to follow, but reconsidered. I peered again through the glass window at the fight below me. The contest was nearly done, the sheriff's men in the toft being now supported by the arrival of the others who had accompanied us to the front door. Two young gentlemen were being pulled roughly from the mud to their feet. Neither of them wore green or possessed a red beard.

I returned to the corridor and opened doors to other chambers until I found a room with an open window, from which the two apprehended in the toft had dropped moments before. Along one wall was a large, iron-bound chest, heavily carved. I entered the room, muttered an expression of disappointment, then slammed the door to the passageway shut while I remained, silent, in the chamber.

I had not long to wait. I soon saw movement. The lid of the chest raised a finger-width. Someone inside the chest was peering through the slit to learn was he alone in the chamber. Pressed against the wall, aside the chest, I was near invisible to whoever it was hiding there. Well, I knew who it was.

A great urge to startle the fellow came upon me. I waited until the lid was raised as high as my hand is wide, then plunged both hands down upon it, all of my insubstantial weight behind the stroke. The lid crashed down and a heartbeat later I heard a muffled yelp. This was most gratifying.

My dagger was yet in my hand. I held it at the ready and lifted the lid. Sir Jocelin Hawkwode lay curled in the chest, sucking upon a finger. The unlucky digit had apparently been caught between lid and chest when I banged down the cover. I felt no remorse. This may be a sin. I must ask Master John.

I believe Hawkwode did not at first know who stood over him with drawn dagger. He cursed me, not an easy thing to do with a wounded finger between his lips, then scrambled from the chest.

"You!" he exclaimed when vertical. He knew then who had brought the sheriff to his door.

"Aye, Hugh de Singleton, friend to Master John Wyclif and bailiff to Lord Gilbert Talbot. The same Lord Gilbert who is friend to Sir Roger de Elmerugg, newly appointed sheriff of Oxford and who, unless I mistake me, is about to return to the house from the toft, seeking you."

Sir Jocelin remembered his disheveled condition and left off nursing his hurt finger long enough to straighten his cotehardie and smooth his cap. A green surcoat was not part of his dress, but I was sure it would be discovered somewhere in the place. It was.

I heard a door slam below me. Moments later Sir Roger bellowed up the stairway, "Hugh, where are you?"

I motioned to Sir Jocelin, intending him to precede me through the door and down the stairs. He had another plan. He spun around, ducked past my dagger, which I was slow to raise, and dove for the open window.

The man was quick on his feet, but so am I. As he went through the window I discarded my dagger and leaped to arrest his flight. I caught one heel with both hands as he straddled the window frame. Momentum caused his body to continue its path out the window while my grip held one foot in place. I braced a knee against the window sill and held tight to Sir Jocelin's ankle. One man had escaped me through a window. I was determined that another would not. A moment later the knight dangled, kicking and squalling, from the window, suspended a dozen feet or so above the mud of the toft.

Sir Jocelin's cries brought Sir Roger back to the toft. He looked up to find the source of the tumult and beheld Hawkwode, heels over head, suspended from a window.

Above the bawling Sir Jocelin the sheriff saw me, my hands clenched tight about the fellow's ankle. This task would have offered Arthur little challenge, but my grip was not so sure, and I was near to letting the fellow fall.

This was too much for Sir Roger. He stared open-mouthed for a moment, then laughed. This became a roaring guffaw. The sheriff slapped his thighs with glee and soon the warder and sergeants were also snickering. Even Sir Jocelin's friends saw humor in the spectacle and grinned.

Sir Roger soon recovered his composure, took stock of the situation, and shouted advice. "Drop him," he suggested. It is always best to obey authorities. I did. And in truth I could hold the man no longer.

Sir Jocelin landed upon his head in the mud of the toft. Two of the sheriff's men were immediately upon him, but their restraint was unnecessary. The fellow was in no mood or condition to attempt escape.

I left the window and hastened to the toft. Hawkwode was on his feet when I arrived. The warder and sergeants were yet grinning at his head-first arrival there.

"This is the fellow?" Sir Roger asked.

"Aye."

"The others?" he asked as he glanced to Sir Jocelin's companions. "Were they a part of this business?"

"I do not recognize them, but it may be so."

"No matter. We'll have them all to the castle and sort this out. Bring 'em along," he directed the warder.

We returned to the street through the house, passing the quaking servant who stood where Sir Roger had left him. Half-way from house to castle I saw Arthur approach, striding from around the Church of St Peter-le-Bailey. I had been so occupied with events that it had not occurred to me that he was tardy returning from his mission to return Kate to Holywell Street.

Arthur glanced from me to Sir Jocelin as he approached. It was clear from his manner that something vexed him. The others continued toward the castle gatehouse while I stopped to greet Arthur.

"You have Sir Jocelin, I see. That the new sheriff?"

"Aye. Sir Roger was eager to favor Lord Gilbert's bailiff."

"Sorry I was delayed. Couldn't be helped," Arthur growled. "Kate an' me got to 'er father's shop an' who was marchin' down Holywell Street but Sir Simon an' a squire. New fella', never seen 'im before. Sir Simon give us a vile look an' says to Kate, 'Takin up with a bailiff is not low enough for you, eh? Is this churl your new love? I'll next see you on Grope Lane, no doubt.'"

My rage was instant. Arthur saw and grasped my arm. "No need to seek 'im," he said, and held out his right hand before me. The knuckles were split and lightly caked with drying blood. 'E'll be more careful of 'ow 'e speaks of a lass henceforth."

"Kate is safe?"

"Aye. Delivered to her father."

"And Sir Simon?"

"Well, I don't know as he's in best of health. Last I seen, 'e was walkin' Holywell Street toward the Augustinian Friars Hall."

"Seeking medical care, was he?" I smiled.

"Aye. 'At would be my guess," Arthur grinned in return. "I told 'im I knew of a competent surgeon who could mend 'is lip. Paid no heed."

Beyond Arthur, where the road through the Westgate circles south of the castle and crosses the Castle Mill Stream, I saw four horsemen appear. Three wore the same livery of blue and black as Arthur. The lord at their head was too far away to identify but I knew it must be my employer.

Arthur followed my gaze and together we awaited the arrival of Lord Gilbert. I was surprised to see him. It is his custom to remove to Goodrich Castle for Christmas and the winter, and this he does by Martinmas or thereabouts, before the roads turn to mire and winter cold is upon the land.

"Hugh," he called out when he saw who awaited him before the castle gatehouse. "You are well met."

The unexpected nature of Lord Gilbert's appearance must have been reflected on my face. He swung down from his mount and explained. "Word has reached Bampton of Sir Roger replacing Sir John as sheriff. Sir Roger is an old friend. I thought to offer congratulations, and see how does your pursuit of thieves proceed."

"You have just missed Sir Roger, m'lord. He has three miscreants in hand we wish to examine regarding Master John's stolen books and other untoward events."

"We?" Lord Gilbert questioned. "You have met Sir Roger?"

"Aye."

"But you've found no books, I think."

"One, m'lord."

"One?" Lord Gilbert raised an eyebrow.

"It was in the possession of a penniless scholar who was then found dead in the Cherwell... but not drowned, murdered." The eyebrow lifted higher.

"And Kate? How does your lass?"

"She is well, m'lord."

"'Tis past time I should be at Goodrich," he explained, "but I delay so as to learn of the recovery of Master Wyclif's books. And Lady Petronilla will not remove to Goodrich until she has seen you wed."

"I am sorry to interfere with your plans, m'lord. I wish to be wed soon, but I am obligated to Master John."

"Well, Sir Roger will be of more aid to you than Sir John, I think. He is in the castle, you say?"

"Aye. With a man I wish to question."

"Let us seek him out, then."

Lord Gilbert strode toward the gatehouse, leaving his horse to be led by a groom. I followed close behind, with Arthur a pace behind me.

Oxford Castle has been enlarged and restored many times. Its passageways are many and crooked and a man might easily lose his way. But not Lord Gilbert; he marched straight to the sheriff's chamber.

Sir Jocelin Hawkwode's henchmen stood beside the clerk's table in the antechamber. The warder stood alert near them, and two sergeants guarded the passageway door. A few supplicants remained in the room, but most had abandoned their pleas for the day. Sir Roger was not in view.

The clerk recognized me and saw that my companion was a gentleman of rank. He leaped to his feet. Not because of me.

"Sir Roger is within," he explained. "Who shall I say...?"

"Gilbert Talbot," Lord Gilbert said, loudly enough that his words surely penetrated to the inner chamber, for the door was ajar. "Tell the knave I've come to see for myself if the King's judgment be so clouded as to put him in this place."

The door swung open and Sir Roger's bulky form filled the doorway. "The King," he replied, "could not decide whether to punish my many transgressions by clapping me in the tower or by assigning me to this post."

Slapping of shoulders and backs accompanied this banter. It was clear Lord Gilbert and Sir Roger were friends. Enemies would not speak so to each other.

"I wondered," Sir Roger said, turning to me, "where you'd got to. You wish to question Sir Jocelin?"

"Aye. And it would be well if you and Lord Gilbert attend the inquiry. A bailiff alone might not pry from a man what a scowling sheriff and baron might, even did they speak no word."

Sir Roger motioned Lord Gilbert and me into his chamber and closed the door. Sir Jocelin sat at the table, but sprang to his feet when Lord Gilbert entered. All semblance of bluster was gone from Hawkwode's features and manner. Here is a man, I thought, who finds himself in trouble he had not anticipated. When in the past I found it necessary to interrogate such men, I discovered it was often best to keep silent so much as possible, and allow invention to loosen their tongues. A man of ripe imagination who thinks on potential punishment due him will often say more than he would otherwise intend, hoping thereby to escape judgment.

Lord Gilbert and Sir Roger should, due to their rank, have led the interrogation. But as they were unacquainted with many particulars they sat in chairs to one side and discharged the work I had hoped of them. They glared menacingly at Sir Jocelin. I watched him chew upon his lower lip in response.

The sheriff had left his chair, across the table from Hawkwode, vacant. He peered at me from under those magnificent brows and nodded toward it. I sat, and took some moments to arrange my coat. Let the scoundrel wait and worry.

"A fortnight past you were toppled into the Thames," I reminded him. "Surely your fine surcoat is much shrunken for the wet."

"Neither I nor my surcoat have been in the Thames," he protested.

"Hmmm. Perhaps another red-bearded gentleman with green surcoat haunts the road to Eynsham. Did Sir Simon pay you well to accompany him Sunday, or did you travel the Eynsham Road with him for friendship?"

"I have not traveled to Eynsham."

"I expect not. The first time I saw you on the road your journey halted at Swinford. Three days ago you traveled only so far as a swineherd's hut in the forest. So you speak true... you have not been to Eynsham. Now, answer fairly: was it for coin or friendship you aided Sir Simon Trillowe?"

Hawkwode glanced beyond me to Sir Roger and Lord Gilbert but found no solace there. "Answer!" the sheriff growled.

"For friendship," Sir Jocelin sighed in defeat. He had apparently decided to behave wisely, as men may do when they see no alternatives.

"Were you of those who came over the wall of Canterbury Hall and seized me and Lord Gilbert's groom?"

"Nay. Knew nothing of that 'til Sir Simon told of the business Sunday morn."

"And what did he tell?"

Hawkwode again looked about the chamber, as if some way of escape previously unseen might appear. I said no more, but awaited a response. When he saw there was no avoiding the question, Hawkwode muttered a reply.

"Said I was to accompany him and Sir William Folville. We were to put a fright to you, he said."

"Why?"

"Sir Simon wished you gone from Oxford. That's why we pursued you on the road to Eynsham."

"When my man dunked you in the river," Lord Gilbert chuckled.

"Aye," Sir Jocelin grimaced.

"To what purpose was I to be frightened away?"

Again Sir Jocelin was silent. So were we all, awaiting his understanding that he had no choice but to answer.

"There is a lass… Sir Simon would have."

"Kate Caxton?"

"Aye. The stationer's lass."

"And for a maid he would threaten harm to my bailiff?" Lord Gilbert scowled.

"What of Robert Salley?" I asked.

"Who?"

"A poor scholar, murdered and found floating in the Cherwell."

"I know of no Robert Salley."

"Perhaps you have forgotten. I will refresh your memory. The lad tried to sell a book, *Sentences*. 'Twas one stolen from Master John Wyclif. Then he was discovered dead in the river. The book he had hidden with a cordwainer, for others also sought it. When I was assailed Saturday eve the attackers said I was not to be found as Salley was. So if Sir Simon knew where I was to be found on Sunday, he knew also who it was took me there in the night and who slew Robert Salley. And whatever he told you, he told my captors I was not to be seen again."

I saw Hawkwode swallow, his adam's apple working vigorously. Perhaps he spoke true and knew not that when he accompanied Sir Simon to the swineherd's hut it was to do murder. Perhaps, but perhaps not. Mayhap his unease was due to discovery, not ignorance.

"If 'twas not you came over the wall of Canterbury Hall, who did so?" I continued.

Hawkwode rested his elbows on the table and dropped his head to his hands. He did not speak, but Sir Roger did.

"'Tis near time for dinner," he said to Lord Gilbert. "You and your man shall join me. This fellow may remain here and ponder his sins and how he may escape punishment for them."

The castle board was an improvement over the fare at Canterbury Hall. The ewerer presented water for washing hands from a brass ewer of cunning workmanship. And though it was a fast day no pottage was served.

The first remove was of eels baked in spices and pike in galantine. The second remove featured roasted halibut and salmon in syrup, a favorite of mine. For the third remove the castle cook provided roasted sea bass, perch in jelly, and fried mussels. A subtlety of spiced baked pears and apples ended the repast. After such a meal I might have preferred a nap, but Sir Jocelin awaited us in the sheriff's chamber, hungry and, I prayed, subdued.

Hawkwode's companions, watched by the warder and two sergeants – who would consume cold fish for their trouble – were seated as they were when we departed the anteroom for dinner. If they were distressed for missing their meal, their bored expressions provided no clue.

Sir Jocelin was also as we left him. I had thought we might find him at the window, but not so. Perhaps he had already visited the opening and found nothing in the castle yard worthy of his attention.

I took my place at the table and Lord Gilbert and Sir Roger again sat behind me. Sir Roger produced an appreciative belch, a response to a good meal. The implication, I think, was not lost on Hawkwode. Did he not provide satisfactory replies to my questions, his future meals might also be in the castle, but composed of stale maslin, cold pottage, and foul water.

"You have had time to consider your position," I

reminded Sir Jocelin. "Before we went to our dinner I asked who it was who came over the wall and took me to the forest if it was not you."

"I knew them not," he muttered. "Lads from Eynsham were sent for."

"From Eynsham?" Lord Gilbert exclaimed.

"Sir Simon sent for the fellows?" I asked. "For the purpose?"

"Aye. He sent for them some days past, as well."

"You saw these men?"

"Aye."

"And 'twas a week past, thereabouts, you did so?"

"Aye," he agreed softly.

A thought occurred to me and it arrived with a vision of a large man, armed with a club, accompanied by a smaller companion, on the road near Swinford.

"Was one of these fellows of great size?"

"Aye."

"His name?"

"Odo Grindecobbe."

Climbing over the wall of Canterbury Hall was a thing this fellow had done twice, I thought. I remembered the thatcher's broken ladder. No wonder a thong broke, was the ladder used by a man the size of Grindecobbe.

But what had Sir Simon to do with thieves? Surely when Grindecobbe clambered over the wall twice, he did so for two different reasons, which I could not see related.

"Did Sir Simon speak of recovering a book from Robert Salley?"

"He didn't speak a name, not that I heard. An' didn't name a book. Just said the fellows from Eynsham was to seek a scholar and recover something that was given to him."

Something that was given to him? Did this mean that Salley had not stolen Master John's books, or been any part of the theft? If so, it was as I thought. And if so, who gave him one of the books, and why? Might a relative have done so? This trail led in two ways, one to Eynsham, the other to Sir Simon.

"What did Sir Simon say when you arrived Sunday at the swineherd's hut and found it empty but for the guard?"

"He was in a rage. Said they'd botched the job twice."

"They?"

"Whoever it was he sent to Canterbury Hall... Grindecobbe and the others."

"Did he speak of the first blunder?"

"Nay."

Sir Jocelin might not have known of Grindecobbe's first mistake, but I did. He, and perhaps some companions, had murdered Robert Salley but not obscured the deed well enough. Did Salley die because he would not give up *Sentences*, or to silence him? Hawkwode did not know, so it would do no good to press him about it.

"The first error Grindecobbe made was to leave Robert Salley where his corpse might be found and his manner of death discovered. Sir Simon surely commanded the scholar's death did he not surrender Master Wyclif's book. We must next visit Sir Simon," I said to Sir Roger, "and learn what he knows. Perhaps he will give different witness than we have now heard."

"I have spoken truth," Hawkwode replied indignantly.

"Mayhap. But men will say many things to escape a noose."

The word introduced a new consideration to Sir Jocelin. His adam's apple again bounced and he was silent while contemplating the thought of hemp encircling his neck. I was convinced the man knew not of Robert Salley's death or Sir Simon's part in it. But an accomplice in murder may hang from the same gallows as he who did the crime. While this understanding washed through Sir Jocelin's mind, Sir Roger spoke.

"Sir Simon would impeach his mother did he save himself from the sheriff's dance."

The look in Sir Jocelin's eyes was one of agreement

with Sir Roger's assertion. I decided to give a small shove to Hawkwode's train of thought.

"We will not get the truth of his actions from Sir Simon. He will scrape himself clean of any offense and scatter the taint on others. So you must tell all you know, or we shall hear Sir Simon's account. I suspect you will not play so benign a role in his version of events as in the version you have presented to us."

"I speak the truth," Hawkwode repeated, rising from his seat.

"Hmm. Perhaps. But have you spoken all of the truth? You sought to dissemble when first brought to this room, and gave answer only when 'twas shown to you that we knew of your lies. What may you tell us of Sir Simon and the monk Michael of Longridge which we have not asked?"

Sir Jocelin had resumed his chair while I spoke. When I mentioned the monk he straightened as if a dagger had pricked him between the shoulder-blades. This was a most satisfying response, and surprising, for I had convinced myself that Hawkwode knew but an outline of the business and nothing at all of the theft of Master John's books. Usually I am not pleased to be in error, but in this matter I was.

Sir Jocelin's posture at the mention of Michael of Longridge gave indication that the monk was known to him, and further, that he had assumed I knew nothing of this portion of the tangle. He could not guess how much or little of the monk's connection to Sir Simon I knew. I waited in silence for his reply. It did not come soon. He churned over in his mind how much, or how little, he must tell to satisfy me.

I was willing to wait while Hawkwode considered his position, but Sir Roger was not. This was just as well. "Who is Michael of Longridge?" he demanded. "What has he to do with this, and to what house is he attached?"

"Will you tell him," I said softly to Sir Jocelin, "or shall I?"

He had been studying stains upon the sheriff's table.

He lifted his face to me and it was apparent that what little fight had been left in the fellow was now vanished. He put a hand to his neck, as if he could feel a cord there already, and spoke:

"Brother Michael is attached to the Benedictine house at Eynsham," he said.

"How is he known to Sir Simon?" I asked.

"They were friends of old, I think... when Brother Michael was a scholar at Balliol and Sir Simon was but a lad."

"The monk," I added, "hired two carters to take a chest to Westminster, to the abbey, but a fortnight after Master Wyclif's books were stolen. The chest contained books. Were they Master Wyclif's I know not, but suspect so. Brother Michael," I added, "and Master John were not friends."

Chapter 15

Silence followed this revelation. In the quiet of the sheriff's chamber we who were there heard agitated voices through the closed door. Excited conversation could be heard from the anteroom. Sir Roger frowned at this interruption and stalked across the room to yank open the door and deal with the uproar.

Even with the door open I could make no sense of the jumble of voices. Several men were speaking at once and each seemed sure it was his words which must be heard. The sheriff's clerk seemed to be the recipient of the tumult. Sir Roger frowned through the open door at the confusion, then quieted the chamber: "Silence!" he roared. He was obeyed.

Lord Gilbert moved to the door and I followed. Even Sir Jocelin succumbed to curiosity and followed, peering between us into the now silent antechamber.

The warder was one of those whose excited babble was halted at the Sheriff's command. Sir Roger looked from him to his clerk, then addressed the clerk.

"What means this prattle?"

"There has been a brawl, m'lord sheriff... at the Canditch near the Northgate. I know nothing more," he shrugged.

The warder, who it was had evidently brought the news, spoke. "Aye, Sir Roger, five or six men, with daggers and clubs, disturbing the peace near to the Northgate."

"Put an end to it," Sir Roger snapped. "Take some men and put a stop to it."

"Aye," the warder replied, and immediately left the room. Sir Roger turned back to Lord Gilbert and looked to the ceiling in disgust.

"Have the miscreants locked up for the night," Sir Roger told his clerk. "I'll deal with 'em in the morning."

Lord Gilbert and I stood back to permit Sir Roger to return to his chamber, but before he could do so another voice and hurrying footsteps could be heard in the corridor leading to the anteroom. All there turned to see who would appear at the door.

It was a burgher of the town, from his dress a prosperous man, unknown to me. The fellow did not hesitate at the door but strode purposefully into the clerk's chamber.

"Sir Roger," he gasped, "'Tis Sir Simon."

"Sir Simon Trillowe?" the sheriff replied. "What of him?"

"He lays in the Canditch, near dead."

Sir Roger glanced back to me and Lord Gilbert, a knowing expression on his face. "Near the Northgate?" he asked.

"Aye."

"Who else?"

"Sir Simon's squire, Sir Roger. More than that I know not. Sir Simon had but a moment before stepped from the Augustinian Friars when four men set upon him in the street."

"Did any restrain the assailants?" Sir Roger asked.

"Nay. 'Twas over quickly and the fellows were gone before aught could be done to stop their battery."

"Was one of the attackers a man of great size?" I asked.

"Aye... a head taller than most an' hands like a porringer."

Sir Roger turned to me: "The servant from Eynsham, you think?"

"Aye. If he lives, Sir Simon would know his attacker."

"And may need a surgeon," Lord Gilbert added.

Sir Roger instructed his clerk to hold Sir Jocelin and his companions to await our return. Together with the puffing burgher we three clattered down the stone steps of the passageway and into the castle yard. Arthur followed close behind. It was but a short way to the Northgate. Neither Sir Simon nor his squire were there.

A knot of men gathered in the Canditch told where the altercation had occurred. The warder and three sergeants had arrived at the scene before us, but stood stolidly in the mud and seemed without purpose.

Sir Simon and his squire had been taken, reported more dead than alive, to the Augustinian Friars. The assailants had struck quickly and then run off down Irishman's Street toward the Hythe Bridge. It was the collective opinion of the witnesses that Sir Simon's purse was the object of the attack. I knew better. But I was not prepared for the truth of the matter when I discovered it.

Sir Roger stalked off toward the Augustinian Friary. Lord Gilbert, Arthur, the warder, and I followed. The porter directed us to a chamber where the afflicted men were laid out upon pallets. The friary herbalist attended them, but had done little but staunch the flow of blood and then stand back to scratch his chin.

Sir Simon lay unconscious, his fur coat yet upon his shoulders. The garment was torn in several places where daggers had penetrated, and drying blood caked the punctures. A small fire spluttered in a hearth at one end of the hall. I asked for the blaze to be refreshed and the wounded men to be moved closer to the flames.

The herbalist frowned at this imposition in his bailiwick until Lord Gilbert informed the friar that I was a surgeon and would take charge of the wounded men. The fellow had already seen that the injuries were beyond his skills, so required no more urging to do as I had asked.

The squire wore a blue cotehardie and black chauces. He seemed not so badly injured as Sir Simon. I required of the herbalist and his assistant that they strip the youth of his torn clothing and bathe his wounds in wine. The squire was alert to his condition and so was able to raise arms and legs to assist his benefactors. A servant brought an arm-load of wood for the fire while I conducted this brief examination of the squire.

Sir Simon was surely the object of the attack, not his purse, for that was yet fastened to a belt about his cotehardie. I asked the herbalist for a table, and when it was produced two friars lifted Sir Simon to it and placed him before the fire. The blaze and a weak afternoon sun which penetrated the chamber windows gave enough light that I could attend the man's many wounds.

I would need my instruments, that was sure. I sent Arthur to Canterbury Hall to fetch them and the pack of herbs from the guest chamber, then bent to a closer examination of the wounded Sir Simon.

A blow from sword or dagger had nearly removed his left ear. It dangled from a strip of gristle and would need to be sewn back to his head. Perhaps the same stroke which took Sir Simon's ear had also left a gash across his cheek. This wound lay garishly open, but did not threaten death. He would go through life with a vivid scar, did not his other wounds dispatch him to the next world. I noted also, with satisfaction, his split and swollen lip, an injury which needed no attention from me.

Sir Roger and Lord Gilbert stood silent while two friars and I divested the immobile Sir Simon of his clothing. He had taken three dagger thrusts. One was upon his leg and was of small concern, but two entered his chest between ribs. If either penetrated to the heart or lungs he must die. Indeed, if one had penetrated to the heart he must be dead already. I laid my ear against Sir Simon's chest and listened. The heartbeat was steady. I opened his swollen lips and saw no blood there, but was greeted with a foul stench. These were good signs that heart and lungs lay unmarred. Not the foul stink. I knew not the cause of that or what it might signify. Perhaps his fur coat was heavy and the dagger thrusts did not penetrate to his vitals.

Several bruises colored Sir Simon's body. A great welt was rising and taking color across his ribs. I prodded the bruise and it was well the man was insensible, for I was sure a rib or two lay broken under my fingers. Such manipulation would surely have brought him agony. I found myself wishing he was awake. It is my obligation to aid all men when they are in distress, as it is for all Christian men, but I felt no duty to release such a man from pain he might deserve.

No man will remain so long insensible unless he has taken a blow to his skull. I ran fingers through Sir Simon's scalp and found a swelling readily enough. This was not so large as to kill a man, I thought. Thomas atte Bridge gave me just such a lump when he knocked me senseless with a beech pole in Alvescot Churchyard.

Arthur arrived breathless with my instruments and herb pouch. I set to work first on Sir Simon's ear and lacerated cheek. This was my first opportunity to sew a man's ear back to his head. It was a more troublesome business than I had imagined. I had misgivings about the task when I was finished. I was not confident the ear would live again, reattached to its accustomed place. Did it not, it would decay and fall away, and Sir Simon would find another reason to wish ill of me.

I next sewed up the gash across his cheek. I used many small stitches, but he would wear the mark of this laceration for what remained of his days.

The punctures in his body and leg were quickly closed, with but two or three stitches at each wound. When I had done I bathed all these perforations with wine and judged myself satisfied. Lord Gilbert, Sir Roger, the warder, and Arthur had looked on silently while I was at my work patching Sir Simon. The warder, I noted, seemed rather green of the face when I looked up from the last sutures on Sir Simon's leg.

The squire lay in his braes upon another table. He shivered though the fire now warmed his corner of the room. He was a collection of bruises and lacerations, but none would take his life, nor did he require a needle and silk thread to close his wounds. His cuts had been bathed. Time would heal his hurts. I told the herbalist's assistant to find some garment for the youth. His chauces and cotehardie were torn and muddy and it would not serve to soil his wounds with such filth.

Sir Simon was yet senseless. Nothing could be learned from him of the attack. The squire, however, had recovered his wits, so when he clothed himself I directed him to a bench drawn near the fire and sought to learn more of what I already guessed.

"What happened in the street? Who set upon you?"

"Don't know. Sir Simon came to this place to find succor after that fellow," he pointed to Arthur, "struck him."

"I treated his wounded lip with oil of ragwort," the friary herbalist commented. That explained the stench when I inspected Sir Simon's mouth.

"We departed the friary an' Sir Simon spoke of seeking aid against another attack. We'd traveled but a few paces on the Canditch when four men set upon us of a sudden."

"Did the men speak, to you or each other, during the assault?" I asked.

"Nay, not while they was at us. But when they was done an' left us in the mud I heard one laugh an' say, 'He'll not be so eager now to seek books, eh?'"

Sir Simon had visited the Red Dragon seeking, I was sure, *Sentences*. Was this the felon's meaning? Or was it me they wished to dissuade from pursuit of Master John's books?

Since my time in the castle gaol I had begun to grow a beard. Sir Simon is above average height, as am I, and possesses a large nose, like mine. He wears a fur coat, and was accompanied this day by a squire dressed in black chauces and a blue cotehardie. Arthur wears the blue-and-black livery of a groom to Lord Gilbert Talbot. Was it me that was expected to lay battered and perhaps dying in the street?

"Was one of the four a large man?"

"Oh, aye," the squire agreed. "A head taller than Sir Simon an' beefy. He swung a cudgel big around as my arm an' caught Sir Simon in the ribs. Took him off his feet an' dropped 'im in the road three paces away from where he'd stood."

That explained the broken ribs. And if the same cudgel caught Sir Simon across the head it would explain his continued slumber.

Sir Roger had listened silently to the squire's tale, now he spoke. "The large man; Odo Grindecobbe of Eynsham, you think?"

"Aye. He and his band were to seek me, but mistook Sir Simon for me, I think."

Lord Gilbert had been leaning against a wall, but stood erect at this assertion. "Why would a servant to the monks at Eynsham wish to harm you?"

"Because one of the monks has stolen Master Wyclif's books, and knows I am close on his trail."

"Monks are forbidden to leave the monastery without the abbot's consent," Lord Gilbert replied. "How could a monk of Eynsham travel to Oxford and return with books?"

"He did not do so. He planned the deed, and sent servants to carry it out."

"What, then, does Sir Simon have to do with these stolen books?" the sheriff asked.

"Somehow Sir Simon and Michael of Longridge learned that they had in common a dislike of me. My enemy's enemy is my friend."

"Ah," Lord Gilbert went to pulling at his beard, a thing which he did when puzzling out a riddle, "but how would an abbey's servants know where Master Wyclif's chamber is, to despoil him of his books and be seen by no other in the Hall?"

"I am certain there is among the Benedictines at Canterbury Hall a man who knows Michael of Longridge and who dislikes Master John and would see him driven away."

"There is friction among the scholars at Canterbury Hall?" Sir Roger asked.

"There is always friction among scholars. But ill feelings at Canterbury Hall run deep. Four scholars are Benedictines and eight are seculars."

"And Master Wyclif is a secular," the sheriff

completed the thought.

"The villains who beat Sir Simon and would have harmed you will be on the road back to Eynsham," Lord Gilbert asserted. "If we return to the castle for horses and men we may overtake them."

Sir Simon and his squire we left with the Augustinians and hastened to the castle. There was no time to call at the Stag and Hounds for Bruce and the palfrey, so Arthur and I found ourselves mounted on horses from the castle marshalsea.

We did not receive the pick of the stables. Lord Gilbert, Sir Roger, the grooms and sergeants galloped on ahead. By the time Arthur and I had passed Oseney Abbey all that remained to show that they had passed were hoofprints in the mud.

We were near to Swinford we came upon a cluster of men and horses in the road. As we closed upon the group I saw that two men lay motionless in the mud. One of these was of great size.

Lord Gilbert stood over the supine form of Odo Grindecobbe. "Did not wish to be apprehended," he said by way of greeting as I dismounted. The man was alive, but a bloody stain upon his surcoat said he would not be so for long. The wound was through his belly, which no man is likely to survive.

Lord Gilbert, Sir Roger, and their party had surprised the miscreants but a few moments earlier. Sir Simon's assailants had made no attempt to scatter or escape, evidently not thinking they were the quarry of the horsemen bearing down upon them. When they learned it was so, two surrendered their weapons meekly. Only two attempted combat. One of these now lay dead, the other, Grindecobbe, lay in the road with his great cudgel beside him. He had made to swing the club at Sir Roger when he dismounted, but the warder saw and ran him through with his dagger before he could complete the stroke.

There was much I wished to learn from Grindecobbe before he died. I knelt in the mud beside him and saw his eyes turn to me. His lips were twisted in pain and his hands lay pressed against the wound in his belly.

"I am Hugh de Singleton. Who sent you to Oxford to do me injury?"

The man did not reply. His eyes traveled to Lord Gilbert, then back to me.

"'Twas Michael of Longridge, was it not?" I demanded.

Grindecobbe slowly nodded his great, shaggy head.

"And he sent you also over the wall of Canterbury Hall to seize Master Wyclif's books, did he not?"

"Aye," he whispered weakly. Perhaps the giant knew that death was near; that speaking truth would not lead him to the gallows. The sheriff does not hang a corpse. And most men would prefer to meet the Lord Christ with truth on their lips rather than a lie.

"And you broke the thatcher's ladder while at the deed?"

Again he nodded, then spoke hesitantly. "Brought a ladder, but seen another an' put both to use."

"You were paid well for this?"

He nodded again.

"Why did you murder Robert Salley?" I was not certain he had done so, but thought the accusation could do no harm.

"Wouldn't say where the book was," the dying man whispered. Blood appeared at the corner of his mouth and left a trail across his cheek as it dripped to the road.

"How did Salley come to have it?"

Grindecobbe was silent for a moment, as if harboring his strength. "He was kin to Brother Michael. 'E knew the lad would try to sell it… an' when you learned of it would set you on the wrong trail."

By the time Grindecobbe concluded this speech his voice had fallen to a whisper I could hear only with my ear near to his lips. I could learn no more from the fellow. His breath became shallow, then stopped. His eyes stared, unseeing, toward the clouded sky. We who yet lived crossed ourselves over the corpse.

The two dead men were hoisted across a horse and

two of the sheriff's men doubled upon another. With the two abbey servants afoot, our party splashed across the Thames at Swinford and approached Eynsham Abbey as the sun touched the tree-tops to the west of the town.

When the porter learned the rank of his visitors he immediately sent for Abbot Thurstan. The elderly monk tottered across the abbey yard a few moments later. He recognized me, and guessed that my appearance with Lord Gilbert and Sir Roger and four of his servants, two now corpses, boded ill for the abbey. He directed the dead taken to the church and ushered me, Lord Gilbert, and the sheriff to his chamber.

The west windows of the abbot's chamber were dark when I concluded my account. Some of the tale he knew already. When I was done he rang for a lay brother and sent the man to fetch Michael of Longridge.

The monk protested innocence when his crimes were set before him. But Abbot Thurstan would have no perjury and soon had truth from him. It was as I had suspected; a monk of Canterbury Hall gave instruction so that the thieves might find Master John's chamber, have the books, and be gone. Brother Hamon had indeed hoped to force Wyclif from his place as Warden of Canterbury Hall.

Brother Michael had withheld *Sentences* when the other volumes were sent to Westminster, for he, like all scholars, admired an excellent book, well bound. Only when he saw I was diligent on the trail of the missing books did he send it to his cousin so as to mislead me when the book should appear in an Oxford stationer's shop. He thought Salley would be able to sell the volume and disappear amongst the young scholars of Oxford before any could trace him. The monk seemed genuinely grieved to know his plan led to Salley's death. Grindecobbe was sent to retrieve the book when Brother Michael saw his plan was failing, and strangled the youth when he would not give it up.

Brother Michael had sought his old friend Sir Simon's aid, not knowing the knight had his own cause to dislike me. And when early that day he sent Grindecobbe and three others to Oxford it was to seek and murder me, not Sir Simon. But as we are much alike in appearance, and Sir Simon's new squire wore apparel of the color expected of Arthur, it was Sir Simon who suffered for my sake.

"What was to be done with the books in London?" the abbot asked. "Surely the abbey librarian would wonder why they appeared."

"I sent word to Brother Giles at Westminster that we at Eynsham had received a legacy. I told him that many of the books in the bequest we already possessed. I offered to sell those, and he accepted. I know how we at Eynsham suffer for our poverty," he continued, as if to justify his crime.

"You will set out tomorrow for Westminster," Abbot Thurstan decreed when Brother Michael had done with his incrimination. "Seek the carters who took the books to Westminster and pay them to accompany you. It is the abbey's responsibility to redeem Master Wyclif's books. Tell the carters I will pay what they require. Has Westminster sent payment?"

"Nay," Brother Michael muttered. "Not yet."

"Then we will not need to take funds. You are dismissed," the abbot said with a wave of a blue-veined hand.

Lord Gilbert and Sir Roger were invited to occupy the abbot's chamber for the night and we other guests were assigned lodging according to rank.

In the grey light of dawn I bid Lord Gilbert farewell. He would return to Bampton and Arthur and I, with the sheriff and his men, would escort Brother Michael on the first segment of his journey.

"Now this business is concluded shall we soon have a wedding?" Lord Gilbert laughed.

"Aye, m'lord. I think so."

"The Lady Petronilla will not set off for Goodrich 'til she has seen you wed. She will know the day, and wills me send her coach for your maid when the wedding day be set."

Master Wyclif greeted the news with mixed joy and sorrow. He was pleased to learn that his books, had Westminster sold none, would be soon returned, but distressed to learn of Brother Hamon's duplicity. The monk, he growled, would be sent straightaway back to Canterbury.

I arrived at Holywell Street at the ninth hour. Kate was pleased, I think, to see me. Word of the brawl on Canditch had come to the shop, and as she had heard nothing from me for a day, worry was gnawing at her. It is not a bad thing when a comely lass is anxious for your welfare.

It was near dark, and time for supper when I concluded the tale of the past days. A simple pottage stewed upon the hearth, but pottage in company with Kate is much to be preferred over similar fare consumed with the scholars of Canterbury Hall.

There was now no impediment to our marriage. With her father we set the eleventh day of January for the ceremony. Advent was now upon us, and no marriage possible until Christmas was past. I told Kate that Lady Petronilla had in mind to send her carriage to Oxford. This pleased her. Few maids will ride to their wedding in a lady's wagon.

It was near time for curfew when I left Kate and walked with light heart to Canterbury Hall. The only man who might seek me harm lay abed in the Augustinian Friary, but footpads might be about, so I kept a hand upon my dagger until I reached the Hall.

Master John was pleased to learn that a date was set when I would become a husband and vowed that he would be at the porch of the Church of St Beornwald for the event.

Next day Arthur and I broke our fast with maslin loaves and ale, retrieved Bruce and the palfrey from the Stag and Hounds, and set off for Bampton. The bells of Oseney Abbey rang for terce as Bruce lumbered past the tower. The bells were pleasant to the ear, but I hoped not to hear them again for many days.

It was the law of Moses that when a man took a bride he would be free from obligation to go to war for a year, nor would he be charged with any business for that time. I hoped Lord Gilbert would remember the injunction but, alas, this was not to be.

Although the fault lay not with Lord Gilbert.

Afterword

Sir John Trillowe was indeed Sheriff of Oxford from July to November, 1365. I do not know if his term was brief due to illness, death, incompetence, or malfeasance. I chose the last of these.

A few medieval Oxford streets, like St Fridewide's Lane, no longer exist. Many other streets have undergone name changes. Here are some examples:

Today	1365
Broad Street	Canditch
Queen Street	Great Bailey Street
Cornmarket Street	Northgate Street
St Aldate's	Fish Street
Magpie Lane	Grope Lane
Oriel Street	Schidyard Street
Merton Street	St John's Street

Canterbury Hall no longer exists, but its location is preserved in Christ Church's Canterbury Gate opening into Oriel Square, at the intersection of Oriel Street and Merton Street.

The conflict between secular and religious scholars was real. John Wyclif lasted only until 1367 as warden of Canterbury Hall.

Salley Abbey is today, like many other monastic establishments, a ruin. Its current name is Sawley Abbey and the remains lie a short distance north of the A59 in Sawley.

The current Magpie Lane was indeed the fourteenth-century haunt of Oxford's prostitutes.

Unhallowed Ground

An extract from the fourth chronicle of
Hugh de Singleton, surgeon

Chapter 1

Shouting and pounding upon the door of Galen House drew me from the maslin loaf with which I was breaking my fast. It was a fortnight after Hocktide, in the new year 1366, and the sun was just beginning to illuminate the spire of the Church of St. Beornwald. It was Hubert Shillside who bruised his knuckles against my door. He was about to set out for the castle and desired I should accompany him. The hue and cry was raised and he, as town coroner, and I as bailiff of Bampton Manor, were called to our duties. Thomas atte Bridge had been found this morn hanging from the limb of an oak at Cow-Ley's Corner.

Word of such a death passes through a village swiftly. A dozen men and a few women stood at Cow-Ley's Corner when Shillside and I approached. Roads to Clanfield and Alvescot here diverge; the road to Clanfield passes through a meadow where Lord Gilbert's cattle watched serenely as men gathered before them. To the north of the corner, and along the road to Alvescot and Black Bourton, is forest. From a tree of this wood the corpse of Thomas atte Bridge hung, his body but a few paces from the road. Shillside and I crossed ourselves as we approached.

Most who gazed upon the dead man did so silently, but not his wife. Maud knelt before her husband's body, her arms wrapped about his knees. She wailed incomprehensibly, as well she might.

Thomas atte Bridge hung by the neck from the limb of an oak, suspended there by a coarse hempen cord twisted about his neck. The cord passed round the branch and down to the tree trunk, where it was fastened at about waist height. The branch was not high – did I stretch a hand above me I could nearly touch it. The man's feet dangled from his wife's embrace little more than two hands-breadth above the ground. Near the corpse lay an overturned stool.

"Who found him?" I asked the crowd. Ralph the herder stepped forward.

"Was on me way to see to the cattle. They been turned out to grass but a short time now, an' can swell up like. Near walked into 'im, dark as it was, an' him hangin' so close to the road."

Hubert Shillside wandered about the place, then approached me and whispered, "Suicide, I think."

Spirits are known to frequent Cow-Ley's Corner. Many folk will not walk the road there after dark, and those who do sometimes see apparitions. This is to be expected, for any who take their own life are buried there. They cannot be interred in the churchyard, in hallowed ground. Their ghosts rest uneasy, and are said to vex travelers who pass the place at night.

"Knew he'd be buried here," Shillside continued, "an' thought to spare poor Maud greater trouble."

That Thomas atte Bridge might wish to cause little trouble to anyone did not seem likely, given my experience of the man. He had twice attacked me, leaving lumps upon my skull. But I made no reply. It is not good to speak ill of the dead, even this man.

Kate had followed us from the house, and now she looked from the corpse to Maud to me, and spoke softly. "You are troubled, Hugh."

This was a statement, not a question. We had been wed but three months, but Kate is observant and knows me well.

"I will call a coroner's jury here," Shillside announced. "We can cut the fellow down and see him buried straightaway."

"You must seek Father Thomas or one of the other vicars," I reminded him. "Thomas was a tenant of the Bishop of Exeter, not Lord Gilbert. They may wish otherwise."

Shillside set off for the town while two men lifted Maud from her knees and led her sobbing in the coroner's track.

"Wait," I said abruptly. All turned to see what caused my command. "The stool which lies at your husband's feet," I asked the grieving widow, "is it yours?"

Maud ceased her wailing long enough to whisper, "Aye."

Another onlooker righted the stool and prepared to step on it to cut down the corpse, when I bid him halt. Kate spoke true, the circumstances of this death troubled me.

I saw a man hanged once, in Paris, when I studied surgery there. He dangled, kicking the sheriff's dance and growing purple in the face until the constables relented and allowed his friends to approach and pull upon his legs until his torment ended. Thomas atte Bridge's face was swollen and purple, and he had soiled himself as death approached. His countenance in death duplicated the unfortunate cut-purse in Paris. It seemed as Hubert Shillside suggested; atte Bridge brought rope and stool to Cow-Ley's Corner, fixed the noose and placed it about his neck, then kicked aside the stool he'd stood upon. All who stood there peering surely thought the same.

I circled the dangling corpse. The hands hung limp and were cold to the touch. A man about to die on the gallows will be securely bound. Not so a man who takes his own life. I inspected atte Bridge's hands and pushed up the frayed sleeves of his cotehardie to see his wrists.

Upon one wrist I saw a small red mark, much like a rash, or a place where a man has scratched a persistent itch. No such scraping appeared upon the other wrist, but when I pushed up the sleeve of the cotehardie another thing caught my eye. The sleeve was of coarse brown wool, and frayed with age. Caught in the wisps of fabric I found a wrinkled thread of lighter hue. I looked up. This filament was much the same shade as the hempen cord from which the dead man hung. Perhaps it found its way to his sleeve when atte Bridge adjusted the rope about his neck.

I stood back from the corpse to survey the place. I was near convinced that Hubert Shillside must be correct. My life would have been easier had he been so. But my duties as bailiff to Lord Gilbert Talbot have made me suspicious of others and sceptical of tales they tell—whether dead or alive. It was then I noticed the mud upon Thomas atte Bridge's heels.

I knelt to see better, and Kate peered over my shoulder. Mud upon one's shoes is common when walking roads in springtime, but this mud was not upon the soles of atte Bridge's shoes, where it should have been, but was drying upon the backs of his heels. Kate understood readily what we saw.

"Odd, that," she said softly, so others might not hear. She then turned to the righted stool and gazed down at it thoughtfully. I saw her brow furrow and knew the cause. I drew her aside so we might converse unheard by others.

"A man who walks to his death will have mud upon the soles of his shoes," I whispered, "not upon the backs of his heels."

"And he will leave muddy footprints where he stands," Kate replied. "I see none on yon stool."

"Walk with me," I said. "Let us see what the road may tell us."

It told us that many folk had walked this way. The previous week there had been much rain, and the road was deep in mud. Footprints were many. Occasionally the track of a cart appeared. A hundred paces and more east of Cow-Ley's Corner I found what I sought. Two parallel lines, a hand's-breadth apart, were drawn in the mud of the road. These tracks were no more than one pace long. Kate watched me study the grooves.

"Did the mud upon his heels come from here?" she asked.

"Perhaps. It is as if two men carried another, and one lost his grip and allowed the fellow's feet to drop briefly to the road."

"How could this be? Was he dead already?"

"Nay. I think not. His face is that of a man who has

died at the end of a rope. But if he did not perish at his own hand someone bound him or rendered him helpless so to get him to Cow-Ley's Corner."

While Kate and I stood in the road, Hubert Shillside and eleven men of Bampton approached. The coroner saw us studying the mud at our feet and turned his gaze there also. He saw nothing to interest him.

"What is here, Hugh? Why stand you here studying the road?"

"See there," I pointed to the twin grooves in the mud. As Shillside had not seen Thomas atte Bridge's heels he could not know my suspicion. He shrugged and walked on. The coroner's jury followed and would have obliterated the marks in the way had not Kate and I stood before them so they were obliged to flow about us like Shill Brook about a rock.

There was nothing more to be learned standing in the road. Kate and I followed the men back to Cow-Ley's Corner. They studied the corpse, the rope, the stool, and muttered among themselves. The coroner had already voiced his opinion that atte Bridge died at his own hand. His companions, thus set toward a conclusion of the matter, found no reason to disagree. When a man has adopted an opinion it is difficult to dissuade him of it, but I tried.

I took Shillside to the corpse and bid him bend to inspect the stained and mud-crusted heels. "The tracks you saw me studying in the road... made by atte Bridge's heels, I think. Why else dirt upon the backs of a man's feet?"

"Hmmm... perhaps."

"And see the stool. If he stood upon it to fix the rope to the limb he made no muddy footprints upon it."

Shillside glanced at the stool, then lifted his eyes to atte Bridge's lolling head.

"The fellow is dead of hanging and strangulation," he declared. "I've seen men die so, faces swollen an' purple, tongue hangin' from 'is mouth all puffy an' red."

"Aye," I agreed. "So it does seem. But if he stood

upon that stool to fasten rope to tree he left no mark. How could a man tread the road and arrive here with clean shoes … but for the back of his heels?"

Shillside shrugged again. "Who can know? But this I'll say; not a man in Bampton or the Weald will be sorry Thomas atte Bridge is dead. He tried to kill you. Be satisfied the fellow can do no more harm to you or any other."

I saw then how it might be. Shillside drew his coroner's jury to the verge and they discussed the matter. Occasionally one or more of the group would look to the corpse, which now twisted slowly on the hemp. A breeze was rising.

Father Thomas, Father Simon, and Father Ralph, vicars of the Church of St. Beornwald, arrived as the jury ended its deliberations. The vicars looked upon the corpse and crossed themselves. Those who yet milled about Cow-Ley's Corner vied with each other to tell what the priests could see; a man was dead, hanging by a cord from the limb of a tree. More than this no man knew. If there was more to know, there were those who preferred ignorance.

Hubert Shillside approached me and the priests and announced the decision of the coroner's jury. Thomas atte Bridge took his own life, chosing to do so at a place where it was well-known that suicides of past years were buried. The stool was proof: Maud had identified it as belonging to their house.

The vicars looked on gravely while Shillside explained this conclusion. The stool and rope, he declared, would be deodand. What use King Edward might make of them he did not say.

Thomas atte Bridge was tenant of the Bishop of Exeter, but was found dead on lands of Lord Gilbert Talbot. The priests and coroner's jury looked to me for direction. Lord Gilbert was in residence at Goodrich Castle. As bailiff of Bampton Manor disposal of the corpse was now my bailiwick. My suspicions remained, but it seemed I was alone in my doubts. Other than Kate.

I saw Arthur standing at the fringe of onlookers and motioned him to approach. While he threaded his way through the crowd I spoke to Father Thomas.

"Will you allow burial in the churchyard?"

The vicar shook his head. Father Simon and Father Ralph pursed their lips and frowned in agreement. "A man who takes his own life cannot seek confession and absolution," Father Thomas explained. He had no need to do so. I knew the observances well. "He dies in his sins, unshriven. He cannot rest in hallowed ground."

Arthur had served me and Master John Wyclif well in the matter of Master John's stolen books. Now I found another duty for the sturdy fellow. I sent him to the castle to seek another groom and two spades.

There was no point in prolonging the matter. Shillside asked if the corpse might be cut down and I nodded assent. It was but the work of a moment for another of the bishop's tenants to mount the stool and slice through the rope. Thomas's remains crumpled to a heap at the fellow's feet. I told the man to unwind the cord from about the limb while he was on his perch. I knelt by the corpse and did the same to the cord which encircled atte Bridge's abraded neck. I then straightened the fellow out on the verge. He was beginning to stiffen in death and it would be best to put him in his grave unbent.

I knelt to straighten atte Bridge's head and while I did I looked into his staring, bulging eyes and gaping mouth. I see them yet on nights when sleep eludes me. The face was purple and bloated, so I nearly missed the swelling on atte Bridge's upper lip. There was a red bulge there. And just beneath the mark I saw in his open mouth a tooth bent back.

I reached a finger past the dead man's lips and pressed upon the bent tooth. It yielded freely. I pulled gently upon the tooth and nearly drew it from the mouth. Thomas atte Bridge had recently been in a fight and had received a robust blow. I was not surprised to learn of this. I knew Thomas atte Bridge. I would congratulate the man who served him with a fattened lip and broken tooth.

But did this discovery have to do with Thomas atte Bridge's death, suicide or not? Who could know? Perhaps only the man who delivered the blow.

Arthur returned with an assistant and set to work digging a grave at the base of the wall which enclosed Lord Gilbert's pasture. Cows chewed thoughtfully on spring grass and watched the work while their calves gamboled about. An onlooker urged Arthur to make the grave deep so the dead man might not easily rise to afflict those whose business takes them past Cow-Ley's Corner. Arthur did not seem pleased with the admonition.

Kate left me while the grave was yet unfinished. She wished to set a capon roasting for our dinner and was already tardy at the task. Her business served to remind me how hungry I was. Some might lose appetite after staring a hanged man in the face. I am not such a one, especially if the face be that of Thomas atte Bridge.

Hubert Shillside approached as Arthur and his assistant shoveled the last of the earth upon the burial mound. "One less troublemaker to vex the town, eh?" he said.

"He'll not be missed," I agreed. "But by Maud."

"Hah. Them of the Weald say as how he beat her regular like. She'll not be grieved to have that end."

"Aye, perhaps, but he provided for his family. Who will do so now?"

"There be widowers about who'll be pleased to add her lands to their holdings."

"A quarter-yardland? And four children to come with the bargain? I think Maud will find few suitors."

"Hmmm. Well, she will have to make do. Perhaps the oldest boy can do a man's work."

"Perhaps."

The throng of onlookers had begun to melt away when atte Bridge's corpse was lowered to the grave. These folks chattered noisily about the death and burial as they departed for the town. They did not seem afflicted with sorrow, but rather behaved as if a weight was lifted from their shoulders. Did Thomas atte Bridge guess this would be the response to his death would he have lived as he did, at enmity with all men, or would he have amended his ways?

The coroner and I were among the last to leave Cow-Ley's Corner. In my hand I carried the hempen rope, now sliced in two, which ended Thomas atte Bridge's life. We walked behind the vicars. I was silent while Shillside spoke of the weather, new-sown crops, and other topics of a pleasant spring day. When he found no ready response from me he grew silent, then as we reached the castle he turned and spoke again.

"The man is surely dead of his own hand, Hugh. You must not seek a felon where none is. And even was atte Bridge slain there is no man in Bampton sorry for it. He was an evil fellow we are well rid of."